SB Sweeney

Educated at Glastonbury, ⸻
thought in Squatsville, eas⸻
committed member of the structurally ⸻
throughout the 80s – specialising in three chord trash rock,
all-night philosophy and breakfast appreciation. He toured
the UK with musicians and artists, promoting political
activism in the 90s and worked on various community media
projects in the noughties. Currently living in the cold heart of
England.

He is assembling a trilogy of novels under the working title of
The Last Days of Albion, of which *Facing the Strange* is the
first part.

FACING THE STRANGE

SB Sweeney

StreetBooks

StreetBooks

First published in 2017 by StreetBooks

http://www.sbsweeney.com

The right of SB Sweeney to be
identified as the author of this work has been asserted by him
in accordance with the Copyright, Designs and Patents Act 1988.

ISBN 978-0-9564242-6-6

StreetBooks
3 Windsor Cottages
Broad Street
Bampton
OX18 2LU

http://www.streetbooks.co.uk

Cover designed by Andrew Chapman
mail@preparetopublish.com

For 'My old fighting partner'

Thanks to all the kind folks who have helped me out over the years – given me encouragement, loaned me money, put me up on their sofa etc – especially: Karl, Murrel, Weez and Jen, Rog the Dodge and Dr Rog, Colin and Clare, Kate G, Helen and Tulip. Thanks also to Rachel at Sayle, Frank at StreetBooks and all the fine writers involved in the OUDCE Diploma class of 2009, notably the excellent and much missed poet, Brian Nisbet – may his spirit soar in the mountains.

Finally, a heartfelt thank you to Miriam who has put up with this for seven years and counting.

This book is dedicated to the lasting memory of KB Sweeney. Save me a high stool at the eternal bar, mate.

A kitchen sink drama featuring a cast of drunkards and deviants; one which tells the tale of Tom Ballindine and his son Dan, a rock musician in decline, who we join one New Year's Eve on the brink of disaster...

Part 1
Three Beginnings

Recipe for an Overdose

Calderdale, December 31 1992

All that matters right now is to stay awake long enough to piece together the last few joins and run the film. You pause to shake a handful of ephedrines out of a plastic tub and then you swallow them dry, one after the other. Although you've started the Tullamore Dew Jessie bought for Christmas, it seems a waste to use it as a pill chaser. You still retain a sense of appreciation, even if you have let go of pretty much everything else.

The task at hand is to piece together a box full of Super 8 films into one feature length reel – and it's almost finished. You have been working on it since getting back from walking the dogs this morning. The idea is to watch all of them in one go without having to change the little reels over.

You have watched the older ones in the box, time and again. The action looks jerky but it's difficult to say whether that was down to the wear and tear on the film, or the projector, or maybe it was just the way people moved back in those days. At least when a hand held cine camera was pointed at them.

The main characters, of course, you know well.

There's Tom, six feet tall and built like the type of athlete who trains too little and enjoys life too much. Usually he'll be well turned out with salt and pepper hair in a duck's arse style, as was fashionable in the late 50s. And then there's Angela, who looks like Jackie Kennedy in her pencil skirts and round topped, short-brimmed hats. She smiles and poses as if she was born to be a leading lady.

The camera once belonged to them. They would carry it around in a double zipped leather case. It was their diary, of a sort, and they had used it well. Then the camera was passed down to you, and the films switch location to mainly in and around the house in Bush Road. They become populated with different characters: Jessie, Frank, Monica and the band.

You've spliced together the whole box of reels in a random order, as each one has come to hand. Right now you want to watch it all, old and recent, in no particular sequence.

You're holed up in the kitchen of a stone end-terrace on the moors of West Yorkshire. Its one conventional source of heat is an ill fitted pot-belly stove, which produces more in blinding smoke than warmth. So the oven has been left alight for two hours in an attempt to take the edge off the chill, you are layered in jumpers and the room is choked. You have two dogs for company and Jessie should have reached London days ago. She, no doubt, is having a wild time.

You complete the final join on the reel and having fixed it to the spindle, you set your work in motion. After gobbing some downers, that is – to take the edge off the ephedrines.

Outside, more snow is falling and the temperature has dropped well below freezing. It would most likely result in a treacherous surface for walking, which rules out making a phone call for the time being. You feel as though you might need to, at some point, but your nearest phone-box is at least a hundred steep yards down onto the valley road. Why struggle in those conditions when you have other options? Why expose what little warmth there is in the kitchen to the frozen winds? The house creaks and groans as if to confirm your thinking.

You wonder what Tom would make of the state you're in. What would he do in your shoes? This Super 8 star who hauled himself up from a poor background to live a reckless and rangy life – surely he'd shrug his shoulders and dismiss it. He'd laugh at the shambles you've made of things. You study him and Angela as they flicker across the wall, large and bright, on a carefree, drunken drive through the north country.

And then it switches to a long panning shot across Ullswater, with a breeze rippling the lake – and now they're inside a pub.

Would things seem this bad if you were there with them, sitting at the bar amongst those old locals, chorusing along with their songs?

You have seen many pubs in these films. You've seen them as grainy, jumping, shadowy places. They are filled with marbled cigarette smoke, occasionally seared by the projector bulb through sections of worn film. Everyone smiles, raising their glasses to the camera, wearing woollen jackets and cardigans, and Tom is always in sunglasses. Life, as you have watched it, was not only a party, it was suffused with certainty.

You are in the some of the older films too – the little lad in a football jersey, rubbing his eyes with his wrists. And this unsettles you. You have peered at that lad, leaning forward in your seat. You have rewound and watched him again, yet it's still like watching a stranger. You recognise the face and the mannerisms, but in the end little Danny Boy is just another character up there, separated from the viewer, so your memory, like the wall, becomes a screen.

Although right now there's only one memory in your head, isn't there Danny Boy? And it won't leave you be...

***

December 26 1992

'There's a wet sleeping bag hanging over a washing line in the kitchen.'

Jessie was up and about. She was wearing knee high woollen socks and a cardigan which barely covered her backside, just the bottom two buttons fixed.

'I wonder what happened?' She continued to pad about the room. There must have been some aim to her activity, but after so little sleep it was difficult to tell. All you could think of was how much flesh she was showing. She must have been chilled to the bone for a start and, if anyone else was about the house, she'd be giving them more than an eyeful.

She paused, expecting a response. You had, sure enough, noticed the sleeping bag and washing line earlier, when you came to on the kitchen sofa. You'd thought nothing of it.

You blinked, not able to raise your head from the pillow while she stood in front of you with her hands on her hips. A Patti Smith poster covered the hole in a broken window behind her, the window you had yet to replace. Jessie was a bit like Patti Smith – her long hair cut to a heavy fringe, the same pale, complicated look. You stretched your arm out to stroke her thigh, as much wanting to rub her warm, but she was just beyond reach and made no move to come closer.

'Hasn't it always been there?' you offered in a croaking voice. You'd only got into bed half an hour or so before and your thoughts were confused.

She laughed and threw an empty holdall across your legs.

'There's been something going on. We don't have a washing line in the kitchen and the bag's wet.' She was speaking in a conspiratorial voice. 'It must be to do with the goings on with Frank last night.'

You felt the breath catching in your throat and your heart began to beat heavily. You wondered why, exactly, Jessie was dressed like that. It had been freezing cold overnight and she would normally wear layers of baggy T-shirts and pyjama bottoms. Why didn't she have those on now? Why had she been naked in bed last night?

When you came to earlier, the house was quiet. It was a dog's wet nose lifting your face that brought you round. You must have passed out during the Christmas party. As you dragged yourself upright you could hear a steady drip and noticed the sleeping bag with a bucket positioned under it. An overcoat had been thrown over you on the sofa, which you slipped into in a daze, and then you stumbled amidst the leaping dogs to let them out of the front door.

There, on the gravel path, you'd been surprised to find a bearded man looking out at the West Yorkshire morning – the first snow flurries of winter were swirling in off the moors. He was vaguely familiar. He said his name was Dave.

As Jessie began gathering clothes from the cupboard, you were wondering what Dave had been doing loitering about the front door. You hadn't seen him at the house before. He said he lived further down the valley road towards Todmorden. But then again, last night had been an open door party. He must have taken it upon himself to drop in – and he must have been one of those 'last to leave' people.

So where did Frank come into the picture? It was gradually coming back to you – a risky car drive through the fog on the moors roads, a few ten pound bags changing hands outside the Labour club.

Last night – you must have been drinking like it would never end. And yet here was the new day and, as you were quickly realising, you had begun it still drunk as well as hungover. You were watching Jessie fold jeans and jumpers, shoving them into the holdall. With all her pacing about the room, one sock had slipped down to her calf. It made her look almost vulnerable.

'Are we going somewhere?' You could hear your own voice asking the question.

Jessie's breasts had swung loose from stooping to pull up her sock and, as she answered you, she covered herself again by hugging the cardigan tightly around her.

'I'm going to London for a meeting with a publisher,' she said. 'The dogs will have to stay here with you.'

***

December 31 1992

...It's easier to try blotting the scene out of your mind, along with a fair few others – like the day you blew out the band. Or at least imagine that they amount to nothing more than a reel or two of film amongst the dozens you have carefully pieced together.

You pour a tumbler full of Tullamore Dew and light a cigarette. Up there on the wall, a boxing match you have seen countless times flickers and rattles. The fight took place at the Preston Flag Market on a murky day. Two pale, bloodied men mauling each other artlessly, viewed through the ropes from the height of the ring floor. It's a dark, heavily scratched piece of film. It was probably shot during the Guild celebrations – you can't remember the story exactly.

You're glad of the dogs being there with you. One rests his chin on your lap. The other is curled up on a three-month old newspaper from Preston – a paper you can't use to light the stove because the front page report is, for some reason, very important. It's a murder and a love story rolled into in one.

The warmth of the dogs as you all sit bundled on the sofa, and the functionality of their approach to life – eat, exercise, stay warm – is what's helping you to keep going. This is because you've been in a daze since Jessie left on Boxing Day. From the moment that she revealed she was going to London. That she had arranged a lift with a guy who was getting paid double time to do a delivery to some art gallery.

That you were to stay behind with the dogs.

And you weren't kidding yourself, she really did say – 'Jessie is pregnant, and no, Jessie doesn't know if Dan is the father' – just like that. It had been her parting shot, effectively, because after that you had become Dan, existing in the third person as she'd put it, struck numb by her announcement. It felt like a hammer blow. You hardly noticed her leave.

And admit it Danny Boy, you've been talking to yourself ever since, with this little voice perched like a sprite on your shoulder. Haven't you?

Jessie's pregnant and she doesn't know if Dan is the father. Does she, Danny Boy?

So you see, Dan sits in the kitchen wishing he'd asked Frank

16

to stay, while he watches two brawlers lurching at each other across his wall. Despite the ephedrine, a warm tide sweeps through his limbs and his head feels like it belongs on a broken doll. But tough luck, he parted company with Frank this morning after giving the dogs a run out, and then spent some time wondering if the shifty dodger might in fact be Jessie's lover.

While the last day of the year grows deeper, Dan is rolling through the Super 8s as more than just a whim. The snow is falling and quickly drifting outside. He has the oven on and a few chopped logs by the stove. It's a good time to review the bits of his life preserved on film. It might help him figure out what chain of events brought him to this sorry state.

Maybe, somehow, that would begin the process of getting himself sorted out.

At least that's the way it seems to Dan – with his head rolling on his shoulders like a beaten fighter, the films running one after the other, back and forth in time, and the thought nagging at him that this time he might have overdone it and should write some sort of note.

Eh, Danny Boy? Eh?

Maybe it's time to write a goodbye note?

The Making of the Front Page Story in Dan's Newspaper

Preston, September 1992

I arrived at my front door and fumbled at the lock. And then I stopped and looked behind me, across to the wood-yard, and then back in the direction I had just walked. The long, straight road from the town centre to home. I must have looked back at where I'd come from for a good while.

Something had changed, fundamentally, but I couldn't put my finger on it. Less to do with the route home, or the look of it, more as if I'd started out the day a different person altogether. As if the road back had taken me beyond the everyday world and out into an unfamiliar place. What kind of journey had I just made?

Maybe it was to do with that old character I fell in with at the Black Horse.

That'd be it. More than likely.

And then, finally, my key made sense of the lock. I turned it decisively and, without even glancing at the neighbour's door, I stepped inside.

'Maggie!'

But something wasn't right. I was met by an unusual silence.

'Maggie?'

I ventured through to the kitchen. This wasn't normal at all. For a moment I was lost as to what to do. I thought about checking to see if she was upstairs, in the bedroom, but ended up stopping at the foot of the staircase.

It'd probably be best if I just retraced my steps.

***

'I can remember slipping through the ropes and climbing into the ring.' The old man twitched and took a gulp from his glass, as if he was again squaring up to his opponent and the drink was for courage.

'I could hear familiar voices in amongst the shouts from ringside. And then the bell rang.'

He looked at me and his face opened into a ruddy grin, revealing a gold cap here and there. His grey eyes were rheumy and veined with the whiskey and Woodbines.

'Next thing I knew, I was regaining consciousness on board the ferry heading back for Pompey.'

I had been sitting quietly at the bar, before he took the stool to my left and struck up a conversation. And now the Black Horse was filling up, the weather an encouragement to a rush of late afternoon custom. Gusty rain struck the stained-glass window panels like brass tacks.

'One of the trainers spoke up first,' he continued, 'a little, punch-drunk fellow, a Cockney lightweight called Artful. He said to me, "By Christ, Doc, you were in an entertaining fight!" He said, "Each time the Scots lad knocked you down, you kept getting back up."'

The old man shuffled on his stool as he spoke, throwing short hooks at shadows.

'He said I must've hit the deck a dozen times in those three rounds but the Scotsman had to settle for points.'

'And you had no recollection of this?' I asked.

'Nothing,' he said, slapping the palm of his hand on the counter, causing the barman to glance our way. 'Nothing after the first punch. But I was told I landed a few good shots myself. Yer man didn't get away with it completely.'

He smiled and shook his head at a memory. Something hazy, probably – skipping ropes, cigar smoke and jazz.

'Wheeew!' I whistled.

'The Home Fleet Championship,' he said looking ruefully

past my shoulder along the bar, 'and me, a ship's doctor, beaten by a hairy-arsed stoker from Aberdeen.

'I was telling ol' Lew Lazar about it yesterday. We were swapping stories at the Wheatsheaf (a good Haringey pub, if you ever find yourself over that way). Anyway, you wouldn't know Lew but he's the gentlest fellow you could meet. He has time for everybody around the bar, but if anyone misbehaves in there...' He slammed a fist into his thick, shovel-sized hand.

He was still trying to catch the eye of the barman who was dealing with the late run of drinkers. I was weighing up whether I had time for another. I'd only stopped in for a quick drink on my way back home. Maggie had gone on ahead, after we watched the parades, to prepare the celebration dinner.

'You know he knocked out Charlie Kray once, and said he never felt so bad about stopping an opponent.' The old man held up a five pound note as if he were bidding at an auction, and then must have received some signal that his request was in hand, as he again turned my way.

'Well anyway, I was telling him about how, when I was a young'un, I listened to his big fight with Ratcliffe on the radio. Lazar v Ratcliffe at Wembley or Earl's Court, it was somewhere like that, an eliminator for the British title. And it was a dramatic fight, sure enough. Ratcliffe was miles ahead on points, running circles around poor Lew and then suddenly, in the tenth, Lew was all over him. He virtually took the bastard's head off.

'And you know, Lew told me that when he'd slumped onto his stool at the end of the ninth he could hear the BBC announcer, the same fellow I was listening to at home, saying: "This is a classic match up where a slick, stylish boxer is outwitting a rough-house East End brawler." And Lew thought to himself – I'm not standing for that bullshit, who's he calling a faacking East End brawler?'

The old man paused to laugh himself into a choke.

'So he went out for the tenth in a fury!'

I finished rolling perhaps the most slowly assembled

cigarette of my life, and lit it. The barman came our way and I reached along the counter for a tin ashtray.

'What'll it be, Tom?' the barman asked

'Let me buy you a pint.' I offered up and the old man looked at me closely before accepting.

'You beat me to the punch,' he said, 'so I'll get the shorts. A Guinness, young Jack, whatever this gent's pint is, sorry I don't know your name...'

'Gable,' I said. 'Gable McGrath, and it's a Double Hop for me.'

'A pint of Double Hop for Gable McGrath,' he continued, 'and two large Jamies.'

What the hell, the old man Tom was one of those characters you don't meet every day. And this was, after all, last orders for the afternoon on the Friday of Preston Guild. Maggie wouldn't mind if I was half an hour or so late.

'Slip a shot in a tumbler for yerself Jack.' Tom winked as he passed over his fiver, and I handed across a couple of pound coins rummaged from my pocket.

With a glass in his hand, Tom stood up from his stool and proposed a toast for Jack and myself to join.

'To Proud Preston and the Guild!' And we all downed our whiskeys with a flourish.

'By God, that's good!' he said, wiping his lips with the back of his hand, and he resumed his perch.

'I guess this'll be your first drink at a Guild?' he asked and I nodded – although I had a vague memory of ghosting about the floor as a child, hands and knees commando-style in 1972, the adults all high-spirited and loud, barely noticing me, let alone my sips from their Martini glasses and Party Sevens.

And I remembered playing a game of soldiers in an attic.

***

So anyway, I was in a haze on a wet, poorly-lit street and thought to myself – Fuck it, I'll walk home. The buses were unreliable into the evening and a walk would do me good. I made for Friargate and through Adelphi, where groups of party-goers were spilling from one pub to another amid roars and the clatter of high-heels.

As I lurched my way past them, through sharp wafts of after-shave and perfume, I thought of my home. I thought of my darling young wife who waited inside for me. And I am certain that I felt as blessed, that I was as sure of my place and time, as a man could be.

All this despite the fact that, even though I had always lived in Preston, I had never felt comfortable here. There wasn't much talk on offer whenever I revealed I was a freelance photographic artist; whenever it got beyond the page three pin-up quips and I explained that I was documenting our disappearing world, that my current project was to photograph the analogue age in all its forms before it was lost to computers, that I took pictures of streets before they were demolished, old pubs and vanishing traditions.

But this evening I felt different. I felt a keen sense of belonging. At least that's what I recall feeling, somewhere along the walk back. Then, without noticing the last half a mile, I found myself at the front door fumbling at the lock with my key.

'Maggie!' I called out as I stepped inside. I could smell the sweet drift of roast chicken in the warm air of home. But no-one, not a soul, stirred.

'Maggie?' I ventured through to the dining table and peered into the kitchen. Everything was quiet except for the buzz and rattle of the fridge. This wasn't what I expected. I felt at a loss.

The dining table was dressed with party cloth and set out with an opened bottle of wine, two glasses, a bowl of peanuts and cutlery arranged for a three course dinner. After checking to see if she was in the bedroom, and finding it empty, undisturbed, I returned to splash some wine into one of the glasses and slump onto the couch.

She must have despaired waiting in for me and gone out. I

didn't blame her. After all, this was Preston Guild and the understanding was that I'd be home hours ago.

***

'...And I filmed the fucking fight from the ring apron!' Tom staggered and chuckled, doing a dance almost, around his stool. 'Yeah, I had an 8mm camera with me, one I "borrowed" from the local newspaper to take shots of the parades, so I filmed it! And Pete did the whole thing for a bet! Right there on the Flag Market, the silly bugger!'

I was doubled up on my stool, hugging my midriff with my arms, laughing so hard the tears bulged down my cheeks.

'Anyway, I had to hand it to the bastard for having the presence of mind to put my money in my shoe, before leaving me in the flower bed that night.' Tom pulled himself back onto his stool.

He slipped a hand around his pint glass as if it were a staff.

'I don't suppose you know the family?' he asked.

'Remind me, what was his name again?' I spoke in gasps, wiping my face with my shirt sleeves.

'He's called Pete Irongate. My old sparring partner...' Tom's voice trailed off.

'That was the Guild of '52,' he said softly.

I decided an answer to his question wasn't necessary and instead sized up the remaining beer in my barrel glass, holding it up to the light.

'Well, I must be going,' I announced, 'I have a lovely lady expecting me home for my dinner.'

'Ah, bollocks you will!' Tom roared, and slapped my back. 'This is the Guild, man! Once every twenty years! You'll be middle-aged next time around, enjoy it while you're young.'

'Last orders was over an hour ago.' I was groping for a reason not to.

'And we've had a few rounds since, and we'll have one more now,' said Tom and he called Jack over from a session he was conducting with a small group at one end of the bar. They had a bottle each of Tequila and Vodka pulled from the optic rack and were swapping rounds of slammers.

***

I was walking, no, stumbling a little… Anyway, I was making my way up the straight road home when all of a sudden I shouted out loud.

'Oooh! Aaah! Gabe McGrath!

'Oooh! Aaah! Gabe McGrath!'

So tell me, Gable, was there a defining moment in your life, a moment that you can pin down and say, 'That was when I realised I would become the most influential artist of my generation'?

In fact, as some would have it, the artist that defined the end of the century?

That is a good question, Mr Parkinson… It's difficult to pick out one moment but, if I had to, it would be the Preston Guild of '92 and a chance encounter I had with a worldly old boxer called Tom Ballindine. When I met him I was still an aspiring artist. I was flat broke and working on the first of my disappearing world volumes. It was as if I needed some direction, and it turned out that meeting Tom opened up a whole new disappearing world for me. It opened doors. After I met him I began photographing people instead of objects. It was not long after that I began my portraits of the forgotten.

Which, of course, led to my commission to document the escalating crisis in Yugoslavia. That's when the big deals started rolling in.

And now? Now I am relaxing, taking a well earned rest in my luxury Haringey apartment – considering my next project. It's been a busy, but rewarding couple of years.

You know, one day I wished upon a star and now it feels like I have woken up and the clouds are way behind me.

And all this, I achieved all this, from a humble home tucked down a side street. Humble, yet warm, with the sweet drift of roast chicken in the air. And always a rousing welcome...

I arrived at the front door, a cosy glow evident through the frosted glass, and I thought of my beautiful young wife waiting inside for me.

I turned the key.

'Maggie?'

But Maggie wasn't there.

My concerns for her whereabouts seemed to disappear once I'd slumped onto the couch. Instead I fell into dwelling upon my drinking session with the old fighter. What a fateful encounter that was! You rarely chance across characters like Tom. He made an ideal subject for my portfolio of work. He was a memory worth keeping.

The only shots I took of him were casual, like family photos, and he was happy with that. He was happy with that and the fact that I could pay for a round. I caught him at the right time. I only cashed my Enterprise Allowance cheque yesterday.

I'd have to go back to the Black Horse tomorrow to find him again and set up a proper photo shoot. But, hang about! The thought slowly crept up on me. Where was my camera now? What had I done with it?

I frisked myself gormlessly.

I had it when I left the pub. How the hell could I have lost my camera? I looked around the room.

How did this happen?

***

'Careful, McGrath, you're spilling most of that good stuff down your shirt!'

I couldn't be sure whether he was rocking and swaying in a pronounced fashion on his bar stool, or whether I was so drunk I was, myself, responsible for all the motion.

'Sláinte!' I said – in fact I probably yelled, it was difficult to tell.

Tom peered as I took some time lighting a cigarette, the end too soggy for the flame to catch.

'Ah, you're not bad,' he said. I watched him down his tumbler of whiskey and reach for the stout chaser.

'You remind me of Danny.'

'Who's Danny?' I asked, fighting the hiccups.

'My son,' he said. 'You may have heard of him. He was in a pop band until recently. They were in the hit parade.'

'Go on, what was the band called?' I was onto my third match.

'They were called the Smokin Joes and the song was something about emasculation, or castration or incarceration – something like that.'

'Rings a vague bell but I can't bring 'em to mind, sorry.'

'Well, they were number one in the hit parade, a year or so back.' He took a long gulp of stout. 'Not my thing, though.'

'And what are they doing now?' I asked. I felt as though I was brushing with fame.

'Beats me. I heard that Danny went off to Yorkshire a couple of months back. Up on the moors. He lives with a bunch of hippie layabouts.' Tom looked at me, but also through me. 'Pity, the lad has talent.'

And then he turned his attention back to his pint.

'Fancy that,' he said. 'Giving up on the one thing you've achieved in life.'

***

So I arrived at the front door of my humble home. Humble yet cosy, a visible, cheery glow through the frosted glass: my launchpad to success and fame. And all this with my darling wife waiting inside for me.

I could only dimly recall walking the last half mile. What kind of stumble had I been in? And here I was, barely able to find the lock with my key.

I had been dwelling upon my chance encounter with that

worldly old fighter and failed to notice my progress past the terraces and ginnels, the cattle sheds and the Big House pub. Although now I thought about it, I had actually noticed the smell of beer, smoke and piss by the Big House and the wafts of cattle muck from the sheds. I recalled registering the thought that this was the smell of my home town. And I felt the firm tug of belonging. At least, that's what I imagined my feeling was.

So, having looked back down the road I just travelled, I took a deep breath of timber-scented air and turned the key, finally, to be met by a rush of warmth, sweetened with the smell of roast chicken.

I looked clumsily around the living room – the dressed table, the dim lighting, some low music I could hear all of a sudden.

Where was Maggie?

***

Jack had come over and was listening in to the conversation, propping his chin in his hand with an elbow on the bar. His drinking group had disappeared.

'...So this was the pub I had my first pint in, and it's the first pub I have a drink in whenever I'm back in Preston.' I noticed that Tom's ring was a Claddagh, which he couldn't quite fit through the handle of his pint pot with the thickness of his fist.

'But each time I'm here it feels like chasing ghosts. The old faces have all slowly gone, one by one, and now no-one even remembers them.'

'So what brings you back this time, Tom?' Jack asked.

'See that snug over there.' Tom pointed into the gloom towards the rear end of the bar.

'That snug was our HQ. There'd be myself and Angela, My brother Paddy and his fiancée Bridget, and then there'd be Pete Irongate and his wife Irene.'

I looked over and could imagine that table lit by a dusty bulb, slung with a paper shade, blue cigarette smoke drawn upwards like the spirit of moths. I could picture a group of young men and women laughing and joking with jazz trumpet blowing from the jukebox...

'I'm here to bury my mother,' said Tom.

And then the tears started rolling down the old man's cheeks and around his nose – a nose which was bent from several short-arm punches. Both Jack and I remained still, watching him until the sobs were reduced to the odd piteous mutter. Then finally he wiped his face dry with the palms of his hands and reached for his glass.

'It's a terrible thing, losing a mother,' concluded Jack. 'But at least she's going out during the Guild. It'll make for a good wake.' And he grinned. 'She must've been lucky.'

Tom laughed heartily.

'I should have been buying her lotto tickets in Cork all this time.'

I looked down at the cigarette I had just rolled. I seemed to have been rolling it forever. It looked like a trampled worm with deathly brown innards spilling from its split.

'There are only a few ways to get rich quick,' Tom declared. 'Win the Irish lotto, do ten rounds with Tyson, get a number one in the hit parade...'

***

I stumbled so badly, in such a pronounced manner, that the cigarette fell from my mouth. I didn't even know if it was lit. I wasn't sure how long it had been since I rolled it and struck the first match.

It was the smell, no, the actual fine, wispy air of beer, piss and cattle muck that brought me out of my thoughts. *What was it about this particular combination of smells that, right now, felt so profound?* I stopped mid-track in the street. I wanted to fully consider the question while engulfed in the aroma of home.

That was it!

I may have hailed my own name to the rooftops at that point. I recall delivering it like a football chant. But the fact was, I realised, I was home. This was my home. I *felt* at home.

With that decided I lurched forward once more, weaving my way towards that little side street opposite the wood-yard which lent the freshness of timber to the clean air of Savick Brook. The air around my small nest in which greatness was being hatched.

And that's what else struck me. He compared me to his son. His gifted son, who was a pop star. Wait until I told Maggie. Her patience seemed limitless, her willingness to sacrifice so much to support my artistic purpose. But surely there were limits? Surely she would appreciate the fact that I'd been recognised as talented by the father of a star. By a man from a generation soon to be forgotten.

Then, without any sort of warning at all, I found myself at the front door. I stood before the frosted glass, swaying to and fro, for what seemed an age.

***

I looked stupidly about the room. Where was Maggie?

Having ascertained that she wasn't in bed (and certainly not with the neighbour, whose overattentive ways bordered on the creepy) I returned to contemplate the table once more. I emptied some wine from the bottle in the general direction of a stemmed glass and most of it seemed to end up in the peanut bowl.

What the hell. Who could blame her for not stopping in? This was the Guild, after all.

I could hear just a buzz and a rattle. And some soft music. Where was it coming from? Had she left a record on repeat?

And then it was as if the world fell away from beneath my feet, as it dawned on me that I'd lost my camera.

How could I have done that? It was unfathomable.

***

Tom rocked forward on his stool, leaning in towards my face, so that he could speak to me confidentially. His breath was over-proof, his voice reduced to gravelly, Louis Armstrong tones.

'You know there's some who will say that the fellow at the Wheatsheaf, who calls himself Lew Lazar, is in fact an impostor.'

My face must have looked blank.

'That, in truth his name is Ronnie; that he was a bit-part actor in the 50s, who now masquerades as Lew, because he's either a hoaxer or deluded.'

'And...' I began to respond.

'And you know what?' Tom said. 'I don't care. He's as real to me as the Ratcliffe fight was on the radio. It's all a matter of faith.' He sat upright again with a look of satisfaction on his face. I realised this was something important to him but, at that very moment, it was lost on me. I was well past my drinking limit.

'It's all a matter of faith,' he repeated. 'And imagination.'

***

I wasn't entirely certain how long I had been upstairs checking the bedroom. I must have staggered about that bed for at least half an hour, checking the linen for wrinkles, for any sign of use at all. And finally I returned to the table, splashed some wine loosely about a glass and slumped onto the couch.

I looked about the room. That is to say my head made the motion of looking about a room, my sight was elsewhere entirely. I was wondering what the hell I'd done with my camera, and from somewhere indiscernible I could hear music playing softly.

Then, out of nowhere, I started singing *Somewhere Over the Rainbow* – but the words completely slipped my mind.

'Daah, daah – da di di da da

daah, daah, daah...'

***

'Gable McGrath! You're all right!' That was the old man's salutation, as we clinked pint pots and downed the last of our beer.

'It's been good to meet you Tom,' is what I meant to say, I may have managed it, the sentiment was there at least.

'Now tell me about your wife,' he said.

'My wife is called Maggie,' I said, probably slurred. 'She's very beautiful. She has black hair and eyes like emeralds. I owe her so much.'

'I'm sure you do,' said Tom.

'Ah, she's too beautiful for me, even the neighbour's got his sights on her. It seems every time I'm away to do some work, I get home and he's there.'

'Well, McGrath, you want to put a stop to that.'

I suddenly felt a little over-exposed. I groped along the bar for my tobacco so I could roll a cigarette.

'Why isn't she here?' Tom asked. 'It's the Guild for Christ's sake. If you can't bring your missus out during the Guild...'

It seemed a fair question. It deserved a better answer than I recall giving.

'I only stopped in for a quick drink.'

There was a lengthy silence between us while I concentrated on the process of rolling a cigarette. The pub seemed almost empty now, even though it had reopened for the evening. Jack was over the other side of the bar polishing glasses with a cloth. From somewhere, it must have been the jukebox, Judy Garland was singing. I was sure the same song had been playing for hours.

'You know what Danny Boy told me?' said Tom, again drawing near. 'He said the guy who wrote this song was stuck for the middle break when, at the point of despair, he heard a police car approaching and as it shot past his window, he

31

started playing the sound of the siren on his piano. Listen, it's the bit coming up now...'

I have no idea how long it took me to roll that cigarette.

***

I was swaying at the front door and all of a sudden I felt beaten, as if I had been in the middle of that Lazar fight and the same BBC announcer Tom listened to all those years back, had just called my shots:

'And Lazar has the look of a desperate man now. He's throwing wild punches, one after the other, at Ratcliffe. Ratcliffe has his gloves up and is swaying to avoid the barrage. And he's down! Ratcliffe is down! And the referee has to push Lazar back to the corner. So eager is Lazar to finish the job, he forgot to retreat to a neutral corner.

'Ratcliffe is up at eight looking dazed but able to continue, and Lazar comes at him again. A tremendous bombardment of punches from Lazar! Lefts, rights, hooks and uppercuts. Ratcliffe is trapped on the ropes, trying to cover up, but Lazar is relentless. Pushing him back into range, landing clubbing punches, and Ratcliffe is down again!

'The referee begins his count with Ratcliffe pulling himself to his hands and knees, six, seven, and Ratcliffe hauls himself to his feet with the help of the ropes.

'And Ratcliffe is down again, and almost through the ropes! A dozen spectators at ringside push him back into the fray! Lazar raced across the ring before Ratcliffe knew he was there and landed a powerful right cross to the side of the head...'

***

Having inspected the bed thoroughly, to check for any stains, indentations or wrinkles, I returned to more or less fall onto the couch, almost spilling my wine.

Fuck it, I didn't blame her. Why wait in for me, when it was the Friday of Preston Guild? She needed to get out there and enjoy it while she was young.

She was expecting me back hours ago anyway. And she already did so much for me, for what reward? I was always broke, usually pre-occupied with my own things. And now I had returned home late, with most of my money spent and my camera lost.

I looked about the room, if you could call it looking, with my head nodding forward involuntarily. The table was like the scene of an accident, peanuts and wine splashed all across it. And I could hear some music in the distance. Or maybe it was nearby, with the volume turned down low.

Inexplicably, I began to sing.

'If happy da di da di da
di dum the rainbow
da di da di daah...!'

Which is when I noticed the flashing blue light. I saw it float past the window and come to a halt out in the street – refracting, just like that rainbow, through the frosted glass of the front door. They were bringing my Maggie home. My sweet, sobbing Maggie, who stepped uncertainly into the house and walked past me as if I didn't exist.

It felt like she walked right through me while I stood dumbfounded with my arms outstretched.

I could see that my camera bag was slung over her shoulder. I couldn't understand how this had happened.

And then, without any semblance of control, I felt myself drift slowly towards the ceiling.

The Beginning of the End

Cork Airport, December 31 1992

Tom was perched up on a stool, staring at the froth trails in his empty glass. He was thinking of the rainfall last night – the way it bounced off the roadside and the smell it released from the earth. To describe the sight of it would be simple. But to accurately convey the quality of its fragrance was beyond him.

Not that he had anyone to swap tales with. A hunched-up glance around the bar revealed the few customers in view as having an unapproachable and self-contained look to them. Ah, fuck it. It didn't matter.

What did matter was that he could die of thirst in this place. All those pumps and optics and not a stir of life from the barman who seemed happy idling over the newspaper.

'I'll have another pint, pal, when you're ready!'

And while his drink was being poured, Tom looked out through a rain-spattered window over the fields and little runways of Cork airport.

It was at a New Year's Eve party, a dinner dance in Victoria, that he first met Angela. And now, over thirty years later, he was off to see in the New Year with her again. He would get there in time for lunch and there were plenty of good restaurants around her part of town. And in the evening maybe they could put on their finest and go out to the Grosvenor Hotel again.

'That'll be two punts sir,' said the barman. A thin, middle-aged man with greasy black hair and a tea towel thrown over his shoulder. There was something familiar about him, but Tom put it down to the Cork-man's face. He'd been long enough in the county to recognise it.

'Will you have one yourself?' Tom asked. And, to his surprise, the barman accepted and poured himself a glass of Guinness. He fetched his newspaper over while Tom settled back onto the stool. He folded it to tabloid size, laid it flat on the bar adjacent to the Guinness pump and, resting his elbows either side of it, he continued to read.

***

The big feller looks like a Plastic Paddy. Probably one of those who's come back to search for their 'roots', which amounts to a nice living for the priests in the west. He seems slightly deranged to boot, knocking back the pints like he's got no clackers – at this time of the morning as well! I'd better keep an eye on him.

Hmm, let me see...

The headlines are all about Princess Diana – and Sinéad O'Connor, still, weeks after the event. Evidently, she burned a photo of the pope in front of millions of Americans. A shameless act, whichever way you look at it.

Turn the page and...

...And there's another story about poor Nan McCarthy's daughter, Maggie.

Poor Nan, she was so happy for Maggie. Pretty Maggie, off to England to live a new life and look how it all turned out. A widow at twenty-two years of age. A pub brawl they say, although it's been three months and they've yet to make an arrest in the case.

***

'You'll be heading for the UK, will you?' The barman barely looked up from the paper with his query.

'Yes, that's right, to London,' said Tom and he took a deep

draught of his pint. 'To see my ex-wife.'

'Ah, a romantic reunion, am I right?'

'Well, I wouldn't call it that so much.'

'So you'll be off there for a business visit...?'

'When it comes to my ex-wife, yes, you could say that.'

Tom ordered another pint and felt the need to explain that he first met Angela at a New Year's Eve party and that this would be a special trip over – one that he hoped would result in a reconciliation.

'She's led an independent life since leaving me,' he said, emptying his glass. 'She's a nurse, she's got her flat and she throws herself into her work.'

The barman had left a freshly poured pint on a bar towel and fallen quiet, his attention drawn back to the paper.

'I think I'll have a large Powers to chase that down with,' said Tom.

***

Thanks be to Christ, the feller's finished his order. Now, where was I?

Services are still being held for members of the Sullivan family from Bere Island who drowned two months ago. The appeal was launched a day after the tragedy, and since then donations have poured in for the poor orphans, the two family survivors who, on that day, chose not to row over to the mainland. Margaret and John Sullivan are now being looked after by...

This is the sort of tragedy that this drunkard wouldn't grasp at all. At least not the effect it has on people in the remote parts. Plastic Paddys. Fuck 'em all! They think they belong here but they don't even come close.

Hmm...

And here's a little piece about the government in the UK announcing measures to combat the latest spate of IRA bombings.

***

'They're talking about a "ring of steel" in London now.' The barman sipped thoughtfully at his glass.

'They need to throw a guarded wall around the whole place and not let any of the bastards out,' said Tom. 'The city went to the dogs a long time ago, like the rest of the God forsaken country.'

The barman let the subject lie.

'Over here on a visit are you?'

Tom looked the scrawny fellow over.

'No, I live in Bantry,' he said. 'I was born in Preston but my father was from Mayo and we only buried my poor mother in September. Her family were from Kerry.'

'Is that so...?' The barman's voice trailed off musically. 'And your wife lives...?'

'Ex-wife. She lives in Pimlico.'

'Ah! Pimlico, London. Now would that be inside or outside your wall?' The barman asked with a grin.

Tom smiled, in an absent way because his thoughts had already turned to the day he met her off the train from Euston. It was a dark November afternoon, the wind was merciless and there she was, stepping onto the platform in nothing more than a cotton dress – as if she was arriving at a West End nightclub. He had to wrap her up shivering in his coat on the bus, until they got to Uncle Bernie's pub, where Mary had fussed over her and dressed her up properly to face the Preston weather.

'She's a survivor, all right,' he said in a mutter, as much to himself.

***

The Irish economy is due for a huge boost once full union with Europe is achieved. This is, in no small part, due to the benefits to be had from joining the single European currency. Despite the political divide that still exists over the question, top economists are predicting good times to come...

***

Angela had once taken him walking on the Thames at low tide. It was a stifling day in early August and, as soon as they were down with the mudlarks, fat raindrops began to hit the ground. Dan was still in the East End with a bunch of squatters, but his band were beginning to make a name for themselves and Angela was in one of her more sympathetic moods. At least, that is until Tom mentioned his own plans.

He thought she would be pleased. He even imagined it would result in them getting back together. But when he told her he was taking up a pharmacy job at the hospital in Bantry, Angela became quiet and short tempered. Despite being struck off over here, he'd been able to land himself a good job in Ireland. After years of scraping by, he thought that being back in a decent earning bracket would help soften her up a bit.

The rain on the river bed had raised a rotten smell like a sewer, and Angela hurried them along to the next set of steps back up to the South Bank. As he watched her lift her skirt to climb the crooked slabs, he realised there was no chance that she would come over to Bantry with him.

'You'll be wanting better weather than this in London,' the barman spoke up. 'It looks to be settling in for the day.'

Tom lifted his head to peer into the little man's face

'It may be pissing down outside.' He finished his Powers. 'But at least the air here smells sweet.'

Part 2
A Few Bush Road Stories

Frank's Part in Doris' Escape

London, May 1985

Pass me one of those beers mate, and I'll tell you a tale about Bush Road. No charge involved, you're quite welcome.

Now back in the good ol' days, ideally speaking, you'd share the same house as your band mates. If you were in a band together, you were in everything together. Completely. Often lewdly. And sometimes, in one way or another, destructively.

Of the seven bands we had living along Bush Road, two of them had record deals and another two were on their way – although, at the time I'm about to recall they didn't know it. They were just a load of hopefuls on the dole with do-it-yourself hair thrashing through endless practice sessions in their front rooms.

There was one house with a pay phone that took incoming calls. It was where the Valley Dolls lived. People described them as post new-wave, whatever that meant. It was just guitars like chainsaws and someone banging a kettle drum, as far as I could tell. Mind you they were an all girl band, buxom and hard-looking, with a couple of tasty ones in their line-up. But the tastiest of the lot, Janie the bass player, was a rug muncher.

And then there was the one house in the street with a television. That was the Smokin Joes, and we all know their story. In those days, the Smokin Joes' gaff was pretty much my home – an ideal location to sell a bit of gear and pull some easy skirt. Good times, all in all.

For those in the street who had anyone who cared enough, the Valley Dolls was their connection with the outside world.

Now and then Janie would be seen running around in her espadrilles to haul someone out from their kitchen or bed or band practice and over to the phone. For Monica, the Dutch girl who hung out with the Smokin Joes, those calls came from South Africa. We would all shout 'Amandla!' as she scuttled out of the door, taking a cloud of chillum smoke with her.

I only had the one bunk-up with Monica. And truth be told, she was strange in bed. She just lay there still, without saying a word, and shuddered when she came, and she carried on shuddering for ages. And then, after an awkward length of time, individual tear-drops began to roll down her face. No sound, just the tears.

Anyway, the band that most of us thought would be odds-on rock stars was a hard driven three-piece from up north called Gang Finger. Their guitar player was a big, spikey-haired geezer, who played his instrument like he was wrestling a wild animal. It was said their gigs were a spectacle, though I'd never seen one. They rarely played live. But they managed to get a following amongst a load of smacked-up ex-punks who were happy just to watch them practice.

So, I was sat around theirs one night, passing a few lines round and listening to Small Faces on the stereo, when first there was mention of some bad luck in the offing.

We were in the downstairs front room where they'd opened up the fireplace and burned whatever wood they scavenged from building sites and suchlike. Sometimes on cold nights visitors would turn up with bits of fence or floor-boards, whatever broken timber they could get their mitts on, just to hang out in a warm, smoky room. But this particular night was quiet with just Dan, Jessie and my good self for company.

Tim, the guitar player, was spilled into an armchair with his hefty legs outstretched. His drummer Max was stoking the fire with a stick. He had a pink mohican, hardly said a word and always wore combats. It was said he once got banged up for hospitalising three coppers during the Toxteth riots. No-one knew much more about him – people just figured he was a violent little toe-rag.

Tim and Dan, as I recall, were in the middle of a debate. Something along the lines of whether there'd be a United States of Europe.

Dan was protesting that it would never happen. 'What about the Soviet Union?' he said.

Dan could never resist Tim's bait. And Tim would usually rip him to shreds – it couldn't be more one-sided if they actually had a punch-up. It would make me feel uncomfortable because I always wanted to look after Dan. Most people thought of him as a stoned hippie but I could see there was a little genius in there somewhere. And in the end I was proved right, wasn't I?

'Bollocks to the Soviets. They're a failed experiment, they don't matter,' Tim said, while I chopped up some lines and Helen walked in with mugs of tea clenched in both fists like knuckle-dusters.

Max thanked her – 'Ta Doris' – but his smile was menacing and he didn't stop stabbing the fire. Helen was his girlfriend, although she was more like the band's housemaid.

'Have we no biscuits Doris?' Max was quizzing her. 'Can you not fetch 'em in?' But Helen had spirit, despite the treatment she got. She sat down heavily and said, 'Get em yer fucking self.'

At which, Tim pursed his lips and said 'Oooh! Language, Doris!' in a theatrical voice.

And at that moment Jessie made the comment about the elephant.

Now Jessie really was a hippie. She even soaked herself in patchouli and dabbled in cards and runes, and all the rest.

'It's bad luck to keep an elephant indoors,' she declared with a knowledgeable air. We all looked at her as she stroked the large carved beast like it was a dog, running her hands up its rearing tusks. It was the only ornamental feature in the room, and a little over-sized I admit, but to call it ill-fated seemed like stretching it.

What eventually broke the silence was the snorting and sniffing that accompanied my first big hoover off the mirror, which I then held out, along with a rolled up fiver, in Dan's direction.

'Fancy a blast of Billy, mate?' I enquired.

And it was some weeks before the elephant was mentioned again.

So to cut to the chase, when this night was happening, I was still trying to work out a scheme to get a hold of Helen. She was pretty, with a sexy poise to her and page boy hair, and I badly wanted a taste. But, obviously, Max wasn't what you'd call generous in spirit. Violence was the only subject that seemed to excite him. So suggesting a two's-up or even a 'slice of the wife' was out of the question. I was going to have to do this one like a back door man.

And the incentive was there. The glances between me and Helen were like electric shocks. She was ripe and ready, I could tell, but even exchanging the looks felt risky. Because, although there was no chance that Tim, Dan or Jessie would have noticed, they were too busy chin-wagging, I was worried about Max. He was shifty and liable to go ape-shit at the drop of a hat.

Then, to rack up the danger, before I left that night I nipped down the corridor to the toilet and when I came out still zipping up, Helen leaped on me like – well, like a seasoned-up hyena. I had to peel her off me, an arm and a leg at a time. But I gave her a wink too, and a little squeeze on the backside so as to assure her I was working on a plan.

You could say Bush Road was a hotbed, pretty much everyone was at it. Tim took on most of his groupies like it was a duty. Often a few at a time, true to the band's name. Eventually he crossed paths with some jail-bait only to discover she was the little sister of a local crime family – and he soon disappeared.

It was said Monica was obsessed with Dan, like she fancied herself as some sort of Yoko from Utrecht. But it was also said that she serviced the whole band. Without doubt, Keith the

Keys helped himself to plenty of Monica's generous support – even bragging about getting in some Double Dutch with her and a journalist from an Amsterdam radio station, one night at a squat gig.

Which was nothing compared to when Monica fell in with Janie. Janie had long since been shagging Kim, who turned up at her door one day, a crop-topped sixteen year old runaway with specs. To most in Bush Road, Janie and Kim came across like a sweet, almost homely couple – but in fact they were well known in their scene for being insatiable, luring in and feasting on stray young birds and blokes alike.

So it happened that Monica was taking a call from Cape Town, while bombed on Lebanese Red, having been called over from a sunbathing session she was enjoying in the backyard of the Smokin Joes'. There she was, mincing about the hallway in a bikini top and a pair of beach shorts when Kim, as she put it to me herself, couldn't fight the urge to strip that horny tart's arse bare and give her a good thrumming (as she liked to say), there and then, while the poor girl was trapped at the payphone, fending off questions from her old man about her future. How could she have known how dirty her immediate future was about to get?

Despite all the goings on with Monica, as far as I knew, Dan never had a dabble. In fact, the only two couples to buck the trend of Bush Road were Dan and Jessie, and Max and Helen. Although, having said that, Jessie had plenty of previous, just that she managed to keep her urges in check for those first couple of years with Dan. At least, as far as I knew.

And with Helen, it was a case of being kept on a tight leash. Or kept as a slave, to be more accurate. Either way, it made my particular task very tricky. Which was why, when my opportunity finally did come, it had more to do with luck than cunning.

It happened to be the night of a big football match and everyone was round the Smokin Joes' watching the build-up on TV. Football was hardly popular along the street those days, but

Dan was a fan and I knew he'd be watching the European cup final. I laid my hands on a few Thai sticks and we had a bottle of Thunderbird each. And then, knock by knock, groups of people began to arrive, calling in by chance as it happens, until we had a full front room.

So how funny was it when full-scale violence broke out between rival fans before the game had even kicked off? For around an hour we were all treated to a live televised riot, thousands of them spilling on to the pitch wearing their football scarves like they were balaclavas. It was riveting viewing – at least until Jessie put a stop to it by wading through all the bodies on the floor and sawing the plug and around a foot of cable off the TV, which left Dan looking like he'd been slapped with an haddock. Jessie wasn't a football fan at all.

About half way through the action, Tim and Max had turned up. Word had got out to them that there was a live riot to be seen on the Smokin Joes' television. They more or less kicked the TV room door down in their rush to see what was going on.

'Scousers!' they roared. 'Fucking mental!'

And after a while, once they'd got drawn in to the violence, I couldn't help noticing that Helen wasn't with them. Through a sweet Thunderbird mist the realisation slowly dawned on me that this was the opportunity I'd been waiting for.

As far as I was concerned, my exit was swift and went largely unnoticed. I hauled myself up to my feet, at the point when a mounted police charge began, and announced to Dan in a voice not to be generally heard – 'I'm just nipping out to the phone box.'

Now 'the phone box' was a code I had with Dan. Whenever I needed a quiet word out of Jessie's earshot, I would invite him out to the phone box which was two turnings up Mare Street, on some pretend call or another.

I don't know why I used that particular ruse as I slipped out of the room, it was the first thing that came into my head. I could have been thinking that Dan would automatically understand what I was up to. Maybe.

When I reached the Gang Finger house and knocked on their door, the last door before the railway bridge, I could hardly have guessed that I would never do this again. Helen opened it a crack – I saw her eyes in the dark, peering around the door edge. Then when she saw it was me, she stepped back into the shadows and let me help myself in.

'Ya right, Frank,' she said, disappearing into the front room. And when I'd shut the door and caught up, I found her squatted at the fire, stoking it into a good roaring flame with a long stick.

It was probably just the sight of her on her haunches that prompted me to go at it there and then with barely an announcement. And at it did we go, like hammer and tongs, in a hot room in front of the fire, until Dan broke his way into the house by fiddling the lock through the letter box. He looked stunned at the sight of us. We'd torn each other's clothes off and were sweating and grunting on an old rug. We stopped mid straddle.

He finally spoke up, saying – 'Mate, you better get out of here. Max is looking for you.' And in a flash I rolled Helen over, leapt to my feet and wrestled my jeans back on.

'Oh, Jesus...' I was muttering.

And she was outraged, leaning on one arm asking where the fuck I was going.

I looked at her, stretched out next to the wood piles with her hair messed up. She looked such a doll – flushed, pouting and panting, with no urge for modesty despite Dan standing about like he'd seen a ghost.

'Darlin'...' I began, but she cut me dead.

'Don't think I won't tell him anyway,' she warned.

There was a sparkle in her eyes, which could have been mischief, anyhow I couldn't leave quick enough. But no-one was in the street waiting for me, like I imagined. Instead all was quiet. I hesitated, looking over at Dan for answers, half thinking I should go back inside to finish off what I'd started with Helen.

'I told Max you said you were going to the phone box,' he

explained.

'So what did he do?' I asked.

And Dan replied in a calm voice, as if he was talking about some old pensioner. 'Well he stayed for awhile, whilst the baton charge was still in full swing. And then he got up and left the house,' he said. 'I suppose he went to the phone box.'

So I asked Dan how he knew where to find me, and I couldn't help but switch my attention to the end of the road in case Max suddenly appeared from his fruitless trip up Mare Street.

Dan looked at me with a dull face.

'Frankie, mate, it was obvious what you were up to,' he said.

And a great surge of panic swept through me. There I was thinking I'd been subtle and crafty. Max must have known too. He was probably getting reinforcements or weapons or some-such.

'Come on mate, let's get back indoors,' I said, hustling Dan down the street. 'Safety in numbers.'

Well, how could we have known that Max was only after some whizz and, having stormed up to the phone box and not found me there, figured I must be at the Valley Dolls house where, upon bursting through their door, he would discover Janie, Kim and Monica at the hallway payphone, in the midst of a show-stopping scene involving some S&M gear, a tall stool and the phone receiver?

'Fucking hell, what the fuck's going on here?' was what I was told he said by Monica, a few nights later when I plied her with vodka, before he offered to replace the receiver. 'Much to Janie's delight.'

'Sure,' Janie apparently told him, 'but only if you wear a set of cuffs and a blindfold.'

It was just getting dark when me and Dan rejoined the football match in time to witness Jessie's big switch off. She held the sawn off plug and the wobbling blade in outstretched arms like a prize, like they were a sword and a severed head. The room broke out in groans and curses.

'You lot are all getting off on bad vibes!' she shouted. And, as everyone slowly drifted away, I began to feel the fear rising up in me. I couldn't help twitching the curtain back for the rest of the night keeping an eye out for signs of danger.

All Jessie seemed worried about was Monica: 'I hope Monica's OK, I haven't seen her since last night,' she said on more than the one occasion.

At the time I figured she'd probably gone off to Stonehenge to fight some Coppers.

'She'll be all right,' I said. 'She's harder than she looks.'

I suppose both Max and Helen went to bed with guilty consciences that night. They both had enough to feel guilty about. Or maybe they'd revealed all to each other in a foul-mouthed row. Either way, they were in bed together when they first caught whiff of the smoke.

To this day I can't help but wonder whether in some way I contributed to the destruction of No. 18 Bush Road, the Gang Finger house. I certainly thought I spotted smoke, and then flames, quite a while before saying anything to Dan and Jessie.

By the time the three of us arrived at the scene, a fair-sized crowd had gathered. We got there in time to find Max writhing about on the street, clutching his left shin. He'd just broken his ankle having leaped from the upstairs bedroom window. The ground floor window was gushing smoke, and flames licked around the frame. We could see Helen sizing up the leap, and looking down at us lot gathered around her man lying sprawled out on the pavement in his underpants and T-shirt. The smoke billowed above and beyond her but she made no immediate move.

Max shouted up at her, his voice gurgling with pain.

'Jump Doris! Jump!'

But Helen carried on looking down at us for a good ten seconds, before she pulled her head back into the bedroom, shouting, 'Fuck off, I'm walking!'

And sure enough, moments later, Helen appeared at the front door with a rucksack. She paused. We all did, I guess – it was a miracle she managed to get down the stairs alive. I suppose to her we must have looked comical, like a pantomime crowd at her doorstep.

And to me she looked like someone who was completely sure of herself. She was glowing and alive – a new person. Although it might have been the flames reflecting off the grime and sweat on her face.

'See ya!' she said. I think to all of us. Then she spun on her heel, and with her head held high, practically skipped out to the end of the street and off towards the tube station. She was wearing a long sleeveless vest, shorts and a pair of espadrilles.

Max was wailing on the floor, the rest of us were buzzing with it all and we could hear the sirens of the fire engines, when all of a sudden Tim staggered through the front door in a cloud of smoke. He was followed by a girl wearing one of his T-shirts. She was tiny, the shirt looked like a shin length dress on her.

Tim was crying. I guess from the smoke in his eyes.

'What the fuck are you lot doing?!' he croaked.

So it turned out that after the ambulance took Max away, we would see neither him nor Helen again. Tim turned up at various addresses for a while until he finally disappeared, leaving behind a confusion of rumours. Some said he ran away with an advance from a record company. But we figured it was more likely his brush with the criminal underworld. Either way, he never showed up in Bush Road again.

Monica? Well, her story went from bad to worse to better again. I'll save that for another time. But I can say that her life took a strange twist when she was found one night carrying a kidnapped baby down the middle of Holloway Road.

And the day after Helen left – when me, Dan and Jessie peered through the gaping hole in the wall where the fire had eaten through the front window, it was obvious how the blaze had taken hold. Like the ashes of a funeral pyre, a pyramid had formed around the charcoaled skeleton of an elephant the size of a Labrador.

Jessie, of course, was well smug.

'Told ya!' she said.

The Making of Frank and Monica

Summer 1984

There's a sign on the basement door, the door into the Smokin Joes' studio, which has a little stick man being struck down by a bolt of lightning – Danger of Death, it says. Then you step inside and you're met by a waft of stale, electrified air. Air thick with old fags, spilled beer and sweat. And the band chop their lines up on top of a PA speaker stack, one that stands about chest height. Picture that and you're seeing what it was like when we first started out at No. 1 Bush Road.

But anyway, to rewind a bit, on this particular occasion I have enough of my fortnight's cash left for a few drinks at the Crowns when I decide to get the night going.

To give you a measure, my giro gets me three and a half grams of speed, a good breakfast, forty fags and enough change for a couple of nights out in the pub. The speed helps me supplement the whole show. Sometimes I can sell a couple of grams, make enough for another three and a half and keep that routine going for the best part of two weeks.

So I've just cooked up my last but one hit of a dwindling supply – earlier than planned, as a warm summer sun is setting and I fancy getting my rocks off – and I tip out a strong one while Exile on Main St kicks out of the stereo.

It takes the whole of side one, but once the rush subsides I jump up, grab my jacket and jog down to the basement. And here I am, in front of the little man getting struck by lightning. I open the basement door to find the band in the midst of a frenzied number. They don't even notice me. Fuck 'em. I need to get moving. And I'm off.

Half hour later and I find myself at the bar of the Crowns, leaning over the counter, looking down the barmaid's T-shirt as she bends into the glass-washer. A blues band is due on but they're still sound checking, which means at least ten minutes until they start, and that's when I feel a tap at my shoulder.

'Awright Frankee!'

And it's little Vinny grinning up at me with his few good teeth.

'Right Vin, 'sappening mate?'

'Good fings, Frankee. Good fuckin fings.' His breath stinks of cheese and onion crisps and his eyes are pinned.

Vinny's an old punk, even his red mohican looks grey at the roots, and I note the bright mischief in his face. Needless to say, I figure ten minutes would be well enough time to get into plenty of useful mischief myself.

'Go on, Vin. I'm interested.'

***

With the weather getting warmer, I'd been keeping a watch over the tree. The branches rode up against the little balcony of my bedroom and, as the mornings became brighter I'd look into them, watching them swell and bloom. The blossoms were beautiful that spring and I figured there'd be plenty of cherries.

The thought of cherry pie, made from fruit I had picked, was like imagining a banquet. Since my parents left for South Africa in January, food had become scarce. They sent money for their 'precious Monica' regularly, but that mainly paid for clothes and nights out, the usual college expenses. Food was about staple dieting – if it was good enough for most of the world's population, it was good enough for me. The fact that there was a cherry tree in the garden felt like a karmic reward.

Over the two months of summer I would open those balcony doors onto the early morning – and sit with my feet on the railings, smoking a joint, while the cherry branches stretched, flowered and finally popped their fruit. The leaves hummed those mornings, while I broke the day in hazily before getting dressed for college. A breeze blew through the open balcony, which would make the hair on my legs stand up, and low sunlight would split between the branches throwing bony shadows across the floor.

***

The last cubicle in the Crowns' gents is known, amongst a select few, as the Doors of Perception, into which slips me and Vin. Whereupon he produces a little foil of top quality brown sugar, just the right thing to balance out the whizz. I'm about to light up a fag to mask the chasing smells, when there's a bang and a clatter and the sound of hasty boots from the bar through to the toilet. Then a leather jacket comes flying over into the cubicle and I can hear the sound of someone scrambling through the window into the back alley.

Vinny is holding the jacket weakly, as if it is some kind of religious object, staring at it and turning it over in his hands.

Next up there's a sound like a herd of startled bullocks storming into the gents. Police, it would seem, judging by the crackle of radios.

'Bollocks! He's out the back!' one of them shouts and I stand frozen and shaking. Whatever they're after is probably in the jacket and here's me and Vin in the Doors of Perception, with a wrap of smack and some freshly burned foil.

But, miraculously, they all exit as quick as they came in and, in a flash, so do me and Vin. Following in their slipstream, so to speak. And as they all scamper around the back, so we stroll, at a fair pace mind you, directly out the front. And we don't stop walking until we reach Vin's flat in Islington.

Once the door is shut and latched behind us, we both collapse with laughter, holding our ribs until it hurts. And then we finally get around to frisking the jacket.

In the breast pocket we find a coin bag swollen with the pure driven snow.

Time to think.

***

Of course, I always played my side of the game and called Mr and Mrs van Der Merwe my parents but they adopted me as a three year old, and that was a fact I grew up with. They were kind to me, in their own way, but the ebb and flow of their own lives always seemed to be more important.

They were academics, both earned good incomes, and they regularly had to attend a talk on politics here or a conference on Third World development there.

By the end of that summer, once I'd become a regular at the Smokin Joes' house, I would get taunted about my parents. But, to tell the truth, I still couldn't say for certain what they were actually doing back in South Africa. Just that they went suddenly, with work to do – and they left me, at eighteen years of age, in charge of a three story town house with a free rein and a modest monthly income.

But I hadn't used and abused the place the way I might have been expected to. I simply let it grow untidy and become natural and, apart from the occasional college friend dropping by, I kept it mostly to myself. Grime had built up on the ground floor windows and the garden had turned into a tangle. I enjoyed watching nature getting a run at the house for a change. It was a different way to look at home, and I had begun to look at the idea of 'home' very differently during that time.

This house was not home. It was a place we moved in to almost two years ago. Utrecht was not home either – it was true to say that it was the city I grew up in, and it contained the streets my natural mother still survived in, as far as I knew. But I felt separated from even the memory of it.

It was one morning that summer, as the cherry branches stirred and scraped at the balcony railings, that I began to find my true home – the place and the people I belonged with.

***

So, in what seems no time at all, we're in Vinny's van and heading down an A road off the M3. It's well past midnight, but we're expected at our destination. Vin made a few calls from the local phone box after we'd sampled the Charlie in the jacket. It fell onto the mirror in little crystals and was as clean as anything we'd ever tasted. We both agreed that we'd stumbled upon a small fortune, if we could find somewhere to offload it.

And half hour after hitting the A road we're sat with Vin's mate, who's called Tony, and a beady-eyed student in the front room of a house in some leafy Surrey town. Tony is carefully razoring a couple of crystals on a small round mirror, when Vin excuses himself to go to the bog.

'Who's yer mate wiv the dodgy Stones?' asks the student, in a strange take-off of a Cockney accent. I give Tony a puzzled glance and he shrugs his shoulders.

'What?' I say.

'You know, wiv all his Mick and Keef missing.'

'Oh, fuck,' I can't help but smile, 'that's Vinny, mate. The last of the Mohicans.'

Tony bursts out laughing and almost blows the lines off the mirror.

I watch as they both have a dab and a snort, and a little squeeze of the packet and then they weigh it up and begin to make their calculations. And I make sure to retrieve the goods while they have a quiet chat by the stereo.

Vin returns to the front room and slaps his hands together, 'What's the SP?' he asks.

'Top quality gear,' says Tony.

'It's the chicken's lips, mate,' I say. I want them to know that we know how good our gear is too.

'It weighs in a few grams over an ounce, so we'll take the Oz for a grand,' says the beady-eyed student, making the first move.

'Nice one mate!' yells Vin, his face beaming with delight.

'Hang about,' I say. 'You can double that at least, when you've cut it up. You're laughing here.'

The three of them are looking me over closely. I don't want to blow this. Five hundred notes from nowhere is a big prize.

'So how about me and Vin get to share a quarter, and you keep the rest for a grand?'

It's no big haggle, I saw the scales hit just under an ounce and a quarter. They'll still get twenty-five gs and without hesitation they agree and begin the weigh out. Vin gives me an appreciative nod, to acknowledge my cool style of bargaining, and the divvying up is concluded before Tony sets off into a session, rolling the joints as fast as the lines get cut.

Some while later, I realise I'm bursting and find my way to the back garden where I merrily piss against the side fence to a noisy dawn chorus. I'm just zipping up when I spot a few ripe cherries in the branches above me and, while I reach up to pluck them, I see the doors open on the balcony next door and out steps a gorgeous bird in a skimpy nightie. She is one tasty package, with pouty lips like Debbie Harry, and I can't resist watching as she settles into a low-slung, cane chair and proceeds to light herself a smoke. With her feet on the balcony railings, and the breeze lifting her nightie skirt, I can see tantalising glimpses of her tidy little minge. Cherry juice begins to trickle down my chin and there's a tent-pole in my combats.

Just then I hear the sound of crashing and wood splintering from inside Tony's house and I jog to the back door to have a shifty. All it takes is a blurry glimpse of blue uniforms pouring through the front door and I'm away, climbing the fence and up into the cherry branches, scrambling as fast and high as possible, when all of a sudden I'm looking straight at the girl on the balcony, who smiles blearily and says, 'Hi!' She's talking in a European accent, I can't make out which one.

'Careful with my cherries,' she says, and I burst out laughing.

'Sorry darlin', sorry,' I say, as I clamber over her railings.

'I've been watching you,' she says, 'you're running from the police, aren't you?'

'Er, seems so,' I say, a little bemused and I duck out of any possible view from next door.

'It's OK, they do it all the time,' she explains, 'Tony says they just take their cut and away they go.'

I notice it's a joint she's smoking, Temple Ball judging by the oily whiff.

'D'you mind if I sit it out, all the same? Rozzers make me nervous.'

'Cool,' she says and offers me a toke.

***

I noticed him straight away, as I stepped out onto the balcony that morning. He was peering over next door's fence, through the branches, and he looked like Ian Dury's younger brother – like a West Side Story gang member. I felt a shiver run through me, imagining his life and wondering what he was doing in Tony's garden. Well, I could guess, but it was difficult to picture Tony hanging out with someone so cool. Then I heard the police arrive with crashes and shouts and I watched as he wrestled his way into the tree for escape.

Next thing, he had hopped onto the balcony and, with an impish smile, he suggested he ride out the raid with me. Once we had shared a smoke he produced some cocaine, which we both snorted off an upturned mirror on my dressing table. Then we drank coffee while he told me about where he lived.

The more I heard, the more I knew this was my future – hanging out with a working band, the rock and roll, all-hours lifestyle. I had to be there. Instead of mock film assignments at college, here was a chance to record the real thing, on my own portable video camera.

After we smoked another joint, I let him stroke my leg for a while. He did it shyly at first, and then he felt his way up my nightie, kneading and fingering. It was enjoyable enough, I hadn't slept with a guy for almost a year. I'd been trying out girls and lately I was with a nice, straight-laced college friend called Ruth, who was very tender and serious. Frank was urgent and rough. He kept flipping me one way and the next, until he finally spent himself and I could catch my breath.

It was some hours later when Frank started up again. He wanted to give me an orgasm, and I didn't resist. It seemed to mean a lot to him, so I looked up at the ceiling and imagined the suddenness of it all. I thought of this good-looking guy climbing up to my bedroom balcony and taking me wordlessly – and then I visualised more. I pictured combinations of bodies, Ruth and Frank and Tony, and my imaginings became so depraved that the orgasm rippled and then washed right through me.

I felt alive and tears of joy slid down my cheeks. Frank was concerned but there was no need. It was something I couldn't possibly communicate to him. He chopped some more lines, as a means of distraction, and I shivered in the knowledge that I had found my place. And that the person to take me there had found me through the cherry tree.

***

It's a day and a half later and with our heads full of Charlie, Monica dishes out the cherry pie. We'd spent an hour riffling that tree for every ripe one we could find and now we're guzzling the results with gusto, served up with piles of blobby cream, until we finish the lot.

We only had the one bunk-up, as soon as we met, but we slept together like spoons from last night to this afternoon and now, having eaten two dishes of pie, we're ready to head back for town.

The warm evening air feels exciting and I realise I'm looking forward to getting home, as we catch a train to Victoria and jump on the 38 from there. The conductor is a rasta, content to stand in his cubbyhole playing the blues harp, and Monica is buzzing at the free ride. Her face looks alight. From our stop at

Graham Road, I lead her across London Fields back home and I shut the door behind us, shouting out a greeting.

There's no reply, but the sound of chunky guitar chords can be heard from the basement and I take Monica's hand and guide her downstairs. We pause at the sign on the door.

'House motto,' I say.

'Oh, so you don't just come to Farnham for your danger then?' she replies, cheekily.

'Some danger,' I say, with all the suave disinterest I can muster. And she raises her eyebrow.

'Arrangements with bent coppers...?' I'm already pushing my way in and there's the band still working on the same number as when I last saw them. The blast of sound feels like a gust of wind.

'Oh, I made that up,' says Monica, casually, as we step in, 'to put you at ease.'

Thoughts of Vinny flash through my mind. I have visions of him being held in some provincial cell, scared shitless. Then it passes, as the band stops mid-number and I introduce Monica as a film-maker. They greet her warmly and she hugs them all like close friends and they use the moment to crack open some beers and have a smoke.

With four hundred and fifty quid still sitting snugly in my pocket, I tip Monica a wink and then nip upstairs to chop a couple more crystals. All in all, I'd have to say, a good result for your average, mid-giro nose around in the Crowns.

Monica's Moment of Truth

September 1986

'When I first pitched up in London I was only sixteen,' said Liam tunefully, almost like he was singing the Pogues song.

'And I did go down the 'dilly, and Leicester Square, and Seven Dials. Or, at least, go down in them. Many times.' He threw his head back as he laughed.

'I've rubbed shoulders and more, with all sorts. You wouldn't believe it!' he continued.

'Some punters give you presents, there's some that give you infections and just a few give you nothing. They're the worst. And the scariest. As soon as they refuse to pay, it dawns on you that they might be after something else. Something more than the deal.'

Monica lit a cigarette and cradled her mug of tea with both hands. She was sitting cross-legged on a council-blue carpet as Liam lay sprawled on a beanbag. These were the moments she was spending before Frank turned up with the speed. She tapped her fingers rapidly on her mug, likewise her right foot on the carpet.

Monica wasn't even sure why Liam was here in the first place. She'd been out with friends last night at a gay club, where she found him in a figure-hugging red dress. She made the mistake of admiring him and he seemed to latch on to her from then on.

'Why are you here?' she asked, and he laughed again.

'For the same reason as you sister, the same reason as you.'

Liam gave her a keen look but she was blank for a moment,

and then it slowly came back to her. Oh, of course – he was after some gear off Frank. But he probably wasn't coming down as badly as she was.

'It'll be good, I promise,' she said. 'Frank always has the best.'

A short rap at the front door stopped the conversation at that point. Monica turned to look out towards the hallway, her eyes sparkling in the low-lit bedroom.

Ruth made her way along a bleak stretch of road – there was an arched brick railway line on one side and crumpled house fronts, the end block of a housing estate and the odd, shabby corner shop on the other. She walked this stretch for what felt like half an hour, dragging along her suitcase with a belt, the evening traffic churning up fumes around her. And just as twilight gathered, at the point where she began to doubt the accuracy of her directions, she came upon Bush Road.

It was then she wondered how Monica would be. She wondered if she'd changed at all. It had been over a year since Monica finally dropped out of college and left Farnham for London. She'd been spending more and more time with some musicians she met. Such a pity. She was a gifted artist in her own right but one that, quite simply, hadn't found her medium.

Before leaving, Monica had told her that any time she found herself in London she was welcome to stay, and to look for her in Bush Road. So, here she was.

Ruth peered down a row of brick terraces, with a narrow strip of footpath to open their doors onto. The road was dissected half way along by the railway bridge. It looked like Coronation Street. She felt a shiver run through her.

Dan and Frank were in the throes of a quick march down Mare Street. Both were elated for their own reasons. Dan had earlier finished a recording session in the basement which resulted in the first fully arranged track of the demo tape, and Frank had just secured some high-grade, unadulterated methedrine imported from Amsterdam at a very reasonable price. They'd chanced across each other at the Crowns, each having stopped in to mark their joy with a pint.

Now they were eager to close the door of No.1 behind them and continue their revelries in the confines of their home. A stiff wind was beginning to whip up, blowing dust and plastic bags into the air. Rush hour was thinning but the drivers were still ill-tempered, all horn and shaking fists.

'What's the betting there'll be some kind of girly gathering indoors?' Frank had been chattering away happily the whole walk back from the Crowns, but Dan had zoned in and out as he reconsidered the final mix and wondered whether, in fact, the drums should have been more 'up front'.

'Drugs and shagging,' thought Dan, 'the man's obsessed.'

'Oh, it's you... wow,' said Monica as she opened the door to Ruth. 'What are you doing here?'

Ruth dropped her suitcase and wobbled just slightly, hoping Monica hadn't noticed, before she recovered herself and said, 'Monica, I've been accepted at St Martin's. I start on Monday. You said I could stay and I wrote you a letter saying I was coming. It'll only be until I find myself somewhere.'

'I didn't get a letter,' said Monica, turning to go back inside.

Ruth peered down a dark, cobwebbed hallway, towards a bare light-bulb way back in a rear kitchen. Monica had veered off into a side room, opposite a staircase that disappeared up into an inky void. Ruth dragged her suitcase in behind her and it slid over a mess of papers strewn across the floor. She glanced around the walls which were covered in posters and home-printed flyers. She thought she could hear some music coming from somewhere in the building – a drum beat, maybe from upstairs. There was a musty smell in the air. Then her suitcase snagged on a heavy rug, causing her to stumble.

Liam kept an eye on Monica's arse as she leaped up and wiggled out to the front door. He couldn't help but watch her.

He'd been watching her ever since he laid eyes on her at around 3 am at the Black Cat. He spotted her as she teetered out of the ladies, a little tipsy maybe, but she held her head high. And she looked cool in her funky heels. She was just the kind of pouting pussy that Liam pretended to be. He was small and tightly bundled too, but he couldn't get that wiggle off as naturally as she could.

He wasn't sure, at that point, what he wanted from her. He simply felt a longing to possess her in some way. To embody her. Perhaps if they were to become inseparable, like lovers, they could merge into a hot little package. Two slightly cracked Bardot sisters for the streets of London.

Liam was sitting upright adjusting his stockings, running his hands down his thighs, checking for smoothness, when Monica came back from the front door and flopped down next to her ashtray. He was about to say something when he heard the thud of Ruth's suitcase toppling over in the hallway.

'I hope Frank gets here soon,' Monica mumbled.

Dan and Frank stumbled through the front door, their boots slipping across piles of junk mail that had been accumulating on the mat. Without a word they made for the kitchen, feeling their way along a blind stretch of hallway with just the bare bulb ahead to aim for. Dan had left his weed on the kitchen table earlier – he remembered its whereabouts as he caught the first whiff of it in the air. He wanted to roll a pokey smoke so badly he began to stagger with the thought, but Monica's voice from the back bedroom stopped him in his tracks.

'Dan – is Frank with you?' she asked.

Before Dan could speak, Frank popped his head around the doorway.

'Allo gorgeous, I've come especially to see you,' he said.

'Oh god, Frank,' she said, 'have you got anything on you?' She looked up at him pleadingly.

'Ah, a damsel in distress,' said Frank. 'Sir Lancelot to the rescue!'

'You have?'

Dan took the opportunity to fetch his weed from the kitchen and put on the kettle.

'Blimey!' Frank spotted Liam. 'Who's this?'

Ruth felt invisible from the moment she stepped into the room where, she found, everything was at floor level. The seating consisted of a bare, single mattress and a beanbag, which at that very moment was occupied by someone who looked like a cheap tart. Ruth couldn't determine whether it was a girl or a boy. The only light came from a dark red lamp in the corner of the room, on the floor. A stereo tape player was next to it with piles of cassettes spewed across the carpet, mostly out of their cases. The one window, which must have looked out onto the rear of the house, was covered over with a black stage curtain.

Monica had barely glanced up at her, instead she rocked backwards and forwards, sucking deeply on a roll-up. The tart exclaimed 'Oooh, what have we got here?' through pursed lips. Ruth gulped, and tucked her skirt under her legs as she took a seat on the mattress.

Monica *had* changed. She was still the same intense-looking, pretty girl from Farnham but she had lost a spark somewhere. And, in arriving like this at her house, it seemed Ruth had upset her.

All of which meant she was glad when the two boys turned up at the doorway. Their grinning, mischievous faces resembled something like normality. And it did the trick of cheering Monica up immensely.

Monica had been completely thrown by Ruth's arrival. It had taken her a moment to remember who she was. This was the last person she expected to see at the doorstep. It was as if someone from another world had followed her into this one. She immediately felt a wave of paranoia. Why had Ruth come? What was she up to? Had she been sent by the Van der Merwes?

Back at art college Ruth had been the class darling, talented and upbeat. She had everything going for her and still managed to carry herself without a trace of snobbery or conceit. Monica couldn't help but respond to the attention Ruth had shown her around the campus. Those were anchor-less days for Monica, her parents had suddenly left the country and she had no place she felt she belonged. But she did have a steady friend – reliable Ruth.

Still, that was the way the friendship should have stayed. Ruth had once been reliable for Monica. There was no way, right now, that Monica could imagine being of any use to Ruth whatsoever, except for offering her some floorspace and a beanbag for a pillow.

'I once got picked up outside Liverpool Street Station,' said Liam, 'and this guy took me to his swish flat in the Barbican. And you'll never guess what he asked me to do!'

'No!' Frank spluttered. 'Go on!'

'He paid me fifty pounds to tie him up in a sack and kick him.' Liam took a very matter of fact sip of tea.

'Unbelievable!' said Frank, 'What a job! I would have done it for a tenner.'

Liam slurped suggestively at the rim of his mug.

'Would you?' he asked, as he watched Frank sift out the lumpy powder onto a mirror the size of a tabloid. Three chunky mounds.

Behind him, by the mattress, the hippie-looking guy was sitting cross-legged chatting to Monica's prudish visitor, while Monica herself continued to rock on her haunches, her head cocked towards their conversation. Strains of Velvet Underground drifted through the house from a room somewhere above them.

Frank paused to accept a spliff, which was passed to him over his shoulder, and he proceeded to draw on it lustily.

Liam couldn't help but wonder whether Frank might be inclined towards a bit of the other, so to speak. He had a cheeky charm to him, and a glint in his eye that suggested he knew his way around the block.

Liam watched closely while Frank tugged the spliff-end a fiery red.

Monica was watching too. She was waiting for him to pass on the joint and get back to chopping up the whizz. The small talk had become pretty much unbearable.

Ruth had been telling one of the boys about her postgraduate place at St Martin's, how she liked to work with three dimensional form, and the importance of texture.

'Ultimately, you should be able to get your hands on a good piece of art,' she told him.

She declined the joint when it was offered to her, but for some reason she took the rolled up ten pound note and leaned in to the mirror. It was as if she did it by reflex. She didn't think anything of it. And, as her nostrils filled up with sour phlegm, she sniffed and wiped her nose on her shirt-cuff like a builder.

He didn't say much in return but he seemed kindly and interested, and Ruth was glad to have someone to chatter away to, although it wasn't long before she felt herself blurting. Then suddenly, in a puff of smoke, the boy was gone.

And Ruth found herself lying down, presumably on the mattress, looking up into three peering faces, their expressions ranging from amusement to concern. Then the strangest anxiety took hold of her, coursing through her limbs like rigor mortis, begging the question of herself – how was she ever going to be able to live a normal life after this? Which was when Ruth realised she would never be the same again. A thought so awful she felt it physically. How could she possibly have her little baby now?

'My baby!' she began shouting, and she could feel her arms being restrained as she wriggled and twisted. She tried to shake the thoughts from her head but instead her mouth filled with foam, which seeped through the gaps in her teeth and spilled down her chin and neck. Cold, trickly rivulets creeping down her neck.

And then she felt herself being lifted and carried away.

***

'In the upshot, the ambulance men stretchered her off to the Whittington.'

'OK,' Jessie was looking at Dan closely now, 'what exactly happened?'

'Well it was like this...'

'Here we go,' said Frank.

'Like I said, it seems she turned up out of the blue, an old friend of Monica's from Farnham. She needed a place to stay for awhile.'

'Straight as a die,' said Frank, 'well boaty.'

'She told me she was a sculptor. Wood and stone, she said. And that she was due to start at St Martin's on Monday. She figured from there she'd find a flat-share with students. It was just for a few days.'

'So what happened?' asked Jessie.

'Well, then I came up here to see you. And when I went back down to make the tea, she was having a fit of some kind.'

'I guess the speed disagreed with her,' said Frank.

'She went into a psychotic fit, they said. She had to be strapped to the stretcher when they took her out to the ambulance.'

'It is, pretty much, pure meth,' said Frank.

'So why did she have some?' snapped Jessie.

'Hey, don't blame me!' Frank raised his hands. 'She couldn't snatch the tenner out of my hand quick enough.'

'It was an awful fucking pity, that's what it was. How was anyone to know something like that would happen? The poor girl is just starting out. She wants to do things.' Dan puffed his cheeks. 'I hope she recovers.'

With that, he leaped to his feet and left the room.

Frank and Jessie were silent, swapping glances. And then Jessie spoke up.

'So what did happen?'

'Well, that's a good question,' said Frank. 'I was distracted by this gorgeous tranny. If I didn't know, I'd have probably given her one. Or him, I should say. Given him one. Anyway, Monica was in one of her usual, gagging to get shit-faced, moods...'

'Yeah, fuck all that,' said Jessie, leaning to flip the album over. 'Tell me what happened with this girl.'

Frank took a deep breath, finished rolling his cigarette and began, just as the chimes of *Sunday Morning* started up.

'Like yer man, Dan, said, she seemed a sweet bird. You know, innocent, she looked a bit out of her depth. Anyway, she was chattering away to Dan for a while, and then I noticed her voice getting louder. She sounded a bit crazy and her laughter was more like a cackle, which made me turn around and I realised Dan wasn't there any more, and Monica wasn't paying any attention. So she was cackling and babbling to herself. Well out of it.

'Next thing I know, she's lying on the mattress, thrashing her arms and legs, screaming about her baby. And we're all asking – What baby? – as we're trying to hold her down. And Monica runs across the road to the pay phone, to call the ambulance.

'It was mayhem. Her face looked blue by the time they got here.'

Frank could see the worry creeping into Jessie's face.

'It's all right,' he said, 'we told 'em she turned up at the door like that.'

Jessie said nothing as Lou Reed's voice faded out with the song.

***

Liam was putting on his stockings, using the hotel room sofa as a footrest. He felt like a performing artist, with classic rock on the radio and a neon Soho skyline as his backdrop. He enjoyed dressing in front of certain punters, and Paul was one of them – it was always a gentle, easy gig with Paul who was now sitting up in bed, smoking. And watching Liam.

Paul was not only likeable, he was also generous with the cocaine. Liam was still sniffing back the residue of their parting line and it was the tinkle of a Velvet Underground song that triggered a memory.

'Did I ever tell you about the girl who went mad after a line of speed?'

Paul chuckled and shook his head.

'Go on,' he said.

'Well,' Liam began, 'this is going back many years, but it happened that I was at the house the Smokin Joes lived in. The band that did *Incarceration* – before they made it, mind you. Not that I knew anything about it. I was there because I'd fallen for a sultry sex kitten I met at a club the night before.'

Liam snapped his garters, and smoothed his dress over the suspender belt before grabbing his make-up bag. He stopped on his way to the mirror and threw Paul a stare.

'This girl was unbelievably sexy,' he said.

'Ooh, a girl! You kinky bitch!' Paul waved his cigarette hand at Liam. 'And then she goes and freaks out on you...!'

'Oh no, she didn't go mad, not then at any rate. Her old school friend was the one that got herself fried on the speed.' Liam was re-applying his lipstick, checking his neck for bite marks.

'She was like Dorothy in the Land of Oz. She was a twee little country girl in her Laura Ashley, who'd come to stay in London for the first time, with her friend, the horny little dyke.'

'And then what?' asked Paul.

'Well, she happened to stumble into a bit of party. The boy from the band had some top quality Thai weed and there was this cute Jack-the-Lad who was dishing out the pure methedrine.'

'I can sense what's coming,' said Paul.

Liam fluffed his hair and wiggled his bra snugly around his breasts. He was proud of his breasts, the way the pill had developed them over the last six years.

'You'd be surprised, darling,' he said, 'she joined in the chit-chat and snorting with gusto, but I guess she overdid it. And it sent her over the edge.'

Liam perched himself by Paul's hip on the bed.

'The thing is, what surprised us all was that it was so sudden. It's like, she was here one moment and gone the next.'

'Just like you, baby,' said Paul. 'Just like you.'

***

Monica opened the front door to the muffled thud of the drum kit from the basement. It seemed early for a practice session. She'd just got in from shopping at Spitalfields, a late run at the veg stalls when the best haggling was to be done. Normally, at this time, any activity in the house would be centred around the kitchen.

She stepped uncertainly on a pile of junk mail which was growing by the day beneath the letter box. The effect of all the paper, well trodden underfoot by a procession of boots and high heels, was like an ice patch. People had fallen over here on arrival, sometimes injuring themselves.

She decided it was time to clear all the rubbish away from the front door, so she dumped her shopping bags in the kitchen and fetched the bin liners. Bills and letters to tenants long gone, menus and brochures, they all disappeared into a black bag under Monica's fierce sweep. That is, until she noticed her name on a letter and drew to a stand-still.

She held the ragged, boot-printed envelope and looked at it for a long while. Just the touch of the paper made her feel weak. It was as if her heart had fallen through her stomach. In the days and weeks since that awful evening, Monica had successfully avoided thinking about 'the visit'. It was like it had never happened. Like Ruth was still just a friend she once made at college in Farnham.

Ruth said that she had written her a letter...

Monica began to shake and she retreated like a robot to the beanbag in her room, holding the envelope in front of her. There was hardly a sound in the house, just the rumble and thud from the basement. It sounded like a warm up, disorganised and disjointed – a cymbal crash.

And then, what the hell, she ripped open the letter, unfolded the paper and read...

Dear Monica,

Hope I find you well – and hope you don't mind me asking you a favour at such short notice.

You once told me that I could come and stay with you whenever I was in London – well, I'm coming this Friday. I'm starting a Post-Grad at St Martin's and I already have commissions for shows. So I hope it's all right if I take up your offer. Just until I get my own place.

And there's more I want to talk to you about. It's best done face to face, when I see you, because it sounds crazy otherwise. But do you remember when we used to talk about how we could bring up a kid together? How we'd show them how it ought to be done?

Well, I just might be.

And if so, daddy's upped and left.

So we may get the chance, if you're game.

I had some idea of a funky house full of artists, and my

sculptures in the garden, and you – Monica – finally accepting that photography is your medium. So, you're busy in your dark-room, and off on photo shoots. And I'm in my studio – a garden annexe. There'll be a rose arch, and herb borders, and we can grow vegetables. And I want framed, stained-glass art-works in the windows.

There's so much we need to catch up on – I'm really looking forward to seeing you.

I know to head for Bethnal Green tube and I have directions from there so I reckon I can find your place. You told me the house at Bush Road has plenty of comings and goings – so put the word out that I'm coming!

We need to talk!

Lots of love, Ruth xx

***

Frank stepped tentatively through the door, expecting the usual slip and slide, but his foot met sure ground. The mound of junk mail was gone. Someone must have finally tidied up. He straightened his waistcoat and took a long stride into the house, throwing the door shut behind him. Within steps of the back bedroom he could smell the smoke. He paused at the doorway and looked in to find Monica sitting on the floor, her head drooping low over a tin ashtray. Flakes of burned paper were drifting in the air around her. The room was quiet, still and in semi-darkness.

'What's going on here then?' he asked, and Monica looked up at him emptily. She said nothing.

'Er, I only ask because I was looking for someone to share a line with, and to come out for a beer after,' said Frank, and

Monica's face began to brighten.

'Because the fact of the matter is, we've got to keep bobbing and weaving, moment by moment. And right now I feel like bobbing with my best mate and sister sulphate.'

And hours later, when they got back, they didn't even think about the certainty of their footing as they both skipped into the house laughing.

Dan and Jessie on Different Roads

May 1988

The tarmac ribbons away through the hills on a late Spring day. This should be a happy moment, thinks Jessie, as she looks out over cloud shadows sliding across green fields. After all, here she is, strolling in a soft breeze with the natural world chirping and rustling all around her. Nonetheless, a sense of unease is beginning to shiver through her limbs and stomach.

The road she's on is empty in either direction. She feels like this could be another time in history. It could be any time. The rural air is fizzing with insects and Jessie can't help but wonder what kind of lift she's likely to get around here.

She should just keep walking anyway. It certainly is beautiful countryside to be walking in.

***

Dan is appreciative of his lift away from the Taunton roundabout. This place is notorious for the police rounds and Dan's loaded up with the band recreationals. It's a bad idea to be hanging around here for too long.

Jessie decided to take a detour at the previous junction. He hadn't felt good about letting her go but she was insistent. She wanted to pick up her friend Babs, from Somerton, and bring her along to the gig. Dan hadn't the time to argue. He had a venue to get to and a pocket full of hash, tabs and powders. And all of a sudden, without Jessie, the lifts had dried up. It had taken almost an hour to get this far.

So, as the little blue escort van skids to a halt, Dan feels the joy erase his worries. He jogs up, holding his guitar case, and sees yellow sunflowers painted along the van sides. A small hippie emerges from the driver's side and gestures at him in an irritated way.

'Get round the back. You'll have to get in the back!' he's saying. He looks like some kind of elf, with his fair pointy beard.

Dan skips jauntily in reverse to the rear of the van and the back doors are thrown open to reveal four squaddies in combat gear. The elf says, 'You'll have to find a space in amongst this lot,' and Dan pauses for a moment, looking at them, before suggesting cheerily, 'Shall I just squeeze in here next to the doors?' – to be met by silence. Not even a flicker of acknowledgement.

Fuck it. Dan crawls in anyway. He needs to get away from the Taunton roundabout. The elf shuts the doors, slides the bolt, bounds around to the driver's seat and shuts his door. A woman is sitting in the front next to him. She has a kindly-looking, round face. Dan can see it in profile as she gazes across at the little bloke. Her eyes are moist and sparkling.

But as she looks on, with the soldiers hugging their knees, the elf, instead of firing the engine and getting their journey going, slams the palms of his hands against the steering wheel, turns around to face them all in the back and shouts – 'OK! That's it! You lot may be cramping my van but I'm not letting you cramp my style!' – at which point he draws out a painted tobacco tin and proceeds to assemble the skins for a large joint.

Dan's feeling of joy has all but vanished.

***

Nobody else is here, so these are Jessie's fields now. Soft, rolling fields so lush the breeze makes waves across them – a breeze that rustles through a sparse copse, and that's the only sound to be heard but for the insects and bird-song. It's a sleepy afternoon and there's still no sign of a car.

She figures it shouldn't take long to reach Somerton and get back out onto the motorway. Depending on how Dan was doing, they might even get to the gig before him. Two girls together, it would be a quick hitch. And surely the first person to come along this road would stop for her.

So why is she beginning to feel a shiver steal through the core of her? It's as if she is inviting the onset of anxiety, summoning it up to clench her stomach. It seems so unlikely, on this beautiful day, while having an adventure on a group hitch-hike to Dartmoor. This should surely feel like freedom. The open roads ahead should be symbolic of Dan's journey with his band – and her journey with Dan.

Yet she is out on her own here, and behind the undeniable innocence of the countryside, Jessie senses something creepy. As if a runaway murderer is about to crash through a hedge, shuffling on legs that are raw from the shackles. She's imagining the shock as he lurches at her, grimy and crazed, just as a pair of crows flap noisily out of an Ash tree above.

She flinches. And then her eyes flit swiftly around the hedgerows.

***

'And what's more, there's a proven link between meat eating and violence,' declares the irate, elfin-like driver, waving his zippo about with a limp wrist. The soldiers, like Dan, seem more interested in the joint getting rolled and resuming the journey. They seem to be as edgy as he feels, a couple of them shifting about and coughing.

'So you people are all fucked up,' he continues. 'First the 'Nam and then the Falklands. You're cannon fodder stuffed full of cow meat!'

The woman next to him has her head slightly inclined, as if she is in the midst of prayer or deep concentration. But a sudden, sharp retort like rifle fire on the van roof shakes her out of her reverie. She shrieks at the top of her voice, causing one of the squaddies to shout out, 'Fuckin' bastard!'

Dan is amazed to see the face of his keyboard player, Keith, pressed up against the passenger window.

'What do you want!?' the elf snaps at him.

'You got room for another?' Keith sounds desperate and Dan decides to speak up.

'He's my mate, he's alright,' he says.

'Dan!' Keith cries out like he's been in the wilderness for years. 'It's you!'

'Man, if you can find any room, you're welcome.' The elf's voice has a resigned tone and he steps out to open the back doors. Dan has to draw his knees up and hold his guitar case at a forty-five degree angle to accommodate Keith and, once they are shut in again, he peers through the back windows towards the roundabout to see if any patrol cars are in the vicinity. It's all clear for now.

'Fuck me,' says Keith, 'that was life and death stuff back there.' He looks shaken as he lays his keyboard case across two of the squaddies' laps.

'What happened?' Dan enquires, as the sermon from the front continues. The subject has moved on to the benefits of psychoactive drug use.

'I got a lift with this German truck driver,' he explains, 'nice enough feller, good sounds, quad speakers.'

'Yes, go on,' Dan urges. He feels somehow as if the length of Keith's story will influence how quickly they get away from this place.

'Well, it was his first trip over to the UK – in fact, it was his first time ever on a driving job.'

'Astral is the best way to travel boys, believe me!' shouts the elf. One of the squaddies bursts out laughing, holding his mouth.

'Yes, go on,' Dan doesn't want Keith to be deflected from his tale.

'Well, it turns out this guy is so nervous about the trip, he

78

hasn't slept for two days. Boris his name is. Nice feller but totally off his head, in charge of a huge, articulated road beast.'

'I see,' says Dan.

'Yeah, so we ended up taking a wrong turn and driving through an ancient little village where we came to a halt at a low bridge. Backing that baby up had all the old 'uns out, I can tell you. We took out one stone wall and damaged a lamp-post, but given the guy was delirious at the time he did a good job.'

Dan is distracted by a glint of blue light on a vehicle back at the roundabout. It could be an ambulance, he figures.

'I jumped out ten miles back while the going was good. The feller's fucked. I gave him my ephedrines.'

It's either an ambulance or a meat-wagon, Dan can't be sure. He should wear glasses but he's too vain. It wouldn't look good on stage.

'And then, worse still, my next lift was with a psychopathic old pervert,' says Keith, shaking his head. 'You wouldn't believe the things he came out with. I had to make him pull over the first chance I got.'

'What the fuck – you guys are all AWOL, anyway. Why not astral?' The joint is finally completed and it looks like a stone-age club. It kicks off a small forest fire of smoke. Dan feels the sweat trickling down the sides of his face.

'So what's the score here?' asks Keith.

***

In what seems like the middle of nowhere, Jessie comes upon a phone-box. It has tufts of wild grass growing from its base, at least a foot high. She can call Babs to let her know she's coming. She finds a ten pence piece in her jeans pocket and steps inside.

When the pips sound she can't force the coin through the slot. It's jammed. She pushes a deep groove into her thumb while she hears Babs' voice saying hello, over and over again. She pushes harder as the sounds of irritation grow from the receiver. Until she slams the phone down and kicks her way back out of the box.

Outside the air hums with the heat of mid-afternoon. She thinks she can hear an engine, some distance away, coming in her direction. She hopes it isn't going to be a psycho. She'd heard a few tales from Dan about lifts with nut-cases along these country roads.

***

Oh lord – it is a meat-wagon. Dan turns to Keith hopelessly.

'It's the filth,' he says, 'our luck's run out.'

But Keith has become absorbed in their little driver's rant, and he gleefully accepts the spliff when it's passed back. Two of the squaddies look sorely tempted, but as a body of men they refuse. Whatever revelries have kept them from barracks, they're over now.

The smoke has become so thick, it is billowing out of the open windows. Dan can see it drift around them from the back. It must look as though the van's on fire to anyone passing by. And here comes a meat-wagon full of police officers cruising slowly towards them.

'Keith, mate, I'm loaded with gear and the filth are coming. We're done for.' Dan needs to speak out his thoughts.

Keith's red face as good as explodes as he exhales a vast cloud.

'Pardon?' he says, coughing out the word, and the elf fires up the engine but it dies. He begins to pump on the choke. The police are within eye-shot now. Dan can see one of them looking right at him, as the little elf shouts out—

'You'll all be gettin' high, man, just off the aroma! The fragrance of sista ganja, man!'

He fires the engine again and the van takes a lurch forward before it settles and he begins, at last, to pull away. However, the police van has drawn alongside and Dan feels as though his world has just collapsed. He knows they will pull over. And he watches as they overtake and they indicate, and he's right. They pull over.

***

Once Dan got a lift with a doddery old guy who wanted to drive
him to the hills and cut off his penis – who told him how
Margaret Thatcher should be subjected to sexual humiliation in
a cage, one that was suspended from the ground somewhere in
public.

Then there were those 'speaking in tongues' Christians who
picked him up because they saw the hand of God over his head
(they would never have considered stopping for a hitch-hiker
otherwise), before attempting to abduct him.

And another time there was that yuppie salesman who
wanted to negotiate a mileage for sex arrangement.

Yes, he'd told her about some strange lifts while travelling
around these parts.

It's a beautiful stretch of road, though. She is walking
alongside a fallow field with a few horses, including a fine white
stallion, grazing lazily. The phone-box is well behind her and
the road ahead bends around a blind, wooded corner. She can
hear the engine of a vehicle approaching.

She mustn't dwell upon weirdos. She should be thinking of
the freedom in motion and travel. She should be thinking about
getting Babs and riding all the way to Dartmoor for a party.

Her lift is one country corner away. She licks her lips,
shoulders her rucksack and sticks out her thumb.

Time to hitch a ride.

***

'It's the Pigs!' the elf cries out. 'Fuck!'

He brings his van to a halt, leaving the engine running, and
twists around to face the back.

'Right,' he barks. 'Speak up! Are you lot definitely AWOL?'
The squaddies look sheepish.

'Yes,' one of them admits it.

'And you two,' he looks sharply at Dan and Keith. 'What are you up to?'

'We're a professional rock band,' says Dan, still quaking, and the same squaddie as before bursts out laughing.

'What!' Keith looks affronted. 'You can fuck off, we're signing up with Sensation Records next week.'

'Oh yeah?' says the elf. 'So why are you hitch-hiking, if you're such big-wigs?'

'The fuckin' camper broke down,' says Keith. 'Symbolic really, just when we finally get signed up, the ol' mother-ship makes its last voyage.'

One of the policemen has stepped out of the meat-wagon and looks to be heading their way. Dan watches on as their driver absorbs the situation and then elects to leap out of the van and bound towards him, in a friendly way, as if he was greeting a close relative he hasn't seen for years. The woman also opens her door and gets out. It's a strategy that seems to pay off as the policeman appears wrong-footed, and the little hippie sets about gesticulating and stamping his feet.

Dan wonders if it might be worth making a break for it out of the back doors while the police are distracted. His gaze has no sooner turned towards the rear windows than the doors are flung open by Keith, who has managed to scramble over the squaddies and out of the front sharpish.

'Slide me keys out, mate, and let's leggit!' he hisses.

***

Babs is curled up in the bunk of the trucker's cab. She's at the tail end of an all-nighter, with the promise of some whizz when they hook up with Dan and the band. It's a neat arrangement back there, cosily laid out with blankets and cushions, decorated with posters of Brando, Bardot and James Dean. And Babs looks like a little doll, in amongst the bedding and the innocence of her dreams.

Things couldn't have worked out better. They're about to get back on the motorway and head all the way to Dartmoor. Boris, the driver, is flying on some uppers he got from his last hitch-hiker and doesn't care where he goes as long as he can eventually park up somewhere. He is miles off target for his delivery anyway. Jessie was able to ascertain this pretty quickly after getting the lift. He didn't take much convincing to come along to the gig, and let them navigate for him tomorrow – Jessie's first two-way ride!

So *Exile on Main Street* is pumping from the quad speakers and Boris is nodding furiously in time as they approach the Taunton roundabout, when up ahead they see Dan and Keith running towards them with their instruments. They look like they're being pursued, glancing backwards as if a crowd should be behind them. Without any prompting, Boris hits the brakes and brings the truck to a skidding halt.

Babs wakes up.

'What's happening?' she says.

The music is belting out from the speakers, it seems much louder now the engine has stilled to a rumble.

Dan and Keith jump into the cab like athletes, swinging their cases over in the back, nearly clobbering Babs in the process.

'Whoa! Man! Boris, still rocking!' shouts Keith.

'Ja! Ja! Cool!'

'Jessie!' Dan looks overwhelmed and slides alongside her.

'What happened to you two?' asks Jessie, as they pull back into the lane. 'And how d'you know Boris?'

Dan is straining for breath and can't get his words out.

'That's a long story,' says Keith, 'and first, to be polite, I must introduce myself to this gorgeous creature.'

'Keith,' he says to Babs, taking her hand and planting a theatrical kiss on her wrist. Babs is still bleary.

'It was crazy,' gasps Dan as they turn onto the slip road. A little blue van and a meat-wagon are a hundred yards or so ahead and, as they pass them, Jessie sees two police officers occupied with their radios while some squaddies mill about on the hard shoulder. In an instant they are beyond the scene, leaving just a stretch of motorway ahead, shimmering in the sunshine.

'I guess those pills'll have kicked in, Boris!' shouts Keith, still holding Babs' hand. And the big German throws his head back to laugh.

'See mate, there was nothing to be worried about after all!' Keith aims a shout Dan's way.

'What's more,' he says quietly to Babs, pulling the half-smoked, monster joint out of his breast pocket, 'we've still got this little boy to polish off.'

And, in no time, Jessie has forgotten the fears of her detour. All that's left in her memory is a phone-box, the sinister hedgerows and some vague impression of a horse in a field.

Three Accounts of the Band Splitting up

July 1992

Keith

What brought me out of my trance, straight off, was when someone asked the question – what was going to happen to Wolfen? I was in a room full of the usual suspects, each looking at the other, most of them already bewildered by events. The chatter died away, and the only sounds to be heard were the slurps of tea mugs and some awkward shuffling about.

Who was going to break the news to Wolfen?

Life as we knew it was about to end – and someone had to tell the urban guerrilla who lived in the attic room. The thought of it helped clear the red mist from my eyes. It fixed my attention on something practical. It saved me from chasing down and grabbing that little bastard Dan by the throat. Why was he doing this? Why now?

So I thought about our strange drummer, who lived an unfathomable, solitary life and was built like a rugby player. He would always be dressed in military fatigues and his comings and goings, from the top room, were secretive, his activities never discussed. It was scary to think of breaking this particular piece of news to him. It ought to have been Dan's job, which is what I said to everybody when the question was raised, and there was a clamour of agreement. But I figured it would probably end up being mine. Dan slammed the front door shut behind him a few minutes before. No-one expected to see him back too soon. And when it came to it, Wolfen's place in the band was, I suppose, down to me.

It was nine years back, when I was a raw sixteen year old, that my path first crossed Wolfen's. His name, in actual fact, was Jason and he occupied the top front room of a squat I found myself in one summer. Everyone else in the house was wary of the feller. They warned me off disturbing him. But late one morning, I could smell some hash drifting down the stairs from his room. I was bored and feeling desperate to get stoned. It would have been out of character if I hadn't knocked on that door.

He was listening to the Clash, full volume (*Brand New Cadillac*, I think), so I had to knock hard and often, but the door eventually opened a crack and I could see his eyes and the bridge of his nose.

'What you want?' He was like security at a Blues party.

'Jason, mate,' I explained. 'I'm just wondering if I might join you in a little of that Afghani magic I'm sniffing about the house.'

So I ended up perched cross-legged on a saggy mattress, while the crew-cutted recluse sat on a swivel stool preparing a bong. He was in front of a large desk upon which, at either end, were two huge speakers. In fact, that seemed to be the purpose of the desk – to sit the speakers on. It was otherwise empty. He wore Doctor Martin ox-bloods, calf length and his combats were cut to fall an inch or two above the top of his boots.

'The name's Wolfen,' he'd told me as he opened the door. 'I never want you to mention the other one again.'

Then he showed me the room with a sweep of his arm.

'Si' down,' he said and there was only the mattress to go for. It didn't take much to figure the stool was his. The music was loud, you'd be able to hear it out on the street, but the sound was crisp and distinct – from high-hat to bass.

'Bruvver, you timed your visit well,' he yelled as he cracked a can of Special Brew. The first chords of *Rudie Can't Fail* were rattling the speakers.

'I like your hat,' he added, using the can to point at my pork-pie and he held his head back to take a long gulp before passing it over.

'Down in one, mate,' he said. 'Can't fail.'

So there I was, perched on his mattress as Wolfen tapped down the mixture in the bong bowl and he gave it a few test sucks, gurgling up the water. I was still gagging slightly from necking half a can of Brew in one go, but I remember thinking the drums were top quality on this album.

'It's a disguise man,' he said. 'Urban camouflage.'

'Fuck, I got this thing in Oxfam,' I replied. 'I play keyboard with a band, I figured Johnny Fingers looked good in a hat.'

'I'm not talking about the hat,' he said.

It took a long time for Wolfen to achieve the perfect draw for that bong, while he told me of the necessity for urban combat-wear and depersonalised identities.

'I move down quiet back alleys, mate, keep out the street lights. Some day soon it's all gonna hit the fan, you wait and see.' He lit the pipe and took a deep lungful just as *Guns of Brixton* began. Before the song ended I was buzzing so hard my head felt like a Roman Candle.

And then we went out and joined a riot in the Square Mile. We stopped the City.

A few months later I met Dan and the Smokin Joes were born. He lived in an end terrace squat and I was round there buying speed off a little Dodger character in a jacket and waistcoat. His name was Frank and he looked like his own best customer – zipping his tits off – so I asked if I could see his gear. I wanted to make sure that his personal stash and what he was selling were one and the same.

He pulled out a large wrap, the sort you'd use for a quarter not a gram, and he had a big grin on his face. His mate Dan was grinning too.

'You're smart,' Dan said and ten minutes later we'd

arranged a jam.

I moved in within a week and between the three of us we sound-proofed the basement and loaded it with a PA and speakers, bass and guitar amps (Dan switched between the two), my keyboard and a drum kit. What we didn't have was a regular drummer. The drummers came and went in quick succession.

For years we played the pub rock circuit in London – from the Beckett's and the Pegasus, to the Falcon and the Bull and Gate. It took a while but we gradually built a following, although one character was there from the start – Wolfen. He turned up at our first outing, a support slot for a Stoke Newington punk band, and he kept appearing at every gig thereafter. He would never stop for a pint or a chat or anything like that, he would just turn up, jump about to our set and then leave.

For a while, in '87, we thought we had the perfect band when we were joined by a jazz-funk drummer called Dave. Then one night at Break for the Border he didn't show up. Fair enough, we were only playing for free beer and burritos but it was a big blow. Dan was announcing the situation to the gathered drinkers, who couldn't have been less interested by the looks of them, when out of the shadows stepped Wolfen. He looked the size of a giant as he settled behind the little studio kit we'd set up. We rolled through the usual song-list and who would have thought it? – Wolfen was a natural, right in the pocket. Out of the blue, the Smokin Joes line-up was complete.

A week later he'd also moved into No.1 Bush Road, and set up in the attic room where he remained as mysterious and distant as ever. If asked about his movements, he would say that he was a long-serving foot soldier for the Department of Stealth and Total Obscurity.

No-one could be sure how old Wolfen actually was – we figured he was a lot older than the rest of us. He said he was twenty-seven, year after year. When it was pointed out to him that his twenty-eighth should be due, he replied that he would forever remain twenty-seven in honour of 'all the dead heroes'.

Even on tour he managed to keep himself to himself, sitting alone in the back of the van reading propaganda pamphlets – left wing, right wing, anarchist, whatever came his way. As soon as he was sound-checked at a venue, he would disappear to walk the streets of whichever place we were in.

A year or so after Wolfen joined us, we were signed up and we saw even less of him outside the business of drumming. With hotel rooms to lose himself in he would slip away after gigs too, leaving the pick of the groupies to me, Frank and the roadie. Dan usually brought his own along – his girlfriend Jessie, who had an air of superiority about her backstage amongst all the excited girls. But to me she seemed no different. She was as much of a tart as any groupie when it came to it. Wolfen, on the other hand, treated her like royalty – he just stopped short of bowing and scraping – and Jessie lapped it up. She had no problem with whatever plots he was cooking, however old he was.

The one person in the house who knew most about Wolfen's activities was Frank, the dealer. Frank more or less lived in the top front room, it was known as the TV room, directly underneath the attic. I say he more or less lived there – Frank was a speed freak, so it would be more accurate to say it was his base camp. The place from which he'd set off on numerous night-time sorties, and to which he'd eventually return, sometimes days later.

It was during one of his nocturnal shifties that he ran into Wolfen, out and about, and he returned in such a state of shock he was unable to talk about it.

'Mate, I value my life too much to tell you,' Frank said, when I pushed him to spill the beans.

'Is it anything we should know about, though? Y'know, if it's something really dodgy that might come back to bite us?' I was worried that we might have a murderer or a rapist in the band.

'You lot've got nothing to worry about,' he said, brushing past me and out of the kitchen. 'It's me whose bollocks are on the chopping block.'

Dan wasn't interested when I told him.

'The man's a perfect drummer,' he said and that was his only worry. He must have noticed the doubt on my face. 'He has never let us down for a gig,' he added.

'Except Dartmoor,' I countered and Dan stopped to look at me like I was crazy.

'If you remember, our van broke down and we all had to hitch-hike to that one,' he said. 'Now tell me this – would you give Wolfen a lift if you saw him by the side of the road?'

The most I could ever prise from Frank about what happened was that he'd stumbled into the wrong lock-up that night, and witnessed things there that he would have been better off never having seen.

So I had to have a couple of drinks to steel the resolve before breaking the news to Wolfen. I was heading for the Crowns when instead I took a detour over to the off licence. I opened a Special Brew on a bench in London Fields and finished it while thinking about the band. And then I downed another as I walked back home.

All of this had started the previous week, after our ridiculous 'tour' of the States. Or, as it turned out, the fight at the airport – which was as close as we got to the USA. That seemed to be the last straw for Dan. At least that's what he told us. I figured there was more to it. Something to do with that cheating girlfriend of his.

Once back indoors I found Frank in a full length red dress, barefoot, with mascara tears staining his cheeks. He looked like a Geisha girl drag act. He stopped me in the hallway before I could reach the kitchen. I could smell burning paper from the yard.

'What the fuck are you doing?' I asked.

'Mate, you don't want to go out there,' he said, ushering me back down the hallway.

'No,' I said, holding my ground. 'What are you doing in the dress?'

'Oh this,' Frank looked down at his feet. 'I couldn't find a girl willing to cash a post office book.' He was leaning on me, holding my left shoulder with his hand.

'One that came my way, y'know.'

'And the tears?' I asked.

'Fire-smoke,' he said, still checking his feet.

'What exactly is going on?' I was puzzled. Only half an hour or so ago, the kitchen was full of people and Frank had been nowhere to be seen.

Just then Wolfen marched into the hallway from the back yard, his face grimed up with soot, sweat pouring from his forehead.

''Scuse lads,' he mumbled as he pushed the pair of us to one side and pounded his way upstairs. Within a minute he was back downstairs and he hustled past us carrying three archive boxes.

'Bit'a spring cleaning, y'know,' said Frank, chirpily.

'Does he know about the band?' I watched Wolfen disappear through the kitchen and out into the yard.

'Keith, mate, what d'you think's prompted the clear out?'

And that was that. It turned out to be an easier gig than I imagined. But there were still plenty of questions left to be answered. And there was also the problem of what to do now the band had split up.

***

Frank

So I set off to see Monica one July morning, like I did most days. She'd been in the nut-house for well over a year and lately she was a lot better than when she first checked in. The visits had become less about talking someone out of their psychosis, and more to do with making plans for when she got out. They didn't seem realistic but it was better to be, y'know, encouraging.

Anyway, little did I realise that this particular day would turn out to be so momentous. Just like that, with no warning at all. It all seemed samey enough as I took a top-up dab from my wrap, glanced around the familiar objects in my room – the mattress, the cassette player, the low wooden table, the TV – and then shut the door. It was the usual quick skip down the stairs and blind stumble to the front door and then, once outdoors and into the late afternoon, the street seemed like it ever was. I suppose momentous days must always start off normally.

But I had barely got a hundred yards up Mare Street when I ran into Scot, one of my more fucked-up customers, who stepped in my way and urged me to have a quiet word under the canopy of a members-only Kurdish café. I was a little nervous about it – the place was called Gulletissory, or some-such, and I'd heard these people were cut-throats. I didn't want to be cajoled into a sale on some gangster's doorstep.

'Fuck off, fuck off!' I shouted, backing away from him with my arms raised, which brought more attention to the pair of us than I'd bargained for.

'I can pay up, pal,' he hissed at me urgently. 'I gottay book.' He flashed the top of a small brown post office book discreetly from his jacket pocket. 'Frankee, man, there's a few ton in there, if you want it.'

I had to admit, my interest was piqued.

'Sweet, mate, and what d'you want in return?'

'Gimme a quarter,' he said. A couple of burly geezers were lurking just behind us at the café door.

'Let's keep walking, mate,' I said and I hustled Scot along the footpath.

We did a deal in the side alley of a pub. I gave him what was left in my quarter wrap, probably more like four or five grams, and he gave me the post office book. I quickly checked it for the balance – he was right, three hundred and twelve big ones waiting to be claimed.

What I didn't notice, until the dodgy Jock had long gone, was that the book belonged to some bird called Emily Jones.

It was after Monica tried to steal a baby that they took her off to the hospital. It blew us all away when we heard about it. She'd never shown any maternal inclinations up till then. I had a sneaky suspicion it was something to do with that bit of posh from the art college that came visiting a few years back. The one who went mental within an hour of turning up. Monica had never really been the same since. But it was tricky to see the link.

Whenever I'd tried talking about it on my visits – y'know, why she stole the baby – she'd clam up. It didn't take long to figure it wasn't a topic up for discussion. So I was left with what I imagined – and I imagined it must have been to do with her art college mate, first and foremost. Why? Because she'd been giving it out about a baby when she had her fit and maybe that stuck in Monica's mind.

But why she would let it all stew for a few years before having a wobbly herself was beyond me.

Anyway, I'd been visiting as much as I could since she'd been in – except when I joined the band on tour. So I figured if I missed this one, it wouldn't be a tragedy. If I was going to get my greedy mitts on the post office cash, it was best done quickly. All I needed was to find someone willing to impersonate Emily Jones – for a small reward, of course.

It should have been easy money – I knew a fair few birds who were short of cash and had no scruples to speak of, but could I find any of them in? Or anyone else remotely willing to dabble in some common or garden fraud?

I was at my wits' end when I decided to try Jessie – not that I thought she'd do it for the sake of it, just that maybe she'd do it for me. As I stepped back indoors and made for the stairs, I noticed a gathering in the kitchen but thought nothing of it. It was probably the usual hangers-on, waiting for one of the band to come up from the basement.

I found Jessie in her room, looking grim as she threw clothes into a suitcase. She was surrounded by piles of bags, bin-liners, books and other junk. Something was going on.

'What's the matter, darlin'?' I summoned up my most reassuring voice, but she burst into tears and flung her arms out for a hug. It took a good few minutes to find out what was happening. Dan, it seemed, had finally snapped and quit the band. He'd been heading towards something like this for a while. Working with arseholes from the music business irked him no end but, according to Jessie, it was also her own infidelities that broke the camel's back. So Dan had decided they would head for the Yorkshire moors, for some space to work things out.

I hadn't a clue what to say, nor what to think. I'd have to catch up with Dan later. I just held Jessie in a tight hug until her sobs became whimpers and eventually her body movement became flirty – and then I held her far enough away to look into her eyes.

'Can you do me favour?' I asked. 'Can you cash a post office book for me?'

Ah well, it was always going to be a long shot. She probably wouldn't have considered it even if she'd been in a good mood. At least I managed to cadge a long red dress off her, and some high heels and make-up, before she slammed the door shut in my face.

This was obviously a job I'd have to get done myself.

It's true to say, I felt like part of the band. I'd been hanging about at No. 1 as long as Dan had lived there, and I helped him and Mr Keys set up the basement. I even toured with the bastards sometimes, sold T-shirts and tapes at the back of gig halls up and down the country – this whole show was a big part of my life. As I walked over to Mare Street I tried to stop myself thinking about it. It needed putting to the back of my mind.

There was some serious role-play to pull off here and I needed to look lively.

I sat down at the bus stop opposite the post office to put the high heels on. I had to virtually break my toes to get into them. Two schoolgirls waiting for a bus laughed openly and pointed at me but I ignored them. This was the way it would have to be done. Apart from Jessie's shoes, I only had steel-capped boots and the dress wasn't long enough to cover them. I threw the boots into my carrier bag and I was ready.

I did pause to wonder why the fuck I was attempting to empty some post office account, dressed like this, when there were more pressing concerns to be dealt with. There was bound to be a chaotic scene back home. And, once it had all calmed down, what next?

But at that point, what mattered more was the three hundred notes waiting just for me, one small counter transaction away. It was time to step over there, get the deed done and walk out with the wedge.

As it happened, I more or less fell across the pavement – the pain in my feet took me by surprise – and the weight of my collision with the post office door practically broke the glass. A set of bells jangled as I felt my way inside, wincing with every step. All four people at the counter turned around to watch my entrance and I made my way through the queue cordon with all the dignity I could summon.

'Yes?' enquired a dreary looking clerk as I reached the 'Please Wait Here' sign. I was holding onto both sets of rope for balance. She had the look of a librarian, peering over her silver wire glasses disapprovingly.

'I wish to withdraw three hundred notes from my account,' I said, putting on my posh girly voice as I handed over the book. I figured it would seem less suspicious asking for three hundred rather than the full three hundred and twelve, but I wasn't really prepared for the outburst of laughter my request would get from, not only the drab madge behind the counter but also the other clerks and even my fellow customers.

'And... And are you Miss Jones?' she asked with tears in her eyes. I spotted a couple of blokes over her shoulder who looked suspiciously like grippers, striding out from the back office.

'Course I am, darlin'. Think I'd trust anyone else with my cash?' I felt affronted. My voice may have slipped a bit when I said it – the woman had to stifle her chuckles again.

I realised I'd made a basic blunder. I should have tried the post office at Stokey. They didn't ask any questions there, they barely looked up at you. It was only because of this dress that I'd gone for the nearer option.

'If you wouldn't mind stepping around the back and talking to one of the supervisors,' said the clerk.

'No offence madam, but fuck that. Just give me my book back and I'll be off.' I made to snatch it from her hand but she recoiled too quickly and then, from out of nowhere, the two grippers came at me.

I had to lose the shoes in order to escape the bastards. They went flying in the air as I kicked up my heels, I think one may have hit someone in the face, and I was out of the dive in a flash.

By the time I got back indoors, and checked to make sure the posse weren't behind me, my plates were in bits. I could barely stand up. I hobbled towards the stairs, thinking if I couldn't make it to mine I could get some rest in Dan and Jessie's. And it was then that I bumped into Wolfen coming down from the attic with a stack of papers in his arms.

Wolfen wasn't an easy geezer to get on with at the best of times. But after I'd accidentally stumbled into a lock-up of his, one fateful night, the understanding between us became stark. There was nothing like the threat of death to focus dealings with a house-mate. If I should ever squeal to anyone, I'd be chopped up and rolled into the Thames in a barrel.

On the day the band split up, Wolfen took me out to the backyard and lit a bonfire from a box full of papers. He then emptied more boxes and bin bags on top of it, with papers flying around in the air. He had me chasing about after any stray sheets, to make sure nothing escaped the burning. He was, without doubt, getting rid of the evidence.

'What you doing this now for?' I asked, and he looked at me in that vicious way of his, designed to scare the shit out of you.

'The band has been a good cover,' was his only explanation.

'And if you ever blab about any of this, mate,' he added. 'Consider yourself fish-food.'

The front door slammed shut and we both turned to look towards the kitchen.

'I'll go and stall whoever that is,' I volunteered, my voice shaking a bit – and I limped back indoors from the yard.

I'd never thought about Keith the Keys and what he may or may not have had going with Jessie. But after I held him up in the corridor, and he'd ascertained that Wolfen knew about the band, his face quickly turned from relief into rage.

'Where's that little toe-rag!' he shouted as he bounded up the stairs and threw open the door to Dan and Jessie's room. 'Where's the little bastard hiding?'

When I caught up with him, he was stood dumbfounded with both fists clenched by his side looking at Jessie who was sitting on the edge of her bed. Behind her was a pile of suitcases and packing boxes.

'It's because of you, isn't it?' he said softly.

Jessie looked up and spotted me and she burst into fits of laughter.

'It's all because of you...' Keith seemed like he was in a trance.

'What do you look like?' said Jessie.

At that stage, I wasn't interested in what I looked like.

'What have you done this time?' said Keith to Jessie, in a way that suggested he knew a fair bit about what she'd done already. She stopped laughing and turned her attention towards him.

'I've done nothing,' she snapped. 'It's not my problem if Dan can't deal with change.'

Keith looked at her with contempt.

'He's making us all deal with a big fucking change now, isn't he?' he said.

'This isn't change,' Jessie spoke slowly, like she was talking to a kid. 'This is defeat.'

I was trying to pull the dress off me in front of a stand-up mirror in my room, one that was broken in a diagonal across the top third, and the smell of burned paper was drifting all about the house. I was still dazed from events, although the thought that I'd effectively given five grams of whizz away to that Jock bastard was nagging at me. By dwelling on that I was probably keeping my mind off what was happening in the house. It seemed a better idea to be riled about getting ripped off.

That was more or less the scene when the door to my room opened and there stood Monica, in black plastic sunglasses, as still as a shop dummy. I think my dress was half way off at the time.

'Jesus fuckin' H Christ!' I said. 'Have they let you out?'

It took a long time for Monica to answer. Or at least it seemed that way. Maybe it had just been one of those days when my adrenalin was worked up so much, time had slowed down.

'Yes,' she said, finally.

The sun had sunk to the point where, late in a summer's evening, it poured over the rooftops, into my room and across a worn-out old rug. Monica stepped forward into the light and I had to squint to make her out.

'Darlin',' I said, 'about time!' But she didn't seem to be in the mood for celebration. She stood still in the sunlight, and I could tell she was looking me over.

'I thought you were coming to give me a dab of speed today,' she said.

***

Monica

It was just a baby in a pram. A sight you'd see every day in the park or outside cafés. I must have walked past dozens of them over the years and not batted an eyelid. Why I decided to kidnap one on that particular day was, for a while, as much of a mystery to me as it has proved to be for the various doctors I've seen since.

It was a dark early morning, thick with a cold mist, and I was walking aimlessly past the Cock Tavern and up Holloway Road. I'd left the house at Bush Road earlier for some fresh air, to clear the cobwebs after a succession of house parties and late-night jamming sessions. I only meant to walk as far as Upper Street but, once there, I just kept going.

I remember being anxious about the future. The band had managed to chart with a song the previous Christmas, a raucous sing-along number. A year later and they had made the top ten. And even though this was great news, it left me feeling more and more alone. I wasn't really sure what part I played in their lives any more, especially since I had stopped making videos. I didn't enjoy it once they'd been signed up and carrying me became something Dan had to justify to the management. I gave up video-making, as much to save him the trouble as anything else.

All this would have been swirling around in my thoughts, I guess, when I walked past one of those 'open all hours' Turkish stores with shelves of vegetables out in front, most of them unrecognisable. Storm lights were hooked to the shop canopy and underneath, next to a display of red, green and yellow peppers, I came across an unattended pram.

That was pretty much the last I remember: a tiny, trusting face and the cold mist and the peppers and those lamps. Next thing I knew I was in a narrow room with an iron bed and a small window.

*

It had been well over a year and my days were spent with doctors and in therapy groups and in my room on the bed reading, when just recently one of the more sleazy doctors gave me a girly magazine after one of our sessions because, he said, it carried a short story by Jessie. The next day he tried to grope me and I locked my legs and screamed until he stopped. It took me some days to figure out that he must have recognised the Mona character as being based on me. In Jessie's story, Mona has plenty of sexual adventures. I'd talked about one or two similar episodes in my therapy sessions.

Until that incident I'd been feeling more and more comfortable in the hospital. I was enjoying the regularity of it all. At first, I admit, it was like a nightmare. My room was on a long corridor with bright windows which looked out onto a courtyard and other corridors opposite on several floors, the whole effect being like a maze. I felt trapped in some sort of puzzle. But slowly, through talking things out in counselling and group therapy, the reason for it all became clear. I had taken the baby for Dan.

Of course I couldn't admit that to Frank when he visited. He wouldn't have understood. He asked a few times, why I'd done it, but I never knew what to say to him. He and everyone else in Bush Road would have come to their own conclusions, I'm sure.

But now the logic of it was so clear, it seemed ridiculous that I had to try stealing a baby, and get myself into these therapy groups, to find out. I adored Dan and would do anything for him. He was in a dead relationship and desperately wanted a baby, and I found myself, one foggy morning, in a position to present him with a done deal, the whole package. It was that simple.

Over time I began to feel a little guilty about how Dan might have reacted to what I'd done. Somehow I felt that, deep down inside, he would have known the purpose behind my actions. I was worried it might affect our relationship. Not to say that we had anything more than a friendship going the last time I saw him, just that it might ruin even that.

It was due to this realisation, in fact it would be fair to say it was due to Dan, that I managed to get better. Frank couldn't believe the transformation. He'd always keep me informed of the house news – his scrapes and adventures, the fortunes of the band – more as a way of talking it all out to himself, I thought. But it didn't take too long before I was able to be interested back and then, after the incident with Dr Hynge, that was it. I was ready to return to the old life. It was like I just snapped out of a trance.

He usually turned up around 3 pm. I knew that visiting me would be one of the first things Frank did of a day. We'd go to the smoking room and buy a coffee each from the machine and Frank would stay for an hour or so, however long we could keep the conversation going.

Lately, in the midst of a heatwave, we'd throw the windows wide open. They looked out onto a back alley, with just a peep of the street if I craned my neck. The noise, together with the smell of hot exhaust, was intoxicating and slightly scary at the same time. The hairs stood up on my arms whenever I held onto the window sill and pushed my face into the rumbling world outside.

One day recently Frank told me about Dan, and the band, and how they were meant to be setting off on a tour of the United States. But a fight broke out at the airport between them and the manager and suddenly the whole tour was abandoned. Frank said he was blown away when he found Keith in the kitchen that afternoon. It seemed Dan completely lost his head after the fight. He refused to come back with the band and, instead, stayed behind at the airport bar. When he did eventually get home to No. 1, he gave everyone the silent treatment before passing out on the kitchen sofa.

Frank said he suspected Dan had also got home to find Jessie 'shagging some geezer', as he put it. This was a surprise to me. I knew Jessie had transgressed now and again – I mean, one of those transgressions was with me. But she said it was only ever at parties, when she was drunk. She would never set out to cheat on Dan. Of course I always suspected this was untrue, I could tell she had lost interest in him a good while ago. Reading her stories only confirmed it for me. She was using all of us, not just Dan. But, to hear this news from Frank, who was loyal as a lapdog to them both, was surprising.

I didn't make such a big deal of it. I asked a few questions, the way I imagined Frank would expect me to. And then we talked about something else. I knew Frank wanted to discuss it more, the situation had him worried, but he backed off when I switched topics a second time.

Instead I left it until long after Frank had gone, until I was lying in bed in the twilight, to allow myself to think about it all – to immerse myself in the thought that maybe Dan would now realise that things with Jessie weren't going to work. It all seemed so timely. After all, here I was – ready to leave this place and go home.

I couldn't really see the sky from my window, the building opposite was too tall, but I swear I could spot the stars twinkling in the glass that night.

When Frank left, I asked him to bring some speed the next time he visited and he told me he would come the next day. I would wait for him with my bag packed and everything would fall into place after that.

Of course I didn't have a bag to pack. I arrived at this place with the clothes on my back and they were long gone. All I had were the jeans and T-shirt I wore on rotation with my other set. And a pair of black sunglasses Frank brought in for me last summer. So that's what I left with.

Which makes the actual exit seem easy and I suppose when it came to it, it was, but I'd waited for over two hours thinking Frank might appear any second before I finally gave up and wandered out into the corridor. And then I walked around that building for a quarter of an hour or more before I found a door to the outside. I passed a few people, in different parts of the building, but no-one challenged me. And that was it, I was gone – out of there.

I wasn't sure which street I'd walked out onto but I kept up a brisk pace in the direction I was headed and didn't hesitate. I just kept walking, taking random turns, until eventually I hit a main road and found myself at Highgate tube. Once I was past the barrier I was as good as home. Even so, everything felt unnatural. The air in the underground was humid and sour, more than I remembered. There was an uncomfortable echo to all the chatter, shouts and laughter.

I got off the tube at Angel and walked directly east. Although things seemed different – a demolished building here, a boarded-up bar there – I knew the direction instinctively. Soon I was back into streets I recognised. Even so, I had a creepy, déjà vu-like feeling shivering up my back. And then of course, near Bush Road, in fact at the top end of London Fields, I completely lost my way. I had to ask an old man, who was out walking his dog, how to get back home.

I was half way across the fields when I spotted Keith at the market end on a bench. He was looking at the ground, with his elbows on his knees. I hovered behind a tree and watched him from a distance.

Was I ready for this?

I thought for a while about my many adventures with Keith. How for years, whenever he was at a loose end, I seemed to be his plaything. Yet all this time I had really been destined for Dan.

In the meantime, Keith stood up, stretched and then opened a can of beer. He took a long, throaty gulp, adjusted his hat and turned to head down the market street. He was out of view when I reached the bench. It was still warm from his backside – at least that's how it felt, it was probably warm from the sun anyway. I pressed the palm of my right hand against the seat before carrying on, slowly, in Keith's wake.

The front door to No. 1 was just the same – the same scuffs and gouges around the door handle and lock. It didn't seem like a year or so since I stepped out with the intention of clearing my head for an hour with a walk over to Islington. And there I was, back again, summoning up the courage to knock, when all of a sudden the door was pulled wide open and I looked up at Wolfen. He stared at me with his mouth open, dropped his rucksack and dragged me into a twirling bear hug.

'Good to see ya back, sister,' he said and then he put me down, picked up his rucksack and walked past me onto the street.

'I'm off,' he called out, and he didn't look back as I watched him disappear onto the main road and away.

So I turned on my heels and looked along the hallway. The house smelled of burnt paper and there was a strange silence hanging like the smoke. Normally the place would be buzzing with activity by now, but it seemed empty. I wasn't sure which room to head for. And then I remembered Frank, and the speed I was promised, and I made my way up the stairs.

As I walked past Dan and Jessie's room and up around to the next floor, I guess I was thinking about the future, my future, one that would inevitably entwine with Dan's. They were good thoughts. I recall feeling happy and excited as I reached the TV room under the attic. But it all drained away from me when I opened the door and saw Frank.

At first I wasn't even sure it was Frank standing in front of me. He was wearing a lot of make-up and the dress he'd pulled down to his waist was a tight-fitting, red one that I vaguely recognised. But it was something else, not the sight of Frank, that stopped me in my footsteps. It was the memory of one night, years ago, when I was hanging out with a cross-dressing boy and an old college friend came to visit. It had been a night full of haze and panic as my friend went into a psychotic fit. Her name was Ruth, and she was pregnant at the time. And Liam, who was wearing a similar tight dress to Frank's, helped me look after her until the ambulance arrived.

As I stood in the doorway to the TV room I realised that the day I took the baby, I did it for Ruth, not Dan.

Part 3
Tom's Tale

Home for the Bewildered

September 1992

Jesus Christ, opening that wine bottle was like a wrestling match, thought Tom as he staggered out of the bathroom.

'That cork was so tight it could've been up a cat's arse,' he said.

His brother Paddy looked up at him with wild, bloodshot eyes.

'It's all fuckin' incidental,' he said, handing up his glass.

'So anyway,' Paddy continued, with his drink freshened. 'The story goes O'Brien hired a taxi to take him on a pub crawl around Dublin. And as the night progressed, he got quietly stocious up at the bar of over a dozen pubs until, when he was in O'Donaghue's, he thought he spotted a familiar face. A sinister fucker sitting in the corner. Some bastard that had been following him around from pub to pub.'

Tom slid the needle across the entire side of an Ella Fitzgerald LP.

'Bollocks,' he said, swaying back from the record player. It was one of those portable ones you can carry around like a briefcase.

'Ah, fuck it.' He bounced the record in about half way through. It landed on a duet with Louis Armstrong.

'Exactly,' said Paddy. 'So O'Brien confronted the guy angrily: "You're fuckin' following me, you bastard!" And the guy held O'Brien steady by the shoulders, and said: "Of course I'm following you sir, I'm your taxi driver."'

The two brothers looked at one another, Paddy's beaming,

bearded face a contrast to Tom's, whose eyes were unfocussed. They were sitting on the beds of a twin room in a hotel in Preston.

'At what God-forsaken time do we have to be at English Martyrs?' Tom emptied his glass and quickly topped it up again.

'I'm sure it'll be a fitting send off for the old girl.' Paddy was keeping it light. 'We've got plenty of time.'

***

'Well,' said Kate, 'I thought Tom looked better tonight.'

She was cutting a plate of sandwiches into quarters, a little snack to have with a cup of tea before bed-time.

'We'll see,' said Mary from the sofa. *Last Tango in Paris* was on the TV and it was drawing her attention away from the open kitchen door. Also, she could feel something jabbing into her backside from in between the sofa cushions and she pulled out the video remote control.

'At least Paddy took him away sober and in good time,' Kate was shouting over the kettle.

'Well I never!' Mary gawped at the TV. The anal sex scene had taken her by surprise and the remote slipped from her hands. 'Well I never!' she gasped, clutching her chest.

'I'll pour us a nice brew too,' said Kate.

'Ooh, yes please,' said Mary without turning her head, and then she winced, shouting out: 'Oh no! No!'

'Bloody well make up yer mind, woman!'

Mary couldn't help but burst out laughing.

Kate brought the butties into the living room just in time to see Maria Schneider shoving her fingers up Marlon Brando's arse. She dropped the plate. Slices of ham and tomatoes, and individual triangles of bread bounced across the carpet as far as the fireplace.

'What the bloody hell are you watching!'

***

They were well in time for last orders, Paddy figured. In fact, as it turned out, they were able to down a good few while they swapped tales and sang songs at the bar of the Black Horse. Paddy watched the pearly cigar smoke cling to the glass racks overhead and, as Tom threw his head back to sing *The West's Awake!*, he thought how it was a shame that more often than not, these days, the good times involved a sad occasion.

'Kate looked a lot better, I thought,' said Tom afterwards, while they stood at the bar with chasers lined up by their pints. 'Less uptight.'

'The thing about this family is they suffocate you with kindness,' said Paddy wiping the froth from his beard. 'It's a fuckin' production line of food and tea.'

'And a parade of their bloody grandchildren,' added Tom. 'I don't recognise half of them.'

They were practically alone in the pub, just a group at the other end of the bar recounting some brawl that had happened recently. It was being discussed in grave tones – someone had been killed.

'Shouldn't they have rung for last orders by now?' Paddy glanced up at the bar clock.

'It's Guild week, so it's Rafferty's rules,' said Tom.

'Jesus, I had no idea it was the Guild,' said Paddy, shaking his head. 'Ma chose a fine time to keel over.'

'It'll make for a good wake.' Tom finished his pint and gestured for another.

'And it's fitting,' he continued. 'Pa died just after the '52 Guild.'

'That's true,' Paddy said wistfully, and he lit a cigarette. 'She managed a good forty years without the old bastard.'

***

Once the carpet had been cleaned, Mary and Kate sat down to

111

their brews while Marlon Brando reeled around a Parisian dining room with a rose tucked behind his ear. They were both silent, cradling their mugs.

Mary was thinking about her mother, about how she had been a strict disciplinarian who demanded order, even in amongst the ashes and coal-dust of a poor life. She hoped everything would go well for the funeral tomorrow, as befitted a proud woman.

Kate was thinking about Tom. They said the news of Ma's death had brought him back to his senses. He'd been let out of the psychiatric hospital a week ago. He certainly seemed on good behaviour tonight, and only drank a few malt whiskeys when they were offered. But Kate didn't trust him. As Ma said, only a few weeks back, both of her sons turned out to be drunken wastrels.

***

'How's Bridget?' asked Tom, tossing his head back to finish his rum.

'Jesus, don't ask,' said Paddy. He had both elbows propped on the bar counter as he looked into an empty glass.

'Well it's good of her to come up with Angela on the train tomorrow.' Tom was in the midst of an order. 'And I'll have two more large ones, pal,' he said to the barman.

'I wish her the best of luck,' said Paddy. 'With Bridget involved they could end up anywhere.'

They both lifted their fresh pints and supped heartily.

'I could never understand why you divorced her.' Paddy wiped his beard with his wrist.

'She divorced me,' said Tom flatly.

'In that case, it makes complete fuckin' sense,' Paddy said, and then he broke into a verse sung to the tune of Nat King Cole's *Don't Get Around Much Anymore*.

'Missed the bowl of the john,

pissed all over the floor!
Cleaned it up with my toothbrush!
Don't brush my teeth much any more!'

The group discussing the murder paused mid-flow and looked over. A little too aggressively for Tom's liking.

'Everything OK, lads?' he enquired, politely.

'Aye,' one of them muttered, a skinny fellow, and then, as if summoning the courage to do so, he spoke up.

'There were a lad murdered last night after drinking here.'

'Fuckin' bad news,' said Paddy, shaking his head.

'You were here last night,' said the skinny man, looking at Tom. 'I saw you.'

'That's right, I was, but I didn't kill anybody.' Tom gulped down some beer to moisten his mouth. Something about this was unsettling him.

'But d'you recall the lad?'

Tom looked the man over. He wore an ill fitting but well tailored suit. A fly-away collar, hush puppies and a cravat.

'I had a few drinks with a spaced-out hippie character. Reminded me of my lad, Danny,' said Tom. 'It wasn't him, was it?'

'Might be, aye,' the skinny fellow seemed thoughtful.

'In the upshot, he was beaten to death outside the Big House pub,' he said and passed Tom a rolled-up Evening Post. 'You'll read all about it in there.'

'Fuckin' bad news,' said Paddy, a second time.

'God rest his soul,' said Tom, and his hand shook violently as he raised the rum-glass to his lips.

***

'D'you think it's just the drinking?' asked Mary. 'With Tom?'

'The man's a drunkard, Mary, he'll not settle for just the one or two drinks.' The ads were on and Kate was watching two animated plasticine cats with moving lips. 'He doesn't know when to stop.'

'I think there's more to it,' said Mary. 'Summat deeper, like depression.'

'Don't talk soft!' howled Kate. 'There is no such thing as bloody depression! There's nowt a hard day's graft, a good feed and a whiskey mac couldn't cure!'

***

Paddy awoke to the rasp of drawn curtains and a face-full of bitter Preston daylight, the first he'd felt for ten years or more.

'Jesus Christ.' He winced. 'What the fuck are you doing?'

Tom was pacing the room wearing a black suit with drainpipe trousers, and a light blue cravat tufted under his chin.

'It's time to get on parade, buddy,' he said, as if there was a hurry on. 'To miss a dawn is to cheat God.'

Paddy pulled the sheets and pillow over his head.

'Parade yourself,' he muttered.

Tom threw him a look of scorn as he left the room.

'Well I'm going for a walk,' he said, slamming the door behind him.

Half an hour later, Paddy was sitting by the grey window that overlooked the ring road with an instant coffee from the complementary tray. He lit a thick Old Holborn roll-up and coughed up phlegm with his first few drags. He was thinking of his mother, the night Pa died, back in the old house tucked away behind the cattle market. He was just a little boy when it happened and it was the first time he'd ever seen the inside of his parents' bedroom.

He'd also seen the gun under a dislodged pillow after the ambulance men carried Pa away. He went and picked it up and took it downstairs to Ma. And what stuck in the memory was the calm way she reacted as she took it off him.

'Your uncle Bernie'll see to that, Patrick,' she said.

Paddy took a sip of his coffee, watching the traffic build up back to the law courts. The rain was beginning to fall in a thick drizzle, gusting in across the Fylde.

Last night Tom told him about his stay in the Shanakeel, the home for the bewildered in which he'd been resident out in the west of Ireland. He'd been going a bit over the top with his drinking, he said, but Paddy knew that wasn't the whole story.

'You've got to get over the old feller,' he'd advised. 'It's not as if you killed him. The man was fuckin' paranoid, living behind some cattle sheds with a gun under his pillow.'

And that seemed to set Tom off. Fair enough, Paddy reasoned, he could have phrased it a little more delicately. But it was the truth – in the heel of the hunt, Tom still blamed himself for driving Pa to his grave. As if the despair had killed the old man off.

At least that's what Paddy figured his problem must be.

Fuck it, he stubbed out his cigarette, why bother with family preoccupations? Why get involved? He'd pay his respects to the old girl and get himself and Bridget back on to the train to London as soon as he could. He felt suffocated.

As he downed the last of his coffee, the door flew open and there stood Tom, wet with the rain, holding aloft a bottle of rum.

'Ol' George still has his basement shebeen!' he announced and his red face was wild with joy.

***

Kate surveyed the scene, as the coffin bearers were called forward. She let her eyes wander over the gathering. This was a colourful family to say the least. There was Angela who was a double for Sophia Loren, with a suede skirt and boots, made up to perfection; and Bridget, who looked as though she'd fallen off a gypsy wagon and young Dan, who'd turned up out of the blue, his eyes like saucers; there was Paddy, looking like a folk singer and of course Tom, dressed up like Dean Martin on a drinking spree to Vegas, with a half empty bottle of rum sitting awkwardly in his jacket pocket.

When Angela and Bridget arrived that morning, and after the coffees were made (Martini for Bridget), they sat down together with the grandchildren and Mary to watch the video their uncle Bernie had sent from the USA. He was too poorly to travel for his sister-in-law's funeral. This was the best he could do.

Kate screamed out loud, as did Angela, when up on the screen popped Marlon Brando's enormous backside grinding away between a pair of splayed legs. Bridget projected a fine spray of Martini across the room and the kids sat with their mouths open. Amidst all the plates of sandwiches and sausage rolls, it was difficult for Kate to spot where she'd put the remote control but she scrabbled about for it. Mary hustled the children quickly out of the room, muttering apologies and, when she came back in, the four women hooted with laughter until the tears ran down their faces.

'Whatever the poor bugger had to say, we'll never know now,' said Bridget, gasping for breath.

***

Jesus Christ, thought Tom, the old ma died well above her fighting weight. He could feel himself struggling across the wet, bumpy graveyard. His footing kept giving way on the sludgy ground, with the effect of lurching the other coffin bearers off balance, tilting the load towards him – which in turn added to the weight he carried.

Truth be told, he was feeling the effects of the weekend as well, and this rainy Sunday morning felt particularly cruel. The cold drizzle stung like sprayed grit in his face.

As he fell over, he thought about the young lad he'd been drinking with on Friday. The lad who'd been out celebrating the Guild. His first Guild as an adult. He'd only known him for a short while, but Tom felt the pain of his loss as if he were family.

And then all of a sudden Danny was standing over him, grabbing for his arms to help him up. The pupils of the lad's eyes looked unnaturally wide, like a doe caught in the headlights. It had been a complete surprise when he turned up at the church – the first time Tom had seen him for almost a year.

'C'mon man,' he said, 'I'll give you a lift up.'

But Danny was just a feeble little fellow and he ended up in the mud as well, as they both slithered, wrestled each other almost upright and then fell together.

Tom could hear Angela cursing and muttering apologies to those around her, as he leaned up on one elbow. Danny was laughing uproariously, face-down in the mud, and beyond him on the soggy ground, the bottle of rum lay on its side.

He cast his eyes across those gathered by the graveside as Ma's coffin was dragged clumsily up to it. He saw a group of children aged between two and twelve and then, standing above them, the family he knew. Amongst them, Paddy and Bridget looking over with amused faces, Kate looking horrified, Mary concerned and Angela, darling Angela, his poor, long-suffering wife, staring daggers at him.

Tom knew from his days in the boxing ring that it was no use trying to get to his feet – his legs were gone. The drizzle had practically peeled the label off the rum bottle, which slid in his grip as he grabbed at it, leaning across Dan to do so. The priest was by the grave, beginning his eulogy, as Tom uncorked the bottle and brought it to his mouth.

'God rest you, Ma,' he muttered.

As Tom watched on, Dan jumped to his feet with his arms out-stretched and he tip-toed, like he was on a tightrope, back to join the rest of the party by the graveside. The boy looked mental.

The proceedings were being wound up when Tom smacked his lips, re-stopped the bottle and laid it back on the ground. His arse felt sodden. Nonetheless, he decided a rebel song would be appropriate for the moment.

'Alas and well may Erin weep, while Connaught lies in slumber deep.

But hark! A voice like thunder spake, the west's awake! The west's awake!

Sing oh! Hurrah! Let England quake! We'll watch 'til death for Erin's sake!'

And he punched the air above his head as the assembled looked on.

***

Bridget had a half bottle of Teacher's in her bag and she poured out a generous measure for herself and Paddy. They were sitting at a table on the Inter-City train back to Euston. Strands of hair had fallen from her beehive, some across her heavily made-up face, some tangled in and around her hoop earrings. She was so drunk she could only speak in guttural outbursts.

'That all seemed to go pretty well,' said Paddy, rolling up a cigarette. 'A nice fuckin' send off for the old girl.'

'Fugghin dizgrays, yer fugggn brudder.' Bridget's eyes were rolling in her head. She was drifting off to sleep.

'Could have been a hell of lot worse,' said Paddy, taking a belt of whiskey.

'They kept their necks wound in, Tom slept it off, we all had a good drink and the old one's safely in the ground.'

Paddy could see a smear of deep red buildings through the rain spattered windows. The smoke from his cigarette added to the gloom. He felt the relief grow, the further away from Preston they travelled. Bridget was snoring before they reached Warrington and once past Birmingham, with the Teacher's emptied, he stood up to go find the buffet car.

Before Going to Cork Airport

December 30 1992

'Thanks be to God,' said Tom, when his pint eventually arrived. 'I thought you must have keeled over while you were there at the tap, you've been so long.'

The barman was in his eighties and he held himself unsteadily by the counter.

'That'll be two punts,' he said, without a trace of humour. The place was virtually empty. Just two burly, muddied farmers at one end of the bar occasionally growling incomprehensibly at each other – probably continuing a family feud that had been simmering away through the generations. The rain outside had firmed up into a steady lash. Apart from that the only sound in the bar was the ticking of the clock.

'God rest the soul of poor Michael Collins!' said Tom, lifting his glass in the direction of John F Kennedy and the Pope, whose portraits were hanging behind the bar. A gust of wind whipped the rain against the door like a slithering rope.

'Fuck ye,' mumbled one of the farmers, the words were audible, before he inclined his head in Tom's direction and spat on the lino floor.

Fuck you too, thought Tom, I'm not scared, I could take you both out no trouble. In fact, to make it worth my while, why don't you round up half a dozen more of you bastards for me to floor.

***

As Tom trailed back to his home above the butcher's, he thought once more about the episode in the bar. Nothing had come of it but some posturing and curses. And, not being one to linger too long in a particular mood, he was soon singing Liverpool Lou and calling for large ones all round, leaving the farmers free to return to their dispute.

Now, back in his flat, Tom was recalling brawls of old that had broken out over beers, pranks and girls all across his life as a young man. He was sitting at a little fold-out table by the window overlooking the main street, with a bowl of corned beef hash, a chunk of soda bread and an opened bottle of Bull's Blood wine.

The rainwater had made meandering streams through the broken tarmac below, flowing past the street lamp and away towards the ditch. The rush of the swollen brook overpowered any other sound in the village. Tom had found a jazz station on the radio, which he turned up loud despite the weak reception. He could live with the hiss and distortion right now to hear some Miles Davis, and he filled his wine glass to the rim.

Earlier in the day he'd taken a trip to Bantry where he collected a parcel sent from his son in Yorkshire. He figured it must be the box full of family Super 8 movies. Dan said he was sending them over. Tomorrow, Tom was off to meet his ex-wife in London for the New Year's Eve celebrations. Their reconciliation had gone pretty well up to this point – although it took a while to patch things up again after his performance at the funeral a few months ago. He'd let his emotions get the better of him and Angela was vexed at the time, but she'd softened her stance in recent phone calls.

So it seemed everything was in hand and taken care of. He was packed and ready to go. It was one in the morning now, he would begin his drive to Cork Airport at 7 am. So, perhaps he had time to dust off his little projector and fold-out screen, and watch a film or two just like he used to in the old days. There was one in there of Pete Irongate boxing on Preston Flag Market.

It was Pete that gave him his first taste of the pub-brawling lifestyle. Tom met him during the Preston Guild of 1952 – the first held for thirty years due to the war. Pete had just returned from his National Service, a two year stint in the desert with a Scottish regiment where, he said, there was little to do but drink and fight. During Guild week all the pubs had extensions, official or not, and Pete had insisted on drinking like the Scots – large whiskeys chased down with Black and Tans. It would take no more than three rounds before he'd begin to prowl the bar in search of opponents.

Tom couldn't help but sway and swing a few hooks, as he recalled some of those street fights, back to back with Pete, dropping big lumbering fellows with body shots because it was easier on the fists. His sight was fixed on the streams of rainwater running along the village main street, as he took a large gulp of Bull's Blood and felt again the crunch of knuckle on rib. And he could hear, as if it were yesterday, the shouts around the bar at the Black Horse.

***

The floor of the Black Horse was made of mosaic tiling and Tom was leaning on the bar counter with his elbows, looking down at it. All the week's excesses seemed at once to have gathered to weigh him down. It was just past midnight and the pub was crowded. Pete had been gone for a while, to the toilet he said.

Tom was attempting to retrace his path through the Guild week up to that point. He could recall first meeting Pete here in the Black Horse, exactly a week ago, after the opening parade. But he had no idea if their subsequent sessions were pre-arranged, or whether they'd happened by chance.

Ah, fuck it, who cares? They'd had some fair scrapes together.

A dispute was beginning to boil over somewhere through the crowd, and he made to heave himself upright from the bar

121

counter. He could hear his father telling him to 'stand straight and walk up looking your best'. And he could smell the gym – the Wintergeen and sweat – and hear the heaving grunts of the boys at the heavy bags.

The barman tugged a short red cord to ring a bell at the bar.

Come out fighting, Tom Ballindine!

He'd have to look after his fists though, they were the tools of his trade. He needed good hands to study medicine and, as importantly, to box. He was due to sign up for the navy after he graduated and he was aiming for the Home Fleet title.

Shouts were being exchanged in the bar.

'Step outside and say that again, pal!' Someone issued a challenge.

Tom felt himself being jostled by the pushing and shoving. He was still attempting a full vertical stance and he hadn't let go of the counter's edge, when all of a sudden the lights began to spin and, with no control at all, his legs gave way from beneath him.

***

Tom picked the box up from the counter that separated his kitchen from the living room. The rain outside began to thicken up again, beating in waves against his window. He was a little unsteady on his feet. It had been a long day and the floor in this place was uneven.

He'd already set up the little fold-out screen and projector. He figured he could spot the reel with the fight on it out of the jumbled dozens in the box. It was older, it wasn't even a Super 8, it was just standard 8 millimetre film. He'd swiped the camera from a local newspaper that published his boxing reports. He hadn't a care about consequences when he strode into the offices of the Preston Guardian, that Saturday in 1952, claiming he needed the camera for work purposes. He'd had a few drinks by then and, after all, it wasn't far off the truth.

Outside the rain was throwing splashes off the road with

some force. Tom opened the sash window a little. It freshened the air when it rained hard like this. He paused with the wineglass to his lips while he wondered what it was about all this that was so familiar. But it escaped him.

The box was bound crazily with thick string, and wrapped with heavy brown greaseproof paper. It was typical of Danny. Messy, complicated and confused like the lad himself. To look at it told a tale.

Tom refilled his glass up to the rim and without thinking began to sing.

> 'Those days in our hearts we will cherish
> Contented although we were poor
> And the songs that we sung in the days we were young
> On the stone outside Dan Murphy's door...'

***

He woke up slowly. At first he fought against consciousness. The bed he lay in felt too damp and earthy, the room too cold, for this to be a gentle awakening. But soon he noticed a misty drizzle in the air and realised this was no bed. It must be a dream. Either that or he was lying in a ditch.

Where was he? He recalled drinking with Pete Irongate, they'd pitched up at the Black Horse after hitting most of the bars along Church Street.

Tom began to chuckle – the chaos they had left in their trail. But bollocks to the lot of them, they'd had some fun. He made to stand up but his legs wouldn't support him. He scratched his wrists and forearms on rose-thorns while he groped and scrabbled in the wet earth. It appeared that he was in a flower bed. He kneeled on all fours and looked about him like a dog and figured that the flower bed wasn't in a garden. He was in a park.

What the hell happened? He blinked as he tried to remember.

The fight on the Flag Market, it started to come back to him, he'd filmed it on a cine camera. He tapped his jacket pocket and felt the film roll still safe and sound. The silly bugger! He laughed out loud. Pete fought a booth fighter for a bet. Five pounds and a sore jaw it cost him.

Tom searched in all his pockets but his winnings had gone. Someone must have robbed him while he was passed out. He cursed aloud and tried to stand up once more but he gave way at the knees. He had no option but to crawl his way out of the park.

So he dragged himself across the spongy, sodden field with the mud and grass squelching beneath his hands and forelegs.

The booth fighter was a fellow from Chorley and was as hard as a bag of nails. He toyed with Pete for a round or two, jabbing him just enough to set his nose bleeding while avoiding the wild hay-makers coming his way. Whenever Pete got close with a punch, the Chorley man would grab him in a clinch and around the ring they staggered like drunks, to cries of derision from the onlookers.

After about five minutes of this, Pete seemed to physically tire and he leaned heavily on his opponent's shoulder.

'Where are you from?' he asked him, gasping for breath.

'Eh?' said the booth fighter, and Pete repeated the question, loudly. Tom could hear him from ringside.

'Chorley.' The reply was almost cordial.

And Pete stepped back as if to offer him a handshake, causing the booth fighter to hesitate, just for a moment but long enough for a tremendous left hook to connect with full force on his jaw – and he collapsed like a pack of cards.

'Well, you can tell 'em back in Chorley that you were knocked out by a Preston masher!' said Pete with great relish and he turned to receive the cheers from the onlookers. It seemed like a glorious moment but, sadly, it was all too brief.

Tom had already begun searching his trouser pockets to see if he could scrape together the five pounds on the bet, when the Chorley man rose menacingly to his feet, strode across the ring to Pete, who still held his arms aloft, and threw an almighty uppercut which lifted him clear off the canvas.

The bet was settled.

Tom was laughing as he crawled and squelched across the boggy field, and then he could see some gas lamps ahead and realised he was near the edge of Moor Park, adjacent to the Avenue. There were benches along Moor Park Avenue, and he decided a bench would make an ideal staging post. Once he reached one he might be able to haul himself back upright.

***

The rain had eased off again and the streams along the Main Street gushed with fresh energy. Hopefully the skies would clear in time for a good dawn, for the trip. Tom's wine glass was empty and he all but drained the bottle for another refill.

He'd been day dreaming, watching the rain splattering against the window and thinking on that fight, the many times he'd seen it. The picture shook badly for twenty seconds while he'd quickly grabbed for the camera to start filming again. It was just at the point where Pete was knocked out. He'd put it down in the first place to search his trousers for money.

He looked down at the box. The knots in the string looked complicated but he couldn't resist struggling with them. If Dan had tied this all up, it surely wouldn't be that difficult to unravel it.

Of course, he would find all the other films inside the box too. He paused to think about it. His life with Angela was in there, packaged in little three minute reels. And then, later on in the sequence, little Danny comes along. In the old days, when they used to have home movie nights, they would try to play them chronologically. Those were the days when they knew which reel was which.

Ella Fitzgerald was singing *I Was Doing All Right* on the radio and Tom took a deep gulp of wine. He was thinking about all the little three minute pieces of his life while looking at the rain run in streams down his window and through the village.

Watching a booth fight in Preston was one thing, reliving the high life he'd once lived with Angela was another.

***

The bench was within a few yards now and Tom crawled with all his might – it had become his sporting challenge. He was using all the last round strength he could summon to get there. Those reserves of energy you must call upon to keep jabbing and clinching, and so see it through to the final bell.

But before he could reach it his hand came to grasp a human ankle. Tom found himself looking down at two sturdy black boots and a set of lower legs dressed in a pair of pressed trousers. He had struck upon one of Preston's finest.

'Good evening, lad,' said the policeman from a great height.

'A good evening to you officer,' Tom managed.

'Are you all right, lad? Do you know where you're going?'

'Yes sir,' said Tom, 'and if you'd be good enough to help me to my feet I should be able to make it there easily.'

'You don't look in very good shape to me,' said the policeman as he helped Tom onto a bench. Tom could feel an uncomfortable lump under his right foot and was untying his shoe laces.

'It's my foot,' he said absently. He took his shoe off and found, stuck to his sock, a tightly wadded five pound note. Tom unfolded it in wonder and then began to laugh. Pete Irongate! Pete must have carried him here after he passed out in the pub. And he'd thought to hide his winnings.

The policeman's face was filled with apprehension as Tom looked up at him and rose to his feet.

'You might want to be careful, carrying cash of that sum around with you at this time of night,' he said.

Tom could feel the policeman's gaze upon his back as he staggered wildly to the top of Moor Park Avenue and onto the Garstang Road, where he turned and disappeared out of view.

He managed to find a couch to sleep on, not far away with a friend of his, but the next morning back at the family home he got such a severe bollocking from his father it still stung him to this day. The old man had only been weeks away from his death, but he seized upon Tom as soon as he stumbled into the cobbled yard and dragged him through the kitchen door. There, he delivered him a tremendous clout to the back of the head. It virtually put Tom's lights out.

'Drink shall be the rock ye perish on lad, if you don't pull yourself together!' And he slapped him hard across the cheek for good measure.

'There I was, hoping that one day you'd make a man of yourself and go back home to Ireland,' the old man muttered, as he let go of Tom's collar to walk out of the kitchen.

The Guild of 1952 was over.

***

Tom had worked apart a knot in the string and was pulling the package through the hole he'd made. He ripped the remaining paper off like a child at Christmas and pulled open the lid of a thick shoe-box – and then he stared for some time at its contents before reaching in.

What the fuck had Dan done now? Tom felt the exasperation rising. Instead of the box full of little film reels he'd expected to see, he found two video cassettes and a note. The note was written on one side of a sheet of paper, torn scrappily from a pad. It was dated December 23 1992. He read it twice.

Dad, I wanted you to have these videos made by a good friend of mine. I thought you might like to watch some of what I did with the band those few years. If you see mum soon, maybe you could show them to her too.

All is well here. Jessie is fine. We have two dogs, both in

good voice. One howls whenever I play the blues, the other growls.

When the weather brightens up, I fancy coming over for a visit.

In the meantime, may the gentlest of breezes fill your sails.

Tom made to pour himself another drink but instead found only a trickle left in the bottle. The Brubeck on the radio sounded a little like the Keystone cops. The streams outside had calmed down to a gurgle.

What use were videos? He didn't even have a machine to play them on.

Tom looked at the two plastic cassette tapes. He must have misunderstood Dan's message about films. He'd assumed he meant the Super 8s. Now he'd have to find someone locally who had a video machine.

He switched off the standard lamp and slumped onto the sofa. He figured he should get a couple of hours' kip before setting off for the airport. It was probably a good idea. And, with the radio still crackling away 5/4 time, he rested his head on a rag cushion and let another day drift to a conclusion.

Losing a Family from Two Points of View

December 31 1992

We had a little flat at the time. Well, a maisonette, they call it. It wasn't a bad place, you could even say it was chic. It had thick-pile, pub style carpets – I remember that – and a sliding glass door onto a balcony. Angela insisted on calling it a terrace, she's always had a knack for talking things up. And I remember that the record playing on the stereo was Miles Davis, Kind of Blue, when it all got out of hand.

It's tempting to look back on it as a genteel house party – a relaxed but polite occasion, the guests dressed in their finest and everything going without a hitch. Angela would certainly have wanted it that way. But I guess I managed to fuck any chance of that up, in some style.

Pete Irongate, myself and a few others had watched Teófilo Stevenson beat Bobick in their Olympic Games fight, roaring on the Cuban as he destroyed his opponent in the third. There was no television at the flat, so we'd dived across the road to a friend of Pete's – a strange, sour little fellow who worked at the post office. His wife was much better value. She poured out the drinks and tipped fresh peanuts into bowls around the room, while swapping jokes and taking the occasional, friendly slap on the arse. It was easy to imagine that in fact she, and not the husband, was Pete's friend.

I played along too, she seemed a lively lady, and I noticed a lad running about the house who looked roughly the same age as Dan. So I invited them all over to the party.

How was I supposed to know it would be the cause of so

129

much trouble? I can't even remember the fellow's name now. Nor the boy's.

The wife was called Abigail.

***

The cine film from the 1972 Guild week has a bleached out look, as if it had all been shot into the sun. Those three reels contain the final segments of family footage in the box and then, all of a sudden, it's the 1980s and the camera has passed on to Dan. Nine scratchy minutes of parades, celebrations, fun-fairs and parties – and then it stops. The decade and the family ends there.

Dan's hands are shaking badly as he tries to join the film. He wants those nine minutes to run in sequence. It's the only sequential section of the feature length reel he's constructing. For some reason it has become important to see them as a whole. Although that's not the reason his hands are shaking. He took five or six ephedrine pills a quarter of an hour ago and they're just starting to kick in. He needs a stiff drink to take the edge off.

He pours himself a large whiskey, drains the glass in three swallows, refills it and opens his tobacco tin. He takes the time out, while having a smoke, to dredge his memories of the occasion but very little comes to mind. He would have been eight years old at the time. He can remember an attic room where the games were, some other boys running about – kids of party guests – and that's about it. Except for recollections of a day when the streets were full of people and floats passed by, with everyone cheering and waving.

Maybe he's confusing two separate occasions. He finishes his second glass and stubs out the cigarette. Who knows? Maybe, in fact, his memories have been made for him by watching the films so often.

He sets back to work with the scissors and tape. He has less than a quarter of a shoe-box to get through before he'll have joined every reel into one feature length film – and all of it, except for these nine minutes, will be in random order.

***

Did you ever see that guy box? Teófilo Stevenson? He was as fast and clever as Ali and he punched a lot harder. When he hit Bobick that night, the big Yank hope fell like a rag doll. Teófilo's opponent for the final didn't even show up, probably scared shitless. What a fighter that guy was – he'd have beaten Ali, in my opinion.

After the Bobick fight, and back at the flat, the drinks and toasts were flowing:

'To Fidel!'
'Viva la Revolución!'

And suchlike. Paddy looked like Castro, he had a similar beard and jawline. He and Bridget had caught the train up from London and brought some of their jazz club mates along. They arrived as if they had been drinking the whole journey, rattling in through the door with a box of bottles and bunches of drooping flowers.

Once the toasts for Teófilo were complete, the singing started up. Angela was passing around plates of cocktail sausages and chicken drumsticks to a chorus of *Whiskey in the Jar,* when a clamour rose for her to contribute. She wiped her hands on a dishcloth and sang to a hushed gathering – the Nat King Cole song, *When I Fall in Love.* Angela has a beautiful voice.

After the cheers died down, Paddy stood up to sing *The Stone Outside Dan Murphy's Door.* And I saw this as a perfect moment to open the first bottle of Jameson's.

We must have been at it for a couple of hours before the records came out and the floor was cleared for dancing. The kids were safely out of the way, playing in the attic, so we could let our hair down a bit. It was the full dark of night outside. From the first floor windows we could see the lamp-heads glowing orange and we could hear revellers passing below in the street, singing and cheering.

***

All of a sudden Dan is in the mood for some Neil Young. He scrabbles around for the tape and sets it playing loud enough to drown out the World Service. One of the dogs laid out in front of the stove, lifts his head, yawns and goes back to sleep. Dan leans over both of them and throws two small logs on the embers.

After the Gold Rush starts up and Dan lowers himself onto the sofa, watching as the flames slowly take to the new wood. The sound of the piano, the voice, the visionary images – this song makes him think of...

What the hell does it make him think of?

Jessie has gone and he can't believe it. Announced she's pregnant, upped and gone – just like that.

The fire spits and sparks in a staccato burst and the dogs lift their heads in alarm. Then they both, as one, turn to look at Dan. His eyes are beyond them, he has no response to give, and they settle back down as they were.

Although he can't deny it, Jessie packing up for London has been on the cards for some time. She's never taken to it up here on the moors. And it seems, while his own fortunes plummet, so Jessie's are on the rise. It makes sense for her to be back in town. In all honesty, he should be as well – but he can't face it. Too much has gone wrong lately. He needs some distance away from it all.

Dan looks up from the stove grate and shakes his head. The dogs are snoring and twitching. The song is just coming to an end – and he thinks about that new home in the sun.

***

I was always of the mind that, presented with a choice of fight or flight, I would always stand – and if necessary, throw punches. I wouldn't, for example, walk in on someone fucking my wife and just turn on my heels and leave. I would drag whichever bastard it was off the woman and batter the bejesus out of him.

I'm not just saying that because I did a bit of boxing in my time. More to demonstrate that I wouldn't have liked what happened, happening to me.

I remember once, staggering back with Pete Irongate to his house in Ribbleton after an afternoon's drinking and we walked in to find his wife entertaining a visitor. They were only sitting, drinking cups of tea with some cake slices on a dish, but Pete pulled the poor guy off his chair and beat him senseless.

He was raging, and frankly it was a bit over the top – Irene, the poor lass, was near hysterical – but I figured I might have done the same myself. It was the cosiness of the whole scene that seemed unnatural. What kind of man has tea and cake with someone else's wife?

The night I overstepped the mark, at least, was an occasion. It was the Preston Guild of 1972. Everyone was in high spirits, I mean the whole town, and the atmosphere was heady. There was a party in our little first floor maisonette. Condensation trickled down the windows, while Brubeck played on the stereo and the floor shook to the treading of dance steps.

I remember the room was in half light. I think whatever light there was came from the kitchen through the breakfast bar. Jackets had been thrown over the backs of chairs and couples were moving together slowly, swaying at the hips.

I remember Abigail grabbing at my arm and whispering, 'Shall we check on the boys?' in such a way as her lips moved wetly on my ear. Even her breath was moist.

Life would have worked out a lot simpler if I'd turned her down.

***

So Dan busily assembles the reels, slicing up Sellotape and trimming film to make the joins as smooth as possible. Neil Young rattles from the cassette player, the dogs are asleep and he has achieved a trance-like state as he works.

He recalls one night in early December when he and Jessie were sat up in bed watching TV. The house was cold and they were both wearing jumpers, holding cups of tea with an ashtray between them. It was a large, bulky black and white TV, positioned right next to the bed on a packing crate. It had to be that close because there was only one plug socket in the room and the power lead was short. Jessie had once sawn it in half in a rage.

They had been watching a documentary about the future of technology. It was predicting many wild and wonderful things, such as the ability for people to send video messages to each other using mobile phones. A future that, to Dan, seemed ridiculous.

The Neil Young album finishes and now it's just tape hiss playing, as he pulls another reel from the box. The World Service is audible again. He's in the habit of leaving the radio on all the time. He finds the muttering voices to be a source of comfort.

The documentary also predicted that soon a majority of the world's population would own a personal computer, and that on the back of the internet, a vast, global media database would emerge. Picture a cross between a library, a high street and a cinema – the narrator spoke like an advertiser. It would be revolutionary because, with so many people able to contribute, it would reflect the sum of collective human intelligence.

Dan turned to Jessie at that point and said, 'Wouldn't it also reflect the sum of collective human stupidity?' And he saw that her face was wet with tears. She had been crying in silence and he hadn't noticed until then.

'We can't go on like this any more,' she sobbed.

Dan remembers being stuck for words.

'Why not?' He felt hopeless for even asking. She looked

hopeless. She looked as though she'd also run out of things to say.

Think of something else, Dan tells himself and he puts down his feature-length reel. The item on the radio is about South Africa and its new found freedom. The voices are joyful. Change has come!

Nonetheless Dan has an urge to immerse himself in the 1970s, and he searches for something else. Another piece of music to suit his mood. He finds a Pink Floyd tape and holds it aloft like a prize-winning ticket.

***

With hindsight, Angela was right to have left like she did. She was a classy lady and she didn't deserve the indignity of the scene. Having said that, when I slipped out of the living room with Abigail, Angela was in the middle of the dancers, whooping and cheering with her arms in the air. The mood was carefree, or at least mine was. I must have thought Angela was in a similar mood.

I met her on the eve of 1959, at a dinner dance in Victoria. The Grosvenor, it was a swish do. And from that night on we lived a good life, in London at first and then, with Danny Boy on his way, we retreated to Preston. We were in our late thirties during that Guild. We had an eight year old boy and a full future ahead of us. That was before I went and fucked everything up.

Abigail was like a she-devil, bewitching me, when I look back on it. I was led along by the leash. She'd probably done this sort of thing thousands of times. But that made it even more of a mystery as to why her sour-faced husband should have reacted the way he did.

The corridor was dark outside the living room. She held on to my arm as we reached the foot of the step ladder leading up to the attic play room. I let her go first up the steps and she wiggled her behind in such a way that was inviting my hand –

just to lend some support, as it were. As she opened the hatch door, she stopped. The boys voices called out in unison – 'Don't come in! Don't come in!' – and I stood below her with a foot on the bottom step.

'All right, love,' she said, 'another ten minutes, then. But after that it's time for your bed.'

And she started into reverse, down the steps, saying that they were playing toy soldiers, had hundreds of them lined up all over the floor. They were aiming rubber bands at them. We stood in front of each other in the corridor. I could feel the heat rising from her and I felt awkward.

'His coat will be in the pile on Dan's bed,' I said and made for the small bedroom. She followed me. And next thing I knew we were up against the wall, pulling each other's shirts off. It was like being in a dream – in a blur of lips and hair. We wrestled each other onto the bed and on top of a mess of coats and scarves.

I could hear bass and trumpet from the front room. It may as well have been from another world.

***

And so Dan reaches the final reel, joins it onto the rest and his feature length home movie is complete. He's lost track of time, it's been dark for a long while. Snow is starting to fall again – he can see flurries blowing across the kitchen window. Icicles are hanging from the guttering on the wood-shed.

The Pink Floyd track has some synthesised barking and howling in it – authentic enough to stir the dogs, who begin pacing about the floor while Dan fixes the reel onto the projector.

Before he sets the film rolling he feels the urge to gobble down a few more pills, downers this time, just to settle himself for the viewing. He rolls a smoke, pours a whiskey and flips the switch. The music is still belting out. Dan figures it'll make a good soundtrack.

As he takes the overhead light off, the images come to life on the wall – his mother and father driving through the Lake District, then across Ireland. And then it leaps to Bush Road, a walk around No. 1 and through to the back yard, the camera zooming in on grinning faces: Jessie, Frank and Monica. Keith the Keys stumbles past the shot wearing a pork-pie hat. It was a sunny day by the looks of it, Frank and Monica are wearing shades. Then the projection turns to flecked white as it reaches the next of his joins.

The music rolls on and Dan refills his whiskey glass. He can feel a deep stupor coming on, five days of pills and booze are catching up with him. He tries to fight it. He wants to see his handiwork in full. He's curious to find out if the random order in which the films have been assembled makes any sense. Although, somewhere in the back of his mind he knows he's doing all this as a way of avoiding the things he should be thinking about.

The dogs have been pacing the floor, letting out the occasional whimper, but now they are settling back down again. One creeps onto the end of the sofa and treads about in a circular fashion on a newspaper, before curling up into a ball. The logs in the stove are in full flame but it's not enough to warm the kitchen. Dan lit the oven earlier as back up – between that and the stove, the chill has just about been lifted.

A new scene begins on the kitchen wall. A dark film full of specks, strands of hair and flash-burns – the oldest in the box. It's of two men in a boxing ring, a windy day by the looks of it. Flags are rippling in top screen. Dan has seen this film many times when he was young, but he only dimly recalls the tale that accompanies it.

At this point he begins to lose consciousness. He tries to keep his head upright but it's like trying to lift a boulder. As he recedes, he feels the grip of panic, albeit a dulled one. He tells himself that this isn't how it's supposed to end. He tells himself to breathe deeply – keep breathing!

The snow works up into a flurry outside as, finally, his chin sinks to his chest.

Both dogs lift up their heads to look at him while the music plays on.

And soon enough the track ends and the kitchen falls quiet – just the tape hiss and rattle of 8mm film and the mumbling radio voices.

***

So that was it, that was the story of how I came to be in this situation. Everyone says that Abigail's husband committed suicide. That was the final verdict from the police too. I heard about it all in London when I went down to talk to Angela – to try salvaging the marriage. I couldn't believe the fellow had killed himself, just for that. There must have been more to it.

Angela wasn't amused in the slightest, even after a couple of weeks away from it all with her parents in Pimlico. She'd caught the first train to Euston the morning after the party, along with Bridget and Paddy and little Danny Boy. I waved them off at the station with tears clouding up my eyes. And then I returned to the flat in Fishergate and drank rum for four days straight.

When Angela heard of the husband's death, she couldn't bring herself to come back to Preston. That's what she told me when I met her in Victoria. Her mind was made up. She was going to find work and a place to live in London – and Danny would live with his grandparents.

It was a long train journey back after that conversation. I'd hoped to be bringing them both home with me. As soon as I stepped off the train and out into the coal-smoke Preston evening, I made for the nearest pub. Some lads were standing at the end of the bar watching the Ali-Patterson fight on a small black and white TV, which was set up on the counter. The landlord eyed me over suspiciously as I ordered a pint. He wiped his hands on a towel tucked into his belt and poured it without a word.

I perched up at the counter as I downed my beer, listening

to the boys cheer and groan as Ali made mincemeat of the poor old guy. This pub was a hundred yards or so away from the maisonette. And it was just a few hundred yards further on, at the Fishergate bridge, where the little fellow committed suicide. They say that he attempted to hang himself but whatever he used as rope snapped as he fell.

I think I was crying, looking down at my pint glass, because the landlord asked me in a whisper whether I wanted to be sitting at the bar in the state I was in.

'Teófilo Stevenson would beat Ali, if they ever fought. Believe me, he'd knock him out,' I said to him, before I got up off the stool and left.

***

'Anyway,' the big fellow finishes up his drink, 'that's about the sum of it.'

Well, I did ask, the barman thinks to himself while he folds up the newspaper. But all I wanted to know was how the wife came to be in London.

The Tannoy sounds with a ping.

'Flight V420 to London Heathrow is now boarding at Gate Two.'

The barman hovers to clear the glasses. This man has been in the bar for nearly three hours waiting for his flight. Now it has finally been called, surely he'll be on his way. Instead, the big fellow looks at his watch before fixing him with a grin.

'There'll be time for a gulper while I let the eejits shuffle along in a queue,' he says and he holds out his tumbler.

Jesus, is there never to be an end to this? What more could he talk to him about? The barman lets the optic refill before forcing the rim against it a second time.

'So, you mentioned you had a son...?' he says, as he opens up his hand for the three punt coins. 'Whatever happened to him?'

An Out of Body Experience

December 31 1992

Strummer threw Pip a glance. He was at that moment spread out flat on the floor while Pip was curled up at the end of the kitchen sofa, which meant throwing a glance involved tilting his head at an upward angle with his jowl pressed against the cold flagstone. Yet he managed to catch her watery eye.

He and Pip didn't need much more to communicate. It was understood. And right now they were both in agreement. Their patience was running out. It wouldn't be long before they would have to resort to one of a few possible courses of action.

As a general rule the two of them made a good team – just on the odd occasion she would go flappy and dizzy on him – but when something had to be done, on the whole, they managed to do it. And for all her flaws, she was an accommodating bitch. He'd often jumped her bones, as he liked to say, and she welcomed it.

Their current problem was that the boss had been sprawled out on the kitchen sofa a little too long for their liking. He had been increasingly prone to these spells of unconsciousness and of late it was a matter to cause Strummer and Pip some concern. They were used to a certain regularity in life. And the central act demanded of them, to maintain regularity, was to make the journey. The daily journey of life.

The fact that this was now overdue, that they should have thrown the door open and bounded out into the evening a good while back, made some imminent form of action inevitable. Which particular one was the question.

140

They could cry at the door, set off a forlorn wailing, and hope a passer-by should hear. But that was always humiliating. Or they could dump their loads over the floor, choose somewhere for maximum impact.

These both seemed like extreme measures, so they decided to try some nuzzling first. Pip could get in there with her long nose and hoist up his head and drop it again with ease. While he could do the licking.

A striking clock lifted Strummer's ear and Pip picked her head up to look around. The radio was on. The embers were low in the wood-burner grate. It was beginning to feel cold.

The light in the kitchen came from a desk-lamp, bent double on a messy table by a wall, and from a small cine projector beamed onto the wall opposite. A beam that just missed a whiteboard with the words 'Dan's Plan' written on it. Next to the outstretched arm of their slumbering leader was a low-slung coffee table, as always cluttered with drinking paraphernalia and a landslide of an ashtray. No cause for serious alarm, yet an unhappy scene. One in which the prospect of bounding out for their evening journey seemed a long way off.

They exchanged one more glance before they both slowly picked themselves up. It was time to get their snouts busy again.

***

The pipes are calling, from glen to glen and down the mountainside.

Yet out on the tops what's unavoidable is the vast expanse of sky, a dazzling blue, which is suddenly filling up with dark cloud like Guinness rolling into a pint glass. Pouring over rock and heather it is swallowing the ground rapidly and you run Danny Boy, you run before the weather should overtake you.

Why is it always in these still, blissful moments that an unwelcome interruption is likeliest?

Nonetheless the moment, whatever it consisted of, is lost. And now you feel yourself curiously low-down amongst the undergrowth of a woodland, panting for breath and scampering erratically. You know the path of protection, the circular gallop that at once guards the herd, or pack or whatever and yet moves the whole party onwards, but this time there's a flappy, dizzy bitch that refuses to form up. Some wet-nosed, persistent flapper that keeps nagging at your face.

The landscape here is dramatic and bleak. Hardly any light makes it down this far, the valley sides are so steep. So each day you make this journey, the patrol that leads through the woodland undergrowth. First through sparse, steep fields, then the wood, then the crags that protrude from the earth like bare working shoulders, all up ahead – a good, neck-tilting look up ahead. Reaching the tops is like reaching heaven with so much sky and vast, empty heathland to climb into.

But just now this terrain has been transformed into a snowscape.

The valley is hushed and white with snow...

That's right, it's snowing outside. You are projecting the Super 8s onto the wall, and the radio is on. The clock's striking and someone is reading out the news headlines – something about the end of the Cold War and the dawning of a new era.

And the shiny, snowbound surface of the steep valley side contrasts perfectly with the black sliver of sky above. But all that changes when you hit the tops. Up where the air is enormous and sweet. Where the world opens into infinite possibilities. So many directions to take, all those potential journeys.

And in the deep dark you rely on the herding circles, those scampering feet and the heavy panting, to keep you moving in the right direction through the woods – which are so thin as to have no trail but thick enough to house mossy glades full of mystery.

Jesus – you feel like a beaten fighter all of a sudden, lying on your back as if having taken a flurry of punches. How did that

142

happen? People at ringside are trying to push you back to your feet, but they keep lifting you by the head. And their long, slippery snouts keep dropping you.

That's right – you were watching a boxing match at a fairground in grainy monochrome. And now it feels as if the crisp white valley floor upon which you lie is in fact the kitchen wall, currently a film screen, and you are that booth fighter sent reeling to his knees. And your ring is the endless white moorland at night, the snow sparkling with starlight, a huge silent arena up there, if only you could get back onto your feet. Get out of your pit and up on your feet, Danny Boy!

The pipes, the pipes are calling. You must go and I must bide.

And you see someone running across the tops, disappearing into the distance. She is skipping across deep set snow, leaving the words ringing in your ears, 'I can't say when I'll be back.'

She's gone and left you out here. The bitch.

And your head hits the ground once again.

The act of herding along a narrow trail is performed in patterns, like Celtic knots, using tight loops around the party. But up on the tops the patterning can range out into wide, galloping arcs – clear distances being easier to cover. However, even on the tops it throws the whole exercise into confusion when the party splits in two.

All of a sudden a flood of black cloud swallows up the sky and the ground ahead, rolling towards you like stout from a tap. So you run and scamper down the valley side as the storm spreads behind and overhead. And into the woods, where you stumble, slip and scramble and sense your pursuer like a hand reaching out towards your shoulder.

The clock strikes the final chime of the hour and it rebounds across the open, empty winter space.

From glen to glen and down the mountainside.

'We will discuss the New World Order of outgoing President Bush's design and what it might mean for Britain.'

You recognise the voice speaking these words. It's the

143

soothing voice of an old friend. But it doesn't help calm your thudding heart as you hurtle towards the backyard and the protection of the wood-shed, the weather sweeping in behind you like a giant net.

You watch, as with each loud beat of your heart she throws another item of clothing into a holdall.

You must... go and... I must... bide.

And she tells you she can't be certain when she'll be back. This sets you off howling pitifully at the door, waiting for someone to pass by and hear. Instead everyone raises their glasses to the camera while children play party games in the background. A boy is rubbing his eyes with the sleeves of his football shirt, which he scrunches up in his fists, and it's you little Dan. That's you up there on the wall.

And is that film burn or the glare of a childhood sunset as the camera moves in close to your blinking face? Never mind Danny Boy, get up on your feet!

The storm gathers up the ground to your rear like stampeding hooves. And there's the backyard, a little tin roof over the wood store – a shelter so close you can almost smell the wood chippings and frosty moss, and hear the drip of the melting ice from the cracked gutter.

'And we'll be discussing the prospects of an expanded Europe with the German Foreign Minister,' says a voice much like your old granddad's.

You recall her smile while you run for shelter, looking into the thick white ground with the padded sound of galloping and panting all around you. She paused at the front door, long enough to let through a chilling draught, before she threw you that smile and said, 'I can't say for sure when I'll be back.'

With the wood-shed now within touching distance you reach forward, chest-out like a sprinter, just the last few leg-wobbling strides, whereupon the storm engulfs you like the earth itself. And then it's all frozen over, pitch dark and silent in the glen except for the disappearing tap of footsteps.

Tho' soft you tread above me...

144

The snow lies deep on the ground, drifting across the tops and down the valley sides. The wood-shed is bejewelled with thick icicles. Through the kitchen window you can see dust floating through a projector beam, a burnt yellow square at the end of it on the far wall. A dog is snuffling at your face, as you lie passed out on a battered leather sofa in front of a small pot-belly stove. Another dog is pacing the room in agitated circles, whimpering and yelping.

There's the click, click, click of the projector wheel, turning a filled-up reel around, and the radio is on. It's the World Service news. The story is about the changing world map.

And your face is being scrubbed roughly with a rasping flannel. A slobbering, rough fleshy flannel.

Jessie's Journal
Part 1

Conceiving Baby Blue

December 26 1992

My name is Jessie Mooncoin and I am a fiction writer. Scenes spill from my thoughts as easily as wine from a bottle – and my mingling of fact and fiction makes for a heady brew. I like to write my stories the way I live my life and therefore I write dangerously, impulsively, intimately – I thrive on relationships, especially when they're spontaneous.

I turned my back on a normal life when I left home and now, over ten years later, trundling down the M1 in a large delivery van, I don't regret it in the slightest. Snow is banked up on the side of the motorway, the windscreen is misting over and it's twilight. A Fleetwood Mac tape booms from the stereo. I met Dave, the driver, for the first time last night. I am alive.

This notepad will now become my mini journal. I am going to spend the duration of this van ride telling you about how I got here so, if this is to be my last journey (and you never know) then at least everyone will understand why I took it. My deadline for a finished piece is the moment we pull up at our destination in London. But truth be told, I struggle with deadlines.

So I could begin by telling you about my childhood. I could tell you about those charmed years, running through yellow fields, carefree and magical. But I'd be lying. It was nothing like that. I was an only child that went to suburban schools and almost everyone I encountered was dull and predictable.

My parents aren't even worth mentioning. They were like grey shadows cowering about the house, lost in the cobwebs of semi-retirement.

So I'll skip the childhood and begin with university. When I hit Sheffield I was ready for it. Riots had broken out across the country and here I was – in the People's Republic of South Yorkshire. But to tell the truth I wasn't much interested in demonstrations or the red flag flying on the Town Hall. I was ready to taste life, to explore and experiment. I studied Literature and became obsessive about the American beatniks and hippies. I howled. I was a cowgirl – a prisoner of the freeway.

I didn't even finish my second year. Fuck it, who needed institutionalising anyway? I fell in with an artist called Gavin within a month of getting there and he took me into a world beyond the campus. A long way beyond. Gavin was my first love, in fact he was my only real attempt at love until I met Dan...

I have to break off to describe the skies over the South Peaks. The sunset spreads between and beyond the crags, throwing pink splashes across a sheet of ink above. Up ahead, all I can see is a blur of tail-lights through the mist and ice on the windscreen. Or is the mist outside? Either way, it's a wonder Dave can see anything at all to drive. He seems chirpy enough though, sliding some Joni Mitchell into the cassette slot. The first song is *Coyote* and I can't help throwing him a smile. I've just stubbed out a small joint that I smoked myself. Dave is smoking his own, which he asked me to roll about half an hour ago. It's easier to smoke our own than to think about passing one between us in the cab, with conditions so bad and Dave having to keep his eyes on the road.

And now, as darkness truly sets in, I have to continue by dashboard light...

The first time that I met Gavin we did acid together. Acid is *my* drug. Others may struggle with suddenly throwing open all their portals to the subconscious, with the shift in time and

150

gravity brought on by coming up, but I revel in it. It makes me want to dance. And fuck. The night I met Gavin, we didn't do much dancing.

His body was breathtaking. I'd never tripped like that before. The desire was instant. And, from that first night, Gavin and I became soul-mates. Over the next couple of years we were rarely apart.

There were three strong themes to my time with Gavin. Sex, art and freedom. He was a photographer and a sketcher. I was often his model. We had no money. We hitch-hiked wherever we went...

I am now writing this wrapped in a sleeping bag in the back of the van. Dave is snoring softly beside me. We are wedged in amongst pieces of sculpture strapped up in boxes. I have a thick slab of candle, waxed onto the van floor next to my head, for light.

Earlier we had to concede that the weather was too poor to go any further. Dave could barely see the road. We left the motorway at the next junction and found a pub car park to pull into. We bought a fish and chips dinner and we toasted Boxing Day. It was a bleak, stale pub with worn through carpet and a few elderly customers, but we didn't care. It was warm.

Dave finally brought up the subject of last night's Christmas party. He apologised, saying that he didn't know I had a man. He'd turned up with a friend of a friend, mid-evening, when just a few people were over and Dan was out with Frank somewhere. As it is, I tend to be over-friendly with someone I haven't met before, but last night I was in full swing to the point where I was probably giving him the come-on.

The party was still going strong when I sloped off to bed. It wasn't long after that, that I was brought out of my dreams by the feathery feeling of being undressed. Someone was in the bed beside me and the certainty and firmness of his touch felt exciting. The room was as dark as pitch, with little in the way of street-lighting near our house. It felt like being blindfolded. I

151

kicked my legs up to help off my pyjama bottoms.

I knew it wasn't Dan. Even while I was willing myself to stay in my dreams, I knew it wasn't him. But I let him explore for as long as it took before he brought his face in for a kiss. And then I felt his beard, yelped and pushed him away.

I sat up holding the duvet to my chest and all I could see was the vapour from my gasping breath.

'I thought you were Dan,' I lied...

'That's OK, I knew you weren't Dan,' I said in the pub. I shouldn't really have said it, but I'd taken some speed earlier in the ladies, which tends to loosen my tongue. I plan on writing all night and figured a pick-me-up would help.

So he asked why exactly I was going to London, the first time he's bothered since we started out, and I told him all about my upcoming meeting with a publisher. I didn't want to discuss my other, more grim, appointment in town, or the fact that I need some space away from Dan.

Later, in the van, as we were settling into our sleeping bags I had to make Dave feel, well, 'comfortable' before he would fall asleep and let me carry on with my journal.

He sees this as our adventure together, he tells me...

I had my first inkling of Gavin's adventurous nature when the subject of earning extra cash came up. Grant money didn't stretch far and Gavin did life modelling, it was easy work. But significantly, the only job he set me up with was a private arrangement – a foppish, well-off teenager from Dore and his three friends who were willing to pay for their sweaty smudges and fantasies (£5 each for an hour's sitting). The poses they wanted me to assume were essentially pornographic but I didn't mind. I was comfortable enough on a mound of cushions, with the boys thumping away behind their easels, and the whole situation threw some light on Gavin's predilections. He liked to share.

I found this out for sure at the end of a long night walking the city, both of us tripped to the eyeballs. Tripping made

Sheffield's steep climbs seem light and we skipped, rather than stumbled, towards our house as the night lifted with the onset of dawn. Inside we found Neil and John huddled under a huge, thick blanket, listening to the Doors. There was a pot of tea, a jug of milk and two cups arranged on the floor beside them. The curtains were closed and all they had for light was an electric coal fire. The bars weren't on, just the bulbs flickering behind orange and black plastic moulding.

I was particularly taken with the tea-for-two arrangement and the notion that they were going to organise it all under a blanket. What I wanted was to crawl under the blanket with them. Gavin pulled cushions from the sofa and piled them all around us while I began peeling off my boots. Neil and John were lost in *Riders on the Storm*, silent except for the occasional outburst of laughter.

It was some while later, when I leaned out of our nest to pour the tea – a process which seemed to take forever – that the fun and games began. First Gavin took hold of me and with a burst of dawn fervour engaged me in athletic sex in amongst the cushions. Once spent, he crawled across the floor searching for his jeans to dig out some tobacco.

I was still getting my breath back when John began stroking my breasts. Before I knew it, he started going down on me and I looked over at Gavin who was sat fumbling with a disjointed roll-up, smiling and nodding. It felt good for him and it felt good for me. So I went with the moment. And I wasn't even put off by Neil, propped up on one elbow fingering my hair and looking at my face closely.

This happened a few months before I found out that Gavin and John were lovers...

OK, I'm writing again after Dave woke up and went mental at my candle. I'd only nipped out for a quick pee, but it seems the sharp breeze not only woke him up but set the wick flickering wildly so that it licked at my sleeping bag.

He said that we were carrying valuable art, created by some

153

young genius. That he'd been paid well to deliver it to an extremely rich private viewer in St John's Wood and to get it there, from Leeds, by December the 27th. If any of it was damaged, loss of earnings would be the least of his problems.

I glanced at the wardrobe shapes strapped to the van sides, covered over with dust sheets. They looked like vertical coffins.

'Oh,' I said. It all seemed an over reaction. The candle was nowhere near the sleeping bag.

He apologised profusely within minutes and then hugged me unexpectedly, but I shrugged him off when he started getting frisky. Enough's enough, I figure.

So now with Dave re-assured and snoring, and the candle re-lit, I can continue...

Promiscuity had become sewn into my everyday life. Not in an obsessive way, just something that happened naturally, every now and again. If Gavin taught me anything it was that true art is truly lived and, as I see it, art is freedom of expression. I just happen to feel good expressing myself sexually.

Freedom and feeling good. As the Tao says: many know the way, few know how to walk it. (And I must say, I have easily wrung several short stories and a novel out of the philosophy. On the strength of which, I have a meeting in a few days' time with Swinford Mason Publishers.

But first there's the clinic at Harley Street to deal with. I keep telling myself: it's barely a life at all...

Anyway, that's all to think about in London. Tonight I am in a journal race against time. I shouldn't digress.)

So, the problem with Gavin was that, even for me, he was a little too out there. By the time we moved to London, I knew he wasn't the soul-mate I yearned for. We didn't split up so much as we untangled. However difficult it was, it left me free to break new ground in a new city. That ground proved incidental, though, until I met Dan.

I used the way I met Dan as a scene in my novel. It was around midnight. I was in knee length stiletto boots, he was in the bath and I stumbled and fell into it. It could have happened to any girl on their way to the loo in a large, rowdy rock and roll house. I found myself slumped across his legs, up to my chest in his bath with my hair dripping wet. I must have looked bedraggled but the attraction was mutual, it was easy to tell. So I introduced myself, formally, offering him my hand. And then we fucked lustily, right there in the tub like two performing seals, splashing suddy water across the lino.

How could I not write that into my story?

Dan was pretty – 'funky little boat-race,' as I liked to say – and he sang in a band. He was different to anyone I had met. He was vulnerable and absolutely sure of himself at the same time.

I'd been seeing an older guy called Kieran for a while, who lived in Bush Road, and I'd spotted Dan around the house whenever I dropped by, which was usually to see his friend Frank the dealer. But I didn't talk to Dan until the day I fell into his bath. At the time, technically, I was still with Kieran, but after meeting Dan I was his. Or, rather, he was mine.

I moved into No. 1 Bush Road within a week and slipped comfortably into the rhythm of life I found there. The hangers on, the drugs, the thud of the drums in the basement at all hours – this was a working house but not one to be recognised by most. Practice sessions happened as and when. If it was past midnight before getting a start, then so be it.

So, the house in which I lived with Dan was known as the Smokin Joes' place. It was a small industry. Haphazard, yes, yet it became a business success, as they like to say now. It took years of playing squats, pubs and parties before the Smokin Joes got themselves a record deal. They would have to wait another year and half before they got a song in the top ten. But from the signing of that deal onwards, my life and Dan's hit overdrive. We toured on and off for a year straight, then we hibernated at No. 1 for eight months recording the album. An unstoppable, full-tilt work party. After which we toured for another year or so – first the UK, then Europe, then we stopped

155

for a writing break before making a hopeless attempt at the USA.

All during this time I was besotted with Dan. He was like a magician. I couldn't have been more devoted – although I have to confess to sleeping with his keyboard player on the odd drunken occasion. (A guy named Keith who isn't good looking at all, yet has a winning way about him.) And then there was Monica, but I told him about that because it was my dabble with lesbianism. And apart from that, oh, and one night when I slept with a funk drummer, but apart from that I was faithful to Dan.

Anyway, it was during the period when he was doing a lot of media work, after the album was released and before the tour got started, that I began to find my voice, my literary voice – and I realised that I was not simply a character in Dan's story, but I was the author of my own. And then I got into thinking, what if Dan's story was in fact just a small episode in mine? Perhaps I was the principal character here?

So I began writing seriously, drawing tales from my life and the people that populate it. I won a highly-rated competition with a short story about an act of arson. And then I began to write kinky erotica and got a few stories published in one of Swinford Mason's top-shelf titles. It wasn't much, but it gave me a positive distraction amidst all the pandemonium of the tour...

So, it seems Dave is an early riser. It's just past seven in the morning and I'm sitting in a service station café while he has a 'a scrub up' in the toilets. I'm glad of the coffee because it's perishing cold outside. My fingers still ache from scraping ice off the van windscreen. And I'm beginning to feel that raw grip of come-down in my teeth and bones.

I thought a lot about my situation with Dan last night. About the destructive path he's been leading us down. Things have taken a turn for the worse since the band split up. I wish I could think of what to do. I need this space to figure it out.

This is an empty café, except for an elderly looking couple breakfasting on eggs and toast. And there's a pair of bikers, padded up in leather and denim, who keep glancing my way. The strip lighting is pale yellow and piped Christmas music is playing through the PA. The staff are wearing burgundy shirts and I can't help wondering where they come from each day, to do their shifts at this faceless station by the motorway.

Oh – one of the bikers has got up from their table and is, right now, walking towards me...

***

Baby Blue – A Lesson in Artifice (Short Story Outline / J Mooncoin / 27.12.92)

Use most of the above, third person, switch names later – and then, from this moment on, everything will happen in a jazz and a jumble, like a car crash on screen, rewound and replayed; where a nine week old life, barely a life at all, will be brought to a juddering end. And the beginning of that end, for Jessie, is in a motorway service station as a blood red dawn streaks across a bitter December morning. She is cradling a cup of coffee, waiting for her new friend Dave who is giving her a lift to London (he has only just excused himself and left for the loo), when a man rises from a table near the breakfast counter and approaches her.

(Or perhaps the end really begins from the moment she swallows down the pill at the Harley Street clinic – a pill that will set about squeezing her insides into a deathly clutch – which would be the more obvious start of an end point.)

Either way she can feel the sharp twinges now, long before she is due to reach London, as she sits doodling her thoughts in a notepad; as she observes the desolation of the motorway café, hardly a soul in the place, except for two bikers by the breakfast counter and an elderly couple with a window seat. Is she having a premonition – a physical premonition – of the pain that

157

awaits her? Or is she simply reliving these moments leading up to it over and over again?

And one of the bikers now sits opposite her and introduces himself – Howard, not a name she would have imagined for him. He has empty blue eyes and his sharp cheekbones are exaggerated by a dark beard and long hair. He is studying her intensely she realises, while making alternative small-talk, you know – festivals they may have crossed paths at, bands in common, the best towns for good pot and blotters. Once Dave returns, the conversation moves quickly onto art. Jessie introduces him to Howard as 'a friend delivering some new work to a private buyer in London'.

Howard questions Dave a little about his cargo and then calls his friend over.

'Charlie knows a thing or two about art,' Howard tells them, as the rounder, hairier biker shuffles over.

And I bet you know a thing or two about bedding women thinks Jessie, her face still flushed from their conversation.

All natural enough and then, a short time later, they are all standing in the van as Dave unstraps one of the larger boxes and carefully peels off the dust-sheet. With Charlie's help, the box is laid horizontally and each side opened to reveal a huge fish tank. At first this is greeted by silence. And then Charlie speaks up.

'Far out.'

Jessie is staring at death – a juvenile doe, fear creased in its stretched cheeks, suspended in something like solid, clear jelly. Charlie says he's sure he's heard about this piece somewhere. Howard remains silent.

'His name's on the tip of my tongue,' says Charlie, 'the artist.'

'It's not who you think it is,' says Dave who, Jessie notices, looks amused as well as slightly nervous. She has become more interested in Dave than she would have imagined when first starting out on the journey with him. He'd given her a lift from Todmorden, in his van, happily heading all the way to London.

And, she quickly decided, she couldn't have hoped for a better one. A fellow free-spirit with a stack of weed for the trip, good music through a stereo sound system, and he was delivering artworks all the way to where she needed to be. It was fated.

He catches her eye as she stares, and she quickly looks away and begins to study the other strapped-up boxes. Although they'd both slept here last night, this is the first time she has seen the goods in anything resembling daylight. They have a sombre presence, like coffins covered in colourless dust-sheets, but they are different shapes and sizes. She stops in front of one which looks like a hat-box, just large enough to house a baby, and this sets her off on a shudder. Dave's scent still wafts from under her T-shirt.

Is this his work? she wonders, and feints.

(The pill has been at work inside her for hours now so she is well into an irreversible process. A concerned looking nurse with a brown bob and spectacles asks her whether she would like a cup of tea. I'd love a pot of tea, she says, for two. And manages a smile.)

She regains consciousness some time later with the van in motion. She is blindfolded and being roughly handled, and it takes a while to discern whether it is sexual or functional. An old boyfriend used to like the kinky stuff, back in her university days, but this was someone sitting up close, grabbing and falling against her whenever the van took a turn or braked up. Her hands are tied comfortably but securely behind her back.

'This has to be some sort of joke,' she says. And gets no reply. Her voice is probably drowned out by the engine. It's difficult to judge volume and distance when blindfolded.

'This has to be a game, right!' she shouts. But instead of the shouted response she expects, a voice leans in close to her ear.

'Best to keep quiet for the time being. But don't worry, all will be well.'

It's her groper yet the voice is reassuring, even though it's only vaguely familiar. Is it Howard? Maybe this is what he sounds like whispering. Whoever it is, Jessie figures it's best to play along and, in around fifteen minutes, the van comes to a halt.

Once Jessie is helped out of the van and her blindfold removed, her eyes blink through tears and focus on a guy standing in front of her who looks like William Burroughs in a crumpled black suit.

'Who are you? What's going on?'

'We are Situationists Miss Mooncoin, of the Theatre of Situations, and you are now part of the artist kidnap performance,' he says, and that's when Jessie sees Howard, and Charlie and a frumpy, grey-haired woman wearing brown plastic sunglasses. They're gathered like a committee of vultures with their heads tilted and jutting. They seem to be searching her for a reaction.

'But you'll both be on your way again soon,' says her captor, after a pause.

'Oh,' says Jessie, 'this sounds like fun.' She can't help wonder where Dave might be. Had he been left at the service station? Surely if they kidnapped artists, he was the one. She suspected he was, anyway. She didn't buy the driving job story.

The next thing she knows, she is being ushered up a set of stairs onto a podium, where she sees a long desk set up with five chairs and, on the floor below, stands a small gathering of alternative press, you know, a few dreadlock crusties with camcorders. And she takes a seat alongside her elderly captors as Dave's art is brought up onto the podium, piece by piece, by Charlie and Howard who then stand alert, ready to be directed.

'This is a hijack,' declares the crumpled suit man.

'A temporary measure. A hold-up and release. We're like anglers throwing the catch back in the river.'

Jessie feels a bit like she did by Dan's side, on tour after the album was launched. She rummages in her jacket pockets for her cigarettes. She used to like smoking at press events. She looked cool with a cigarette.

'What's the point?' shouts one of the crusties.

'The point, ladies and gentlemen, is to hold the first

exhibition, however brief, of 'A Sleepless Death' by Dave Kinsale, before it loses its artistic virginity in East London!' The crumpled suit man rams his fist on the desk causing Jessie to twitch.

Howard and Charlie whip back the dust-cloths one by one, to the odd murmur from the floor.

'In so doing we demonstrate to the rich collectors of this world how easy it is to not only steal their art...'

And the final dust-cloth reveals Dave, naked, standing awkwardly in one of his fish-tanks with a black blindfold covering half of his face.

'But also their artists!' The crumpled suit man sits back in his seat, heavily and theatrically, and turning to Jessie adds, 'And of course, ladies and gentlemen, their gorgeous companions.'

A smattering of applause breaks out amongst the assembled, before they disperse and the performance is over.

So Jessie is surprised to find out, a few hours later, following some particularly frantic sex in the back of the van, that Dave isn't the artist after all. They pull over in the next service station down the M1 after the Situationists reload the van and release them. And, once parked, they barely speak to each other while spilling into the back amongst the cargo, like drunken workmen – their strangled screams emptying into the roar of the roadside.

'The joke is,' says Dave afterwards, still breathless, 'that I'm not even the artist. I'm Howard Smith! The guy who said he was Howard is Dave Kinsale. He thought it'd be a laugh to prank the Situationists! We'll be meeting up in London later...'

He sees a faraway look in Jessie's eyes.

'Sorry,' he says. 'I was in role.'

And Jessie feels betrayed. She feels invaded and it's a response she struggles to rationalise. She felt a similar confusion that day when Dan burst through the door on her, in their dim, smoky bedroom heavy with the musk of sex. The horror on his face as he told her he was quitting the band. Just like that. No comment about what he'd walked in on.

(She doubles-up now as though she has been kicked in the stomach, a convulsion takes a hold of her and tears are forced from her eyes, tickling her cheeks. She thinks of a song lyric, she can't even remember where it's from – something about putting pain in a stranger.)

'I thought there was something strange about that biker,' says Jessie. And she smiles in her new ex-lover's direction, but her thoughts go well beyond him. Then she suggests a coffee and a freshen-up in the services, before they continue their journey to London and to her arrival at an unavoidably messy end.

***

...I watch him as he crosses the floor in my direction. He has handsome, sharp features. He hardly breaks his stride as he walks past me, brushing the lino on my table as he does – and he heads out towards the exit while my fellow traveller slides onto the seat opposite and with a smile says, 'Come on babe. We've gotta keep moving. We have our creations to deliver.'

On our way out of the service station I pop a postcard into the mailbox. It's for Dan back in Yorkshire. Inspired by *Coyote*, it says:

No regrets, Danny Boy. It was time I had to get away.
Think of me as a hitch-hiker. A captive of the white lines
on life's highway.

Then we drive into London in a blur of steel and concrete – and I resolve to swallow that killing pill in honour of all those in my life who could have been the father, before I reach a final decisive full stop.

Part 4
Dan's Tale

Arriving at a Bad Decision

June 1992

Dan pulled the door shut again. Carefully, softly, as if in doing so it would be like he had never opened it in the first place – as though he hadn't just laid eyes upon a scene of lust and debauchery. He could hear his heart thudding in his chest. The images and aroma of the room were swarming his senses. Had they seen him? Had they noticed the shaft of stairway light through the open door? Did they hear his heavy breathing in amongst their moaning and slaps?

God, the room was shuttered with the little red lamp on. And, without doubt, that was the latest Smokin Joes demo tape playing on the stereo, very low. It was a hot, pungent little scene and it reminded Dan of a film. Not just the atmosphere of the room, but his own horror at the witnessing.

Apocalypse Now.

He was numb.

***

Probably not the best moment to recall a childhood fear but that's exactly what Dan did as he sat in the bar at Manchester airport, wondering what his next move should be. He held his beer glass with both hands and stared straight at it as much to avoid catching anyone's eye.

He was thinking about the fine edge along which he'd tip-toed all his life – how he had always been one piece of bad luck away from disaster. And then he recalled his childhood solution to bad situations, which was to retreat home, wherever that may be, and the resultant fear that things at home may well turn out to be worse.

He had his guitar with him, on the floor next to the table. His personal guitar, that is. His back-ups had gone already in the band van, along with his luggage. His coat was thrown over the case as if it were a military coffin. He'd just stubbed out his third cigarette and was reaching in his pocket for another. Primal Scream was playing from somewhere within earshot.

It was then that he noticed a woman with long, black corkscrew hair. He looked up just as she walked into the bar dragging a heavy looking suitcase behind her. She must have been aware of his stare because she met it, briefly, and her eyes were green. She was a beauty. She paused long enough for it to register, and then Dan looked back at his glass and tugged a Marlboro out of the packet.

***

He hesitated outside the bedroom door. Should he knock?

How ridiculous. It was his bedroom too. Why should he knock to go into his own bedroom?

Nevertheless he dithered at the door for some while. Long enough for his heart to gather pace and to detect feint, muffled sounds of activity from within the room. He thought he could hear one of his songs playing. The rest of the house was still. The staircase behind him fell away into darkness.

It seemed unnecessary, they'd lived together for over five years now, but he felt awkward about arriving home when he wasn't expected. On his way up, he'd stepped heavily on the creaking stair to try and sound some warning.

And now, at the bedroom door, he wondered whether he should knock.

Although, what was he expecting? If she was in there with a lover, would she tidy herself up and usher him out of the window before shouting the all clear? And then would he walk in to find her innocently reading one of her manuscripts, lying belly down on top of the bed with her legs crossed in the air? Would the only clue to her infidelity be the curtain flapping at the open window?

***

It had been a long, difficult journey that brought Dan to this point, cradling a pint-glass, considering the consequences. But the upshot was that he'd just been humiliated. All of them, the whole band, had been humiliated – by a little upstart from the record company. It happened in public, here at the airport. They'd been lucky not to get arrested. It had all been one huge fuck-up.

So Dan chose not to join the rest of them on their drive back down to London, but to stay behind at the airport bar and settle his head with a drink. He needed to figure out what his next move should be. At this point, he could be as expansive as he liked. He had his passport in his breast pocket and Jessie wasn't expecting him home for six weeks.

But he'd probably end up going home anyway.

This was the only time she hadn't joined him on tour since they first set out in a camper van, years back. She was a writer now, and wanted to stay behind to concentrate on her novel while the Smokin Joes embarked on their grand tour of the USA. Perhaps she'd be disappointed to see him back within two days. Of course she'd be disappointed.

The beautiful woman had taken a seat at the table alongside, just within his peripheral vision. He could see the address tag on her suitcase. She was going to Cork. Maybe he should go there too. His dad lived in Cork and it had been a while now since they'd got together for a drinking session.

Dan finished the last of his beer. He glanced across at the woman who was engrossed in some papers, probably her flight documents, and he decided on another pint. There was never any sense in having just the one. Especially when there was a decision to be made.

***

He wondered if her hair would be tangled and sweaty, as though she hadn't been out of bed since the evening before. Yes, he could imagine it. And she would be half asleep, her head leaning into her lover's shoulder. They would both be drifting off after their most recent bout of lovemaking. The room would be shuttered and they would be unaware of the full blaze of morning – of the air outside crisp with the bustle of business.

And then, as he opens the door, allowing a shaft of light to fall diagonally across the bed, he would see her remain blissfully adrift, while her lover stirs for a moment, blinks, looks up and sinks once more into their slumbered embrace. A tangled, sweaty embrace.

And the door would be pulled to. Softly. So as not to disturb them. Despite his heart pounding like a jack-hammer and his legs giving way beneath him. Leaving him standing outside the bedroom. Numb, as though a tiger had just leapt out of the jungle at him.

***

Dan watched the Guinness settle in his glass until the separation of black stout and creamy head was complete. The barman had sculpted a little shamrock shape into the top for a decorative flourish and it seemed a shame to spoil it with a first swig.

On the occasion of his only previous visit to Cork, he'd found his old man in the midst of some turbulent scenes, the most recent being a run in with the Garda. Literally – he had driven his battered old Ford into a parked patrol car along the road to Bantry.

'The little gurrier!' he cried, as he fired up the badly dented vehicle at Cork airport. 'It's got me into all kinds of scrapes.'

Dan managed to take a good draught from his pint without disturbing the head too much. His shamrock was intact. He wanted another Marlboro to go with it, but the little foil ashtray on his table was spilling over. It was hardly any bigger than a milk bottle top. Six cigarettes had filled it. He looked around to see if he could find a replacement.

The woman next to him wasn't smoking. He could ask her if she didn't mind him taking her ashtray. It would be a way to say hello, to acknowledge that he'd noticed her. But she was engrossed in reading through her travel documents. And what was he thinking anyway? He should be getting back home. Regardless of whether Jessie would be expecting him or not, it was the only thing he could realistically do.

***

He grabbed the door handle, as if to be decisive, but hesitated. Perhaps it would be better to call out first. It would be more polite. All was quiet from within the room. All, that is, except for the muffled sound of moaning and slapping. And some music – was it the Smokin Joes demo?

And there he stood, frozen like a dummy, his right hand engaged in a firm grip of the bedroom door handle. The rest of the house was quiet. That wasn't surprising. It was around mid-day and this was a late rising household.

Why hesitate? What would be the worst he could he find?

The shaft of light from the opened door would fall diagonally across a bed, the duvet writhing with not two, but three bodies. And in the midst of the pillows, and the animal rise and fall of the bedding, would be a mess of tangled, sweaty hair and a flushed face, blissful and oblivious to the intrusion. To the sound of his breathing as he stood inhaling the humidity of the scene. With its little red lamp and the odd sense of déjà vu, as if he'd felt all this in a film.

That would be the worst of it, surely. And by expecting the worst, hadn't he just taken control of the situation?

So he turned the handle slowly, quietly and inched the door open, almost changing his mind in the very act.

***

And then he'd backed his car through a shop window in Clonakilty, so he said. Dan's father had picked over his recent trail of chaos while they'd each enjoyed a pint in a Dunmanway hotel. But what had been most alarming for Dan, was the discovery that the old fellow was in residence at a psychiatric hospital.

'They let me out to work every day, though,' he said. 'It's more like board and lodgings.'

Dan knew his old man was a drunkard, but mental as well? Perhaps that accounted for those crazy, sleepless moods that sometimes took him over. Dan had always just figured he was a bit of a wild-man – like Oliver Reed – but it seemed there was more to it.

He'd been waving his unlit cigarette about while recalling his trip to West Cork. He grew aware of the woman next to him looking up from her papers. Her eyes looked feline, the green was so deep. Here was an opportunity to talk to her. He could ask if she minded him taking her tin foil ashtray. It would then give him the chance to acknowledge that he'd noticed her when she walked in.

A last call for an Alitalia flight crackled through the Tannoy and she quickly gathered her coat and suitcase and hustled out of the bar. As he watched her go, Dan felt like he had missed out on something. He felt at a loss. The empty table and skewed chair only emphasised her sudden absence. And then his gaze fell upon the small foil ashtray. He retrieved it and lit his cigarette in between cupped hands.

Strange how priorities make themselves. Here he was, considering giving up all he had worked for, turning his back on the life he had made for himself, and all of a sudden he was more interested in a woman he had briefly laid eyes upon in an airport bar.

***

He shut the bedroom door and stood outside on the landing. He felt numbed, the horror so complete that he may as well have been drifting up a jungle river surrounded by purple flares. That's what this feeling reminded him of. It reminded him of that film, its wilful expedition to insanity and its cautionary motto: *Don't get out of the boat...*

Perhaps he hadn't stepped on the creaking stair with enough force to sound an audible warning. If he could arrive home all over again, he would step on that stair as if it was the head of his worst enemy – as if it was that little creep from the record company, who called himself a manager.

But what use would that have been? It's hardly likely that she would have ushered her lovers out of the window before he reached the bedroom. Even if she had heard him.

He hesitated. The sounds from within the room, the moaning, the slapping and the music were still audible through the door. They probably hadn't even noticed him. Why would they? They were in the midst of a humid, tangled scene in there. And the music would have drowned out any noise he made in opening the door.

He felt as though he should have been noticed. Maybe he should open the door again? Maybe this time he should step inside boldly and manfully. He should boldly step inside and lay claim to his territory, his bedroom and his lover.

Yes, that was it! He felt the adrenalin pump through his limbs as he reached for the door handle. It was time for decisiveness.

***

It was supposed to be their attempt at 'breaking the American market'. Dan hadn't liked the idea from the outset. They had

171

got this far largely on graft and good luck. Only Keith could be called a top musician. America was way over their heads.

But Andy from the record company insisted the time was ripe for the Smokin Joes to take on the States – a fan base in the States may persuade the bosses to go with the latest album, he reasoned. We would set off straight after a warm-up in Manchester and, once over there, hire a tour bus for six weeks building up the gigs and the reputation on the road. Andy turned up at the airport looking like some yuppie from the City with a mobile phone. We all laughed at it – it resembled a walkie talkie with a long, wobbly antenna – and we took turns grabbing it, shouting, 'Buy pigs' bellies! Buy! Buy! Buy!' into the mouthpiece.

Andy said it was essential for communications while the band was in transit. But it turned out that although he'd thought to bring along a phone, he'd forgotten to arrange the visas. Keith took this news the worst, but at least he'd saved them all some time by bringing up the subject while they queued for the departure lounge.

'And you've sorted the visas, haven't you?' Keith said to round off an itinerary check, and Andy looked at him, at first with humour and then with an expression of fear growing in his face. The colour drained from him. Dan, as he watched on, felt his own fear grow simultaneously.

For Dan though, it was a more profound fear. It had to do with the whole purpose of his life. The fact that all the work he'd put in for the past nine years had culminated in this. That it had all resulted in this company idiot controlling their every move.

As Dan looked on, Keith leapt for Andy's throat and the anger spread along the line and through the rest of the band entourage until airport security were forced to intervene.

It was a complete fuck-up.

***

This was a late rising household. Dan found himself tip-toeing up the stairs, he didn't want to wake anyone up with any banging or clattering about. But midway up the staircase, at the point where he reached the creaking stair, he paused. He stood on it forcefully to sound a warning for Jessie. He barely gave a thought as to why he should want to do this. He had a vague notion that she would hear the creak and hurriedly clear her bed of lusty, sweaty lovers.

And then he found himself at the bedroom door. Should he knock? Or maybe call out? The idea seemed ridiculous. This was his bedroom. What was he expecting? What would be the worst he could find?

He stood still on the landing, the house was quiet despite the full bustle of the day outside. Nothing could be heard except a steady dripping sound from a distance away and some music turned down low. And there was some heavy, rhythmic breathing and groans of pleasure in there.

Maybe everyone in the house was in bed with Jessie. It would be like a Roman orgy, a Bacchanal in the bedroom. As he opened the door he would be met by a scene of writhing, moaning bodies all tangled and flushed. And there'd be music playing on the stereo – the latest Smokin Joes demo. They had all waited until Dan was on tour and then the whole street had converged on Jessie in their bed. Now he came to think of it, he was surprised he hadn't seen a queue forming around the house on his way in.

He grabbed the door handle and his legs almost gave way as he considered the woman he loved engaged in a mass orgy with all-comers. He could practically smell the heat and musk from the room through the merest crack and see a shaft of light spreading across the bed, which was churning like an eel tub. Like the duvet had a life of its own.

He was still holding onto the bedroom door handle. He could hear the grunts and sighs from inside the room, there was no point kidding himself. The horror made him feel numb, as if the will to live had been punched out of him. It was just like

173

when he saw that film.

Perhaps he should call out first, he thought, but he was already opening the door.

***

Dan had taken some downers earlier as matter of routine, not being a good flyer, and now having finished his second pint at the bar, he was beginning to feel the bendy effect – like life in a vapour trail. It was as if each time someone walked past him, they kept on doing so for seconds afterwards.

He had to try concentrating his mind on what he was going to do. Someone hovered by the table vacated by the beautiful, green-eyed woman – a confused looking bloke in a shambolic suit, but he ended up opting for a window seat. The woman's empty chair was still twisted in Dan's direction. It took awhile, but he realised his head was beginning to drop towards his lap as he stared at it. He pulled himself upright. He had to focus.

Although, in the upshot, he already knew that was the end of it with the band. As much as he hated admitting it, the fact that the record company had turned down his latest album demo still burned.

'We don't want to be churning out product for the Woolworth's bargain bucket,' was the explanation offered. 'Lo Fi rock, New York Dolls style – however you see it – it's dead. The scene's moved on, Danny. You need to write something new – reach for a bigger sound.'

That had to signal the end in itself but the problem for Dan went deeper. It was about being controlled by idiots on Charlie. He might as well be working in a bank. And it was the fact that they were now in danger of being pushed in whatever direction the company wanted. There were two albums left on the deal – which would take a few years at least, the way things were going. To Dan, with or without the band, another few years of this seemed like a prison sentence.

So what was the next move?

He squinted in the direction of the bar counter and could make out a blur of glassware and reflections, with bottles lined up on optics like piping. It was almost midday – time to make a decision and head back for London.

He thought about the film he'd watched on the hotel TV the previous evening, and the soundtrack: *beautiful friend, this is the end* – and he thought about the boat, the one vessel of safety in an insane environment.

He brought himself to his feet and bent his knees to pick up his jacket and guitar. He'd decided. His safe boat was with Jessie. It was time to go home and tell her about quitting the band. It was time to leave it all behind for awhile. He had a few friends in Yorkshire, they could rent a house up there and Jessie could get some space to do her writing. Maybe, once away from London, she'd be more open to the idea of kids.

With that, he made his way out of the bar, weaving in a pronounced fashion through the tables and out towards the taxi rank.

***

Dan looked wearily up the staircase. It was as if he was arriving home for the hundredth time that day. The house was quiet. Although it was mid afternoon, not a stir was to be heard. He wondered where Keith and Wolfen were. They should have got back a couple of hours ago. Everyone else was probably still asleep. It was that kind of household. Late to bed, late to rise.

He tried to tread softly as he took it a stair at a time. He didn't want to disturb anyone. But wait a minute, Jessie wasn't expecting him home. Or maybe she was? Maybe she'd seen Keith? No, of course she wouldn't have seen him. She'd still be in bed. Dan felt awkward about arriving home when he wasn't expected.

As he came to the stair with the creak, he decided to step down hard. He should announce his arrival in some way and this was the best he could do. He dug in his heel as if he was crunching the skull of a beast.

And then he found himself at the bedroom door. In an instant, the palms of his hands became slippery with sweat and he felt as if the life was draining from him. Jessie had his demo tape playing in there. He could hear it. But he could also make out the sounds of sex. The rhythmic creak of the bed, the moans of pleasure and urgent, almost violent grunting and slapping noises.

His hands were so sweaty he could barely get a grip on the door handle. His legs felt as if they were going to fold under him. If he knocked, or called out or something, maybe they would stop. Maybe it would dispel it all. Or perhaps, if he went back downstairs and came back up again he'd find that the whole scene was a figment of his imagination.

In fact he would find her lying flat on her belly, kicking her legs in the air, reading the latest draft of her novel. The curtains would be open and the full blaze of the day would wash the room in light. And she would look up and see him and her face would beam with joy. And then they would sit on the bed and discuss the future in a mood of optimism and camaraderie.

Maybe.

But he stood at the door paralysed, and he felt surrounded by the smoke of purple flares. It was insane. Tigers were leaping out of the jungle at him. And he kept telling himself – for God's sake, don't get out of the boat! While a voice muttered hazily in reply, 'I thought *you* were in charge.' And the walls of the landing spun crazily like rotor blades until he realised that was it.

The End.

And he opened the door slowly, to see a shaft of light spreading out wide across the bed.

The Funeral and the Fortune Teller

September 1992

Dan had spent the last few minutes looking at his own reflection in the train window while the green-wooded valley sped past in a blur. He had been staring into the blank sockets of his own eyes, retracing his weekend when, all of a sudden, the train slowed to a halt and rabbits began to hop about by the tracks. He pulled away sharply from the window, thinking – 'Where the fuck did they come from?'

He was still feeling the effects of the mushrooms and booze, and the sight of bunnies jumping out of his reflected face was alarming.

He uncorked a rum bottle, about a third full, took a gulp and banged it shut again. His dad had given it to him after the funeral, as a parting gift – a half drunk bottle of rum and a copy of the Lancashire Evening Post. Dan chuckled to himself as he thought about the state his father was in. He turned up at the church looking as though he'd been on a week-long binge. He looked as rough as Tom Waits waking up in a gutter.

Mind you, Dan seemed to have raised a few eyebrows himself just by showing up. It seemed no-one expected to see him at his grandmother's funeral. He didn't blame them, in the normal scheme of things he probably wouldn't have made it. But it worked out to be a good ruse to get away from Jessie for a couple of days. He needed a break from her moods.

So the aunts and uncles nudged one another and nodded their heads in Dan's direction. A few of them even acknowledged him with smiles that seemed a little too wide. It may have been that they sensed he was high as a kite. Dan was pretty sure he wasn't doing anything weird enough to attract attention, but he was well aware that he'd overdone it after stumbling into some festival in a local park the previous evening. So either he was, in fact, acting weirdly or people were surprised by the mere fact that he'd shown up.

He figured it was more likely to be the latter. What would they know about tripping?

***

Indian incense was wafting about Marie's table while she sat idling the time between customers. She flipped the cards over, one after the other. One, two, three. Cups, fool, lovers. Business had been slow for the last hour or so and she'd been amusing herself with the Tarot. A breath of breeze rippled the canvas flap inside the small events tent and blew two cards from the top of the pack.

She smiled as she picked the magician and the tower up off the grass floor. This was some rare clarity she was bearing witness to right now. It had happened before, that she'd been idly turning the cards when a pattern revealed itself from nowhere. On that occasion she saw the vision of her nomadic life as a new-age fortune teller. At this moment in time, she was sensing something much more immediate. The cards were telling her that she was about to receive an interesting visitor.

Marie spread the entire deck across the felt table top, and gathered it up again in one hand. Festival folk were walking to and fro past the doorway of her tent, she could see them mostly from the chest down. The next band on stage were being introduced by the MC. There was a perceptible whiff of ganja in the air, despite the police officers patrolling the site.

There wouldn't be much longer to wait before her visitor turned up – and she already knew at least some of the answers he'd be looking for.

***

Dan was gathering up items of clothing and travelling essentials from around the room, throwing them all into a hold-all. Jessie was lying on the bed watching him, chattering away, when suddenly he felt a strong wave of déjà vu.

'Has this happened before?' he asked Jessie.

'What?' she sounded incredulous.

'This whole scene, us talking like this while I'm throwing some stuff together. This has happened before,' he explained. 'I'm sure I'm having a déjà vu here.'

'Have you been listening to anything I've been saying?' Jessie was speaking with a tone of outrage.

Dan returned to picking through his notepads spread out on the floor. He was looking for a particular one.

'Yep. You're not happy. This place is driving you crazy...'

He found it. It was a small green schoolbook in which he'd penned some folk lyrics, years back – inspired by The Pogues. Dan fancied returning to it. He held it out in front of his face and studied the handwriting on the cover before throwing it into the holdall.

Jessie sat up in bed.

'Too fucking right,' she said. 'And more to the point, you're driving me crazy too.'

Dan didn't answer. He didn't know what to say. So instead he rummaged about the bedside table for the dope tin.

'Where are you going, anyway?' asked Jessie.

'My Grandma's funeral in Preston.'

'Well, let's hope it does you some good.'

Dan was all too aware that Jessie was struggling with being cooped up here on the edge of a moor, so far from London. Suddenly she was taking umbrage at all sorts – like, of all the things, the rate of his drug-taking. Things just weren't working out the way Dan had hoped when he suggested they move up here for some space.

He felt himself burning in the face as he broke off a chunk of the black and slipped it into his jeans pocket, handing the tin back to Jessie. He zipped up his hold-all and got to his feet.

'I'm sure it will,' he said. 'Us Ballindines know how to give someone a good send-off.'

***

Marie was recalling the night when she laid out the Tarot in the shape of her own future. She was a ward nurse at the time, working at the Royal Preston. It was her twenty-eighth birthday – June 19 1990 – and she was in the midst of her Saturn return.

It was as if the cards turned themselves over.

Up until then for Marie, reading the Tarot would only reveal sets of possibilities, whichever layout she used. That night on her birthday they presented a clear course of action. Her inner and outer journeys would now have to merge.

She set off for Glastonbury festival the next day, joined up with the peace convoy in the free field and never went back to the ward. Instead she wrote a letter, which she posted from Pilton, informing her colleagues that she'd decided to move on. It had been over two years since then, in which time she had travelled all across Europe following the mysteries of her true vocation.

So to Marie, being back in Preston at this festival had seemed nothing more than nostalgic, until she turned over the fool, those cups and the lovers. And finally death. And then a breathy gust blew the magician and the tower across the tent and she realised, at that moment, that this was meant to be – that she was supposed to be here. The cards had taken her away and now they had brought her back.

She was dwelling on all this, when the flap of her tent was swept aside and in stumbled a disorganised looking man of around her own age.

'Oh,' he said, ''scuse me. Do you mind if I just hang about in here for awhile?'

He was glancing shiftily back through the tent flap,

clutching a hold-all as if it were his bag of loot.

'Sure,' said Marie. 'Take a seat.' She gestured towards the only one in the tent – the chair opposite her own on the other side of the card table.

***

Dan had been weaving in and out through a column of trudging human traffic since he'd turned up at Avenham Park some time ago. He wasn't sure when that was. It must have been a good few hours back, although it still felt like he was inside the crowded, rattling train carriage. And he could still feel himself blinking as the sunlight bounced off the carriage floor and bleached out the seat across the aisle – (it was like a strobe light whenever they passed a stand of tall trees). Yet now he found himself on a festival site, amongst a large trudging throng. He should concentrate and keep moving.

The guys on the train who told him about the festival produced a tobacco tin, one of those with a fantasy scene painted on the outside. When Dan peered into it, he saw half a dozen dried, stumpy pieces of mushroom that looked like wood – and felt like wood to chew.

Now faces were zooming in and out of his line of sight, while the space in front of him became squeezed by shuffling bodies, only to open up again like a concertina. He felt nervous and pursued as if there were a group of agents on his tail. Small and elusive agents that seemed to be everywhere he went yet just out of sight. Obviously they were throwing a wide net. But he figured if he could make it over to where the travellers had set up, he might be able to lose himself in amongst their vehicles.

So here he was, sitting in a tent that felt like the inside of a balloon. The breeze billowed the canvas and there was a musky perfume in the air. The gypsy opposite him had a slightly lop-sided face, as if she suffered from Bell's palsy, and her right eye held his own in a tight stare. The cards she shuffled were large and had an elaborate Celtic design on the back. Her fingernails

181

were red.

'What brings you here?' she asked, and Dan watched her hands as she placed the deck on table, turned the top card over and produced the fool.

***

The fortune teller was right about one thing, that's for sure – Dan was stepping onto the platform at Hebden Bridge as the last of the day's sunlight fell across a row of hanging baskets – he was fighting a hopeless battle when it came to Jessie. The fact was, it was impossible to get a clear idea of what she wanted. She was having wild mood swings lately. Maybe she needed to be back in London, fair enough. For Dan though, he needed some peace and quiet to think in.

The bus pulled into the station forecourt and it shook like an old man as Dan paid his fare and took a seat.

While travelling along the valley road, the reflection in the bus window seemed not to be of his face but the fortune teller's. Her loaded, bloodshot, witch-like stare. Of course, things were pretty heightened at the time. Well, to be truthful, he was tripped to the eyeballs. But the whole scene, as she laid out her cards and delivered her predictions, was as vivid as a nightmare.

Her voice was deep and she spoke in a monotone. All except when she started back from one particular card and gasped, as if she'd been expecting all the others to come along but this one had surprised her. She said it was about death. A violent death that had taken place just recently.

'We're talking hours rather than days.' She looked grave.

'Within a year you'll meet a widow,' she spoke up after a lengthy pause. 'And you will be the first to bring light back into her life.'

Her voice was hypnotic. She was speaking rhythmically, in a possessed tone, as if someone else's voice had taken over.

It took Dan a long time to gather himself. At least it felt that way. The day was darkening all around them. She said more but some of it was muttered and indiscernible. Most he'd forgotten.

'In turn, it'll save you too.' He remembered that, and the stuff she said about Jessie – 'Your present problem.'

'She'll leave by the same door through which she came in,' was the gypsy's verdict and he understood her completely when she said it.

A rubbery bass line had been thudding out from a PA nearby for at least ten minutes. The breeze flapping at the tent entrance was perfumed and cool. The last of the setting sun cast warm orange light across the pair of them through the canvas walls.

By the time Dan stepped out of the tent, she had for a long while been muttering like a crone and busying herself with her cards. It was dark and the moon looked full as strands of cloud parted and re-sliced it. Camp-fire smoke was drifting through the air. Dan turned around to look back at the fortune teller sitting in lamp light, the tent-flaps held open by fluttering ribbons. It seemed as if she was the length of the park away.

The bus came to a juddering halt across from the Waggon and Horses and Dan leaped up to his feet. The sun had already passed over the valley and he stood in late afternoon twilight as the bus rattled away along the road.

Just a hundred yards or so up a steep lane and he'd be back home.

***

We've met already, he said. He seemed very certain. Sometimes, in altered states, people could tap into a seam of insight, so Marie paid attention as he explained that he'd been in a period of sustained déjà vu since that morning. As soon as he set foot in her tent, he recognised the whole scene – the felt-topped table, the waft of musk, the festival sounds outside and, of course, Marie.

You've already told me everything you just said and I've lived this whole day before, he claimed. *And will keep on living it. And, to prove it, you're now going to tell me something I have always known.*

Marie turned over a second card. The four of cups.

'Well,' she said, 'it doesn't matter how often you have lived this scene, believe me, this time will be the first.'

It's my dad, isn't it? You're going to tell me about my old man, he said. His father's presence was all about, for sure, but Marie couldn't have anticipated turning over the hermit at this point. It took her completely by surprise.

'In a way, yes. Yet his influence isn't what you think. It's distant.' She held her voice steady.

Nonetheless, she could see that the father was playing a hand in forging the future for his son.

'A death has taken place,' she continued. 'A violent death...'

At first he laughed. It was the drugs, most likely. But then he settled into a more quiet, contemplative mood as Marie set about investigating every possible turn of events this incident could bring into being. She used layout after layout like she was an archaeologist, slicing up sections of the earth to build a picture. She was getting an eerie feeling the widow in question was her old workmate from the Royal Preston. The young Irish lass, Maggie McCarthy. This reading was reminding Marie of one she did for Maggie years ago – it was turning out to be the conclusion of it.

So the future for this lad sat opposite, at a dead-end in his own life, was going to be the saving of her? Marie looked at him. He was a sorry sight, wasted and bedraggled. He lifted up his head to meet her gaze.

Have you ever properly noticed how everything connects together? he said, and his eyes were like Catherine Wheels.

***

From the doormat, beyond the leaping dogs, Dan could see

Jessie at the kitchen table with a coffee mug in front of her. She was scribbling in a notepad, probably working on another chapter of her novel. Whenever he read her short stories, they made him feel uncomfortable. Her scenes and characters were all too familiar. But she'd kept the novel secret – she didn't want anyone to see it until it was finished.

'So how was the funeral?' Jessie put down her pen and made for the kettle.

'I think it probably went fine,' said Dan, throwing the newspaper on the table beside the rum bottle.

'You don't sound too sure.' Jessie ran the tap while she looked over her shoulder.

'Well,' said Dan, 'the old man didn't distinguish himself...' He hesitated, he felt too tired for this. Jessie turned and looked at him closely.

'You look like you've been dragged through a hedge backwards,' she said. She glanced over at the almost empty rum bottle.

'It's a long story.' Dan held his hands up. Jessie was standing with her arms crossed like a schoolmistress.

'M'dad turned up at the funeral looking like he'd been drinking for days.' Dan could see her face darkening.

'And then he fell over in the graveyard while he was carrying the coffin,' he continued. 'And when I tried to help him up, the sheer drunken weight of the feller pulled me over.'

Dan was hoping for some laughter, but Jessie busied herself with the coffee jar.

'Hence the soiled look.' Dan gestured at himself with his hands, as if he was modelling the finest clothing. 'But anyway, the rum was his parting gift at the station. He'd already drunk most of it.'

Jessie used the newspaper as a place-mat for Dan's mug.

'And what state did you turn up in?' she asked.

Dan blew over the surface of his coffee. He hadn't the energy to make a story up.

'It so happens,' he said, 'unbeknown to me, that it was the

Preston Guild. A once every twenty year, town festival.'

Jessie looked unimpressed.

'Anyway, I got talking to this hippie couple on the train and they told me about an alternative festy, with bands. And then they produced a tin of Mexican mushrooms.'

Jessie started shaking her head, laughing, looking down at the table.

Dan rolled a cigarette. He let the tale end there. Jessie would have no problem imagining the rest.

Ten minutes later, Dan gulped the last of his coffee down so he could head for bed. Jessie picked up the newspaper and glanced over the front page.

'So what's the news in Preston, then?' she asked, idly.

'I don't know, I didn't read it.' Dan got up from his seat and stretched. 'Not much, probably.'

A story caught Jessie's eyes. She was holding the paper still and her lips were speedily mouthing the words. Dan was beginning to creep away when she looked up.

'Well they've got something to read about,' she said. '*Man brutally murdered after Guild Parade* is the front page headline.'

Dan shrugged his shoulders. 'I always said it was a tough town,' he replied and turned to leave the room.

He could feel Jessie's stare on his back as he made for the staircase.

Jessie's Journal
Part 2

The Interview

December 30 1992

There's a cup of coffee, with frothed milk, on a lino table in front of me and I'm looking out of a grimy café window onto the market street where an old lady is talking to a beggar. She's smiling up at him as she puts a coin in his hand.

Random acts of kindness in amongst the harsh bustle of everyday life, I like to focus on those. Of course, the tales I write are strewn with cruelties too. Fiction feeds off cruelties. And, at first glance, mine would seem crowded with all manner of them. Read closely, however, and you'll see my tales also contain small moments of kindness.

Take the latest little story – of my meeting just now at Swinford Mason Publications in their swish offices in Fitzrovia. I walked into that building an aspiring novelist and I have come away with an entirely different proposition.

If I was to write it up as a piece of fiction it would happen like this.

***

I was sitting on a soft leather sofa in a shaft of sunlight as Swinford Mason paced about for a while. His office occupied the whole top floor, which had three large windows along one wall. I had to squint to follow his progress around the room.

'I have been giving your novel a lot of thought, Miss Mooncoin, a lot of thought,' he said, and he continued to pace the room. He spoke with a loud, commanding voice.

189

'A couple of general comments,' he went on, 'one, it needs sexing up, your characters demand it; two, you've got a great series of adventures, but where's the cork that requires removing from a Nairobi man's arse? Do you follow?' He was gesturing with one hand as he trod his restless path.

'I'm not sure I do,' I said – well, more like whispered under my breath.

He finally sat down on the sofa alongside and turned to face me. He had his back to the window, so I had to shield my eyes.

'These tales are auto-biographical, are they not?' He was speaking softly all of a sudden.

'Well...' I hesitated. For some reason I hadn't been expecting this. I wasn't sure what I'd been expecting. 'I suppose, you could say that some of it is true, but it's all fiction, really.' I realised I was stammering.

Mason shuffled in his seat – that is to say, his silhouette moved enough for shafts of sunlight to jab out from around his head.

'Tell me about your characters,' he said, 'tell me, for starters, about Maggie. Where did you get her from?'

'Oh, I put her in at the last minute. She's from a newspaper story.' I wondered where he was going with this.

'A local newspaper Dan brought home...' Mason's silhouette was silent and still. 'From Preston, when he went to his grandmother's funeral.' I felt ridiculous all of a sudden. 'The murder's a true story. Well, based on truth. The report included a picture of them both. It's safe to say she's pretty.'

'And how about Monica?' he finally spoke up.

'Ah, well. Monica, that's a different story...'

***

Victor was sitting in front of half a dozen monitors, idling the time reading a magazine that he found at the control desk. Or, to be more accurate, he was scanning the headlines. The stories didn't interest him at all. It was a trade magazine and, as much as Mason had attempted to enthuse him about the publishing world, it just didn't grab him. Victor enjoyed the more organic side of production.

But then a story did catch his eye. Someone called Berners-Lee was inventing a new system for the internet. Victor had heard Mason talk a lot about this lately.

The article was imagining how the technology could progress. It said that eventually the system would enable someone to move graphically from one screen of information to another, almost as if they were flipping to random pages in a magazine. Ultimately it would have the capacity to carry streaming video and live broadcast media. Victor stopped reading and looked up to the ceiling.

When he turned his attention back to the monitors, he saw that little had changed up in the top office. Except that Mason seemed to be priming himself with some Charlie and the lighting had altered. It had become darker around the bar area. A set of blinds had been shut.

Victor set Mason's clip microphone to record. As much as he hated to admit it, the old bastard knew his stuff.

***

So I told him about the real Monica, not the one in my novel, and he stood up and began pacing about the room again. I told him the whole story, right up to the other day at the Christmas party.

'So, she's real. How about Frank?' He drew a set of blinds across the middle window of the three, before leaning over a mirror on the bar counter to snort a line.

'More or less, but it's fiction,' I protested.

'Oh, and is Dan fiction?' There was a gentle mocking tone to his voice, and he held out the rolled up £20, inviting me to join him.

'I use a word processor for my writing, I'll change the names later with the push of a button,' I said, growing more uncomfortable by the second. He was right. These characters and their adventures were, more or less, the true story. I stood up to accept his offer.

He looked at me directly as he continued to hold out the £20 note.

'So what puzzles me is this: why Maggie?'

I stepped out of the sunlight and into the shadow across the middle of his office.

'Why throw in a character drawn largely from your imagination?'

It took me a few moments to answer. I felt like a small girl all of a sudden.

'Dan deserves a happy ending,' I said. 'Maggie is his destiny.'

'Ah!' he said. 'You only gave me ten chapters – how does it all end?'

I took the note from his hand.

'I want it to splutter out like a firework that doesn't go off,' I said. 'Until the readers peer at it closely.' And I leaned in to the mirror. 'Then I want it to explode in their faces.'

At which point I grew up again with two short, thick lines of cocaine. One for each nostril.

***

Of course, it's worth pointing out that Victor's side of the story is largely imagined. But the rest of the fiction here is drawn from fact. It's also worth pointing out that, since I last reported, the beggar has been spat at and had his hat full of coins thrown around the street by a group of boys.

***

Victor glanced up at the wall clock. Still another 30 minutes until his 'library' shoot. He could sit back for a while and watch the old bastard try to snare another hopeful artist. This one he'd heard of. Victor had read some of her erotica. He was a Smokin Joes fan, so reading their adventures was a must. And Jessie Mooncoin was the girl on the inside.

He was interested in seeing how she got on with Mason. And he was, of course, expected to record the action, should any get going on the office sofa.

***

I was sitting in shade up at the bar with a band of sunlight each side of me. Massive Attack was playing through some speakers that were built into the office walls. This was the high life – the coke crept through me like anticipation and Swinford handed me a tall spritzer with a bent straw in a glass rattling with ice cubes. He came round to join me on one of the high stools and we toasted Mason Publications. What the hell.

'Your novel is not what I want to talk to you about,' he said. 'But we'll publish it anyway, when you get the rest of it to us.'

Just like that, casual and offhand, and a deal was made. But of course, there was more to it. He lit a cigarette and continued.

'But the way it'll really sell is if you join us in our brave new publishing world.' He offered me a cigarette and passed over the lighter.

'Go on. What do you mean?' This felt exciting. It felt like I was arriving at the big time.

He looked at me closely for a moment, stood up from his stool and wandered over to the far side of the office, muttering to himself, before returning to the conversation.

'You've heard of the internet, I presume?' he asked, tipping more coke out onto his little mirror.

'Yep, sure.' I didn't fully understand what it was about, but I knew it involved computers connected through the telephone system.

'Within a year we'll be using the internet for a communications medium that's going to turn publishing on its head.' He slid out a razor blade from an inner flap of his leather

193

wallet.

'And I can tell you Jessie, Swinford Mason Publications are ahead of the game.'

I hit the bottom of my glass with a loud slurp.

'By creating a library of material for launch date,' he said, slicing up the crystals. 'We're ready to hit the ground running.'

'I can't see people reading a novel on a computer.' I didn't get it.

'Not novels, darling,' said Mason, cosily. 'Think of it as a magazine. And soon it'll be a magazine with little TV screens on each page.'

He held out the mirror and the rolled-up twenty.

'Come and join us as a contributor. Help us populate this new world.'

All of a sudden I could see him as a villain in a James Bond film. He was a villain and I was the girl he wanted for his decoration, hovering between the straight life or going bent.

I took the mirror from his hands.

***

It wasn't the fact that he wanted sex on the office sofa that threw me, I expected it (and felt horny myself in fact, cocaine always does that, but I was still pretty uncomfortable downstairs from a 'procedure' two days previously). What threw me was that his proposition amounted to nude modelling.

I would be a staff writer, penning my erotic short tales from the kinky underworld, but there'd have to be some accompanying photographs, nothing too hard-core, just mood-setters. I tried to imagine this – on computers – but I couldn't get beyond 'Reader's Wives'.

'You want me to be a nude model in a computer magazine?' I asked.

'Believe me Jessie, within ten years erotica will be the mainstream. Everyone will be at it. There is big money to be

194

made here.'

'As a nude model?' I wasn't convinced.

'As an artist,' he replied. 'As a personality.'

I fiddled around in my bag for my tobacco tin. Mason offered me one of his.

'And if you're a personality on the internet, it'll make it easier to sell your novel,' he said. 'All over the world.'

He pulled up tall on his stool. 'Which is, in the end, what we both want.'

He paused for his answer. I lit the cigarette and avoided his stare.

'Can I have a day to think about it?'

***

And here I am thinking about it, in a café just around the corner from the squat where I'm staying. I'm stirring my second cup of coffee and looking out of the window onto Chapel Market. It's starting to get dark even though it's not yet 4 o'clock. The murk seeps through the street, and the traders begin to clip electric lamps to the frames of their stalls. There's a waft of coals and roasting chestnuts in the icy air as the café door opens and in bundles the beggar.

'I'll have a nice cuppa tea!' he calls out in a strange, snarl-like voice, probably not helped by a face numbed from a day in the cold. He has a beard, a tatty great-coat and fingerless gloves. He is shuffling on his feet, trying to bring the life back to them, and rubbing his hands together.

He smiles at me and nods.

'Where are you going today?' he snarls.

***

Victor had just stepped out of the edit suite into a narrow, carpeted corridor, holding a small digital video camera in his hand, when I bumped into him.

195

'Oh, sorry!' He leapt back as if he'd touched an electric fence.

I was equally surprised. I'd been in a daze since leaving Swinford's office and had become completely lost around a maze of corridors and staircases. I'd been looking at the deep thread of the pale blue carpet and hadn't even considered that anyone might appear in front of me.

'Victor,' he said, holding out his free hand. 'Head of Production – or, to be more accurate, Mason's media dogsbody.'

He was smiling kindly as I shook his hand, but I couldn't help glancing in to the room he was just leaving. Banks of screens and a control desk with sliders and knobs.

'I'm Jessie...' I began.

'I know,' said Victor, 'I'm a bit of a fan of your fiction.'

'I've just had a meeting with Swinford Mason...'

'I know,' he interrupted again. 'We've been looking forward to you joining us here.'

He still hadn't let go of my hand and I had to gently disentangle it from his grasp.

***

The beggar is proud of the way he's packed his worldly goods into a shopping trolley. He points out a half drunk wine bottle as an example – carefully wedged upright in the back corner, so nothing spills. His name is Dennis and he looks me over thoughtfully as we walk along Chapel Market. His trolley rattles over the cracks in the pavement. His fingers are blackened almost up to the frayed wool of his gloves.

'You're a writer,' he muses. The trolley continues to rattle. 'I'm an actor, you know.'

It occurs to me that while we were in the café, I'd done most of the talking. He'd told me little about himself beyond his name.

'Well, I was an actor,' he continues. 'There's not much work for me now.'

He pulls up to a sharp stop, and begins to gesture theatrically.

> *To be, or not to be; that is the question:*
> *Whether 'tis nobler in the mind to suffer*
> *The slings and arrows of outrageous fortune,*
> *Or to take arms against a sea of troubles,*
> *And, by opposing, end them. To die, to sleep—*
> *No more, and by a sleep to say we end*
> *The heartache, and the thousand natural shocks*
> *That flesh is heir to—*

He gives a bow, as I clap and cheer, and passers-by push past us muttering and cursing. We are on a busy corner of the market. Vapour rises from his great coat and his beard is glistening in the street-lights.

'That was amazing,' I say. 'When were you treading the boards?'

'Oh, years back.' He hauls his trolley around and begins to trundle down the street towards Angel. 'In the good times – with Harris, O'Toole and Reed.'

His voice is becoming less of a snarl, more of a booming baritone.

'Those were wild days in Soho. Do you know that part of town? Wild days.' I can see he's using his trolley as a kind of battering ram as he progresses through the busy pavement traffic.

'Too wild for me, in the end.'

We are crossing the road towards Angel station.

'I should have got out while the going was good,' he says. 'TV, that's where the money is now.'

We stop and look at each other under the station canopy. A cold breeze whips up from the street.

'Where do you go from here?' I ask.

'Wherever my trolley leads me,' he says. 'And you?'

'I'm not sure – either back to Fitzrovia, or just a hundred yards further down the road.'

'Fitzrovia, yes, where your big publisher is. And what's in the Angel for you?' he asks.

'My old life.' I say it without thinking.

A couple in my line of sight are kissing and hugging as they part outside the station. The Standard seller is wrapped up warm in a hat, coat and gloves, shuffling on his feet.

'Well,' Dennis offers a grimy handshake in my direction. 'Times change.'

I take his hand firmly, with both of mine.

'Now, would you have a pound to spare?' he asks.

I give him a big hug and a five pound note, and turn to head for the escalators.

Part 5
Maggie's Tale

The Story that wasn't in Dan's Newspaper

October 1992

First it was a straight fight – a punch-up. It happens everywhere, all the time. He didn't stand a chance as it was, nevertheless the violence escalated as more lads spilled from the pub, drawn by the skirmish and shouting and, like wild dogs bringing down the weakest of the herd, they joined in the demolition of Gable McGrath.

As he fell it was as if his shape had already shifted. As if he had already become human mist and disappeared into the damp, orange-lit night.

***

Maggie sat up in bed in a state of alarm. She'd been dreaming. Something about pennies – and a fountain. Not a sparkling, cool fountain shimmering with coins but something dull, warm and disgusting – like the gushing insides of a freshly killed pig. And then she was chased along a street lined with shops. A street that looked familiar but wasn't quite right.

Her room was in twilight. She wasn't sure whether it was morning or evening. The pillow felt damp under the palms of her hands. She looked down beside her, to the empty part of the bed, just as she had been doing for days, or perhaps it had been weeks. It must have been weeks by now.

Her right hand was tingling and hot again and she shook it loosely. It had become a part of her waking up, to such an extent she didn't notice it any more than the time of day.

201

Sleep provided her a sanctuary of late whereas, before she was given indefinite leave from work, sleep had been a luxury to slip into between rotating shifts and emergency call-ins. As Gable used to say, 'It's all the same day, man.'

So it seemed easy to return her head to the pillow and rejoin the dreams she'd briefly left. After all, she was giving in to a natural pattern – at least that's how she understood it. It was the way things were now. And in no time this particular wakening was forgotten as her thoughts retreated into darkness.

***

So, pretty Maggie, you're back again. And awaiting your first flicker of the eyelids, that first slide (or is it flight?) under the canopy of consciousness, is an old hag beckoning with her finger. An old hag with a large mole on her face and her ill-stockinged feet in a pair of ragged slippers. A hairy mole and socks with big, round holes at the heels and shins.

'Come here, little Mags, and I'll do your hair,' she is saying, all the time beckoning and foot-tapping.

You feel your hair twisted and tugged and eventually gripped by rubber bands into pigtails so tight they make your eyes water. The undersized school clothes are equally uncomfortable. And then you feel a cold, heavy penny pressed into your palm.

'Be careful with your dinner money, girl,' the hag moithers.

You know you'll be careful with it. It will be safe with the rest of the pennies you have saved this week so that, by Friday, you actually will have enough money for a dinner. And you slip your right hand into your skirt pocket, place the penny in with the others and make your way to school.

How strange then to find yourself walking out of the door, not of a house, your house, but a shop, and to find yourself next to a busy main road. You look back through the glass of the shop door and see a face, indistinctly, peering and leering. Why does this make your heart race and prompt you to break into a run? For whatever reason, you run and run but the road changes shape, becomes sticky underfoot. You realise you have no skirt on. And the shops don't look quite right.

Then it's dark. A fine drizzle wets the air. You shuffle along the middle of the street, pulling your shirt down to your thighs to protect your modesty, until you trip over something soft and weighty. Losing your footing feels like drifting in the air, as helpless as a balloon floating upwards towards the rooftops.

You see a broken body lying in the street below – twisted out of shape, under an orange street-light which reflects off the puddles. Steam is rising from the nearby cattle sheds.

***

A muttering conversation intruded upon Maggie's sleep. She thought the voices were in the room with her, two doctors discussing a patient, but soon realised they were coming from somewhere around the back ginnel. She recognised Bob's, a growling sort of voice, talking about the weather.

She could feel the weight of Bob's body pressing hard upon her, against a rough wall that tore and frayed her cotton dress. Sweat began to trickle down her chest and legs. Her heart was racing. He smelled of beer and carbolic soap.

And then she woke up with a start.

Only now she was downstairs, at the table, sitting in her dressing gown with a lukewarm cup of tea cradled in her lap. Some of it had just spilled on her thighs. Photos were strewn across the table-top.

The phone was ringing, and it soon triggered the answer machine. She heard Gable's hesitant voice on the old, worn tape – 'Leave us something... funny... or weird, after the beep.'

Her mother began to speak, addressing her in the third person as she always did when leaving a message.

'This is Nan, Nan McCarthy, leaving a message for Maggie. Would she please give me a call, tomorrow at 11 in the morning, to the telephone at DeBarra's bar. She knows the number. I'll be waiting. I'm very worried about her. She didn't seem well at the funeral, and I haven't heard from her much since. I do hope her lovely friend from work is looking after her. What was her name? Eileen? Anyway, please could Mags call me on the telephone at DeBarra's tomorrow at 11 am? Thank you.'

Her mother's messages used to make them laugh. She probably felt she should direct her words at Gable, in response to his answer phone greeting. But who did she think she was talking to now?

Maggie scribbled a note to herself: Phone mum at DeBarra's, tomorrow 11 am.

A week later she would find that note and not be able to remember when she'd written it. She would then phone DeBarra's to discover that her mother had enjoyed a glass of Guinness, the day she'd stopped in for the phone call, but for the life of her the landlady couldn't remember which day that was.

***

Just when you thought you were safe, drifting into a gentle, reviving slumber, you find yourself perched reluctantly on a step-ladder, afraid to look around. Tins, jars and boxes are standing in columns on the shelves before you. Rather than get off the ladder, it feels like a better idea to keep climbing. But you have run out of steps. Then you feel yourself being tugged sharply backwards.

The hag has you in a firm grip by the crude, knotted pigtails she has just wrung out of your hair. She drags you over to the kitchen table where she's counting out pennies – stacking them in tall, precarious piles. For all the world, you pray that those pennies remain undisturbed and not suffer a bump to make them collapse and scatter noisily across the lino.

'Mind the table,' you find yourself saying, despite understanding that it's wrong to speak up so boldly.

'Cheeky little minx.' The hag leans in towards your face to say this. 'What do you think I am? Retarded?'

She pulls back with her hand raised, as if on the verge of delivering a slap when, not just the penny stacks, but the whole house collapses.

All of a sudden you are out in the middle of a dark street with no clothes on, walking with your head held high. Not out of pride but out of a strong sense of what may be lurking below your eye-line. You are anticipating the dead-weight, the trip, the drift into the air. You long for it, in fact. Instead you feel yourself being roughly manhandled.

'Let go!' you shout. (Bob, next door, hears this and is alarmed. It's mid-afternoon, why would Maggie be shouting?)

But your assailant ignores you, takes it for play-acting, and forces you up against a rough wall that scrapes at your back.

'Let go!' you shout again. 'I haven't begun flying yet!'

You feel somehow incomplete by not drifting into the air, up there with the cattle steam and misty rain, above the twisted, broken body.

You aim punches at your captor's head.

***

A sharp knock on the door brought Maggie suddenly out of her sleep. She was on the couch, looking up at the ceiling in a dark front room. Was she dreaming? The door sounded again – a loud, urgent rap of the letter flap.

No, this was real and she hoped it wasn't Bob. He did this once before (was it yesterday?) after he'd heard her shouting out in her sleep. He told her that he thought she was being attacked. He was concerned. Maggie slammed the door in his face after calling him a hypocrite.

It made her face burn thinking about it. Why did he have to turn up and remind her of what happened that night? What audacity to shoot round like that, full of care and concern, at the first peep. And what *did* she shout out during her sleep?

She'd been dreaming, something about lying – and a playground slide textured like a rough concrete wall.

The door sounded again, and Maggie could hear whoever it was lifting the flap to look in. She didn't move. She barely breathed. All they would be able to see was an empty staircase, the couch was just out of view. She hadn't even picked her head up from the arm-rest.

Eventually she heard footsteps walk away from the door and up the street towards the hum of the main road. Maggie continued to lie still until her eyelids grew heavy and she quickly gave way to their weight. Why fight it?

***

'Come here you little brat!' The hag stands by the table tapping her slippered foot like a demented rabbit.

'Come here and open your hand. Show me what you've got hiding in there.'

You look into her eyes which seem silver at the moment, but you know they're really a cloudy grey. Her teeth are bared as she speaks, and they are brown. You notice that she's wearing fingerless gloves and a cardigan which is at least a foot too long, so that it trails on the floor around her. The mole seems to twitch independently to the rest of her face. You feel the dread building up inside as if you're about to explode.

'No! I have nothing in my hand!' you proclaim.

And then you're in the back of the butcher's shop, in an icy room holding something that feels like a stocking, as a burly man carefully tips a bucket of blood into it. You watch your frozen hands stain red with the spillage and enjoy the warmth of the blood on your numb flesh. While at the same time you feel sickened. The pig had barely stopped squealing.

'That is how we make a black pudding,' says the burly man, leaning towards you with his handlebar moustache, but you're now climbing a ladder so tall you can't see where it ends. Nevertheless, it feels more sensible to keep climbing than to stop or, worse still, go back down. You wonder what may be at the top.

When you do run out of rungs, you simply begin to float adrift in space. Effortlessly, but with no real control. You wave your arms and legs in the air like hopeless propellers but they refuse to steer. And that's when you remember that, at this point in the proceedings, you're supposed to look down.

***

'Where was I?' Maggie asked aloud, which woke her up unexpectedly. The standard lamp was on, while at the same time sunlight split through the blinds. She was sitting at the dining table, with her head resting upon her arms on top of a scattering of photos. As she lifted herself back upright, a few of the photos stuck to her sleeves.

She wondered how long she'd been sleeping at the table. Her back felt stiff.

The answer phone was rewinding, with a steady beep building up to the caller's message. But there wasn't enough tape left to leave one. The answer phone was full. It simply clicked off dead on the caller, who then hung up.

She thought about who it might have been: her mother, her work-mate Elaine, or Bob...

Bob left her a message the morning after that night. He may as well have saved his breath.

'Er... Maggie. Um, I don't know what to say... uh, I'm sorry. I'm so sorry.'

She'd been surprised he could talk at all after the punch she'd landed on his jaw just twelve hours earlier.

She hauled herself up from the table, squinting through shafts of sunlight. The kitchen was even brighter, with the strip-light on. She groped her way over to the kettle and flipped the switch. Her pills were on the counter and, as she popped a blister, she imagined it was Bob's eye.

Back at the table, with a mug of tea cradled in her hands,

she looked again at the photos. These had just come back from the developer. Gable took the last of them on the morning he died – the morning they both went to watch the Preston Guild parades. Maggie stared at herself, smiling and waving in amongst the crowds. She looked like a stranger.

And then there were a few photos of a man, probably in his sixties, close-up studies showing every wrinkle, the veins in his eyes, the misshapen nose. Who was this? The background looked like the Black Horse, which is where Gable said he was going. He must have met this fellow while he was there.

Oh, God.

Why hadn't she just insisted he come straight home with her from the parades?

The phone had been ringing and Maggie decided she ought to answer it. But just as she lifted the receiver, the call hit the answer machine. She could hear someone on the end of the line breathing unsteadily as they waited to leave their message. Rather than speak anyway, Maggie carefully replaced the receiver. She wanted to listen to Gable's voice. And she wanted whoever was calling to hear him as well.

As Gable 'ummed and erred' his way through the greeting, Maggie crawled over to the couch and clambered on. Before the tape had rewound, she was fast asleep.

She didn't hear the machine click off dead. Nor did she hear the caller's voice through the speaker saying – 'Hello? Are you there? Hello?' – before hanging up.

***

'You're not leaving this house until you show me what you've got in your hand!' The old hag is pacing back and forth in a tight pattern, just a few steps in each direction, her cardigan tangling about her ankles.

Why does this vindictive midget insist on tormenting you?

You are about to turn and run when, all of a sudden, you're jerked back by the arm. She may be small but she's strong. You keep your fist clenched while she holds your right forearm in a tight grip. With her mole twitching like a cat's whisker, the hag raises a ruler and delivers an almighty swish down upon your hand. Pennies fall and scatter across the lino like crashing cymbals.

'Now that'll do me fine for a trip to DeBarra's,' she says, scrabbling about the floor.

You are in shock. It feels like your whole world has collapsed. You begin to wave your hands frantically and kick your feet. And, when you least expect it, you begin to lift from the floor and hover above the scene around cupboard height.

You find an open window and you're out, soaring above the treetops, swooping over the roofs and chimneys. The air feels fresh. Sunlight shimmers on the trees, their leaves are trembling. You curve and duck under power lines and lampposts. You feel a sensation in the pit of your stomach similar to that still moment when you have reached as far back on a playground swing as possible.

Then, without willing it at all, you find a perch. The top of a step-ladder as a matter of fact. You are faced with boxes, tins and packets all brimming with desirable produce. Strange, but you feel a wicked longing for some of those packets. You feel like helping yourself. Just a quick snatch with the right hand. You lean forward and...

Huuugh! The breath is drawn out of you like a vacuum. Grabbed again, but this time not by the pigtails.

'And this is how we make a sausage young Maggie.' The moustachioed butcher leans in towards your face, leering and wagging his finger.

Only now it's not a shelf full of products, but a counter you stand in front of. You can barely see over the top. You strain on the outermost tips of your toes, lifting yourself by the counter-edge, until you come eye to eye with... come eye to eye with...

Bob!

You run and run down a street full of shops. A busy street, although no-one gives you a second glance. But you barely make fifty yards in... oh... minutes. And then you notice you forgot your skirt. How ridiculous. You had it when you flew out of the hag's window earlier and now, here you are, stark naked from the waist down. In a crowded area. With some creep in pursuit.

To cap it all your feet stick to the floor. You look at them to see if they have sunk into quicksand or wet concrete and, when you look back up, it's night-time. There's a fine drizzle in the air. More like a mist – like a thin, sharp mist propelled from a shower. You feel drenched, your face wet. You're tugging at your shirt while stumbling along the middle of a road. And then you trip.

***

'Where am I?' Maggie sat upright suddenly, looking about her. The pillow felt damp to the touch. Her right hand was tingling and hot. A cool breeze lifted the net curtains by the open window.

She must have been dreaming. It was something about – wings and ladders. And a strange, little old lady rummaging about the floor on her hands and knees.

She wondered what might have roused her. Her senses were keened, listening for the door or the phone. But all she could hear was the gentle rustle of nets on rolled cane blinds. It sounded like a spirit leaving the house to soar beyond the rooftops and clouds. It pricked a memory of her dream, which soon gave way to sleepiness. And as she relaxed, her head sank backwards, inevitably, deep into the pillow.

Another forty winks would do no harm.

***

You look square into the hag's bright silver eyes. She is slapping a ruler firmly into her rump over and over again.

'You're lying,' she says, 'now open up your hand and hold it.'

She looks at you evenly.

'Go on, just think of it as a sausage. You can squeeze it too if you like...'

'What?' You can hardly believe your ears.

She leans in towards you, spitting through her jagged teeth. 'Don't be shy little girl.'

'You're not supposed to say that,' you splutter. 'The man in the shop says that.'

'Don't be inventing stories, you little slut.'

These aren't stories, you think, while you strain on the tips of your toes, peeking over the counter. The pervert, of course, remains seated, his moustache beaded with fat dewdrops. He points over to a tall step-ladder, five shelves high. You follow his finger with your eye, and gulp.

As you teeter on a rung adjacent to the top shelf, reaching out for the flour packets, you ask yourself why he isn't doing this, given he's the shopkeeper and knows exactly where to find the flour. And then you notice his breath. The smell surrounds you, the smell and the rasp of his breathing.

'Here, let me hold these steps steady for you,' he says.

You try to climb but you're all thrashing limbs and make little progress up the ladder. It's no use, you'll never escape. So you hold out your right hand, palm up, in resignation and turn around. But he's gone.

Out on the street, you run until your heart beats furiously yet somehow the shop is never out of sight. You must have been going around in circles all this time. You keep running, pushing your way past ever increasing crowds, until you can only stagger. The bodies around you have thickened to such an extent that you're forced to claw them apart to progress. That is, until you break into a clearing. A crowd has gathered around a strange little ragged figure, scrabbling and snuffling about the pavement. There's something familiar about this creature and you scratch your head to remember. That's when you realise everyone in the crowd is now staring at you.

At you – standing there with your fingernails tangled in

your pigtails. And, of course, you've lost your skirt. How ridiculous.

You glance downwards to check if your shirt-tugging is in fact protecting your modesty and, when you look back up, the day has become night. The crowd has disappeared and you are walking hesitantly up a street. It is a familiar walk but you can't quite recall the occasion, or, in fact, why it's familiar at all. And then finally, out of the blue, you remember.

You trip, you stumble, you scream. With a mad flailing of arms and legs, some motion is eventually achieved. But, rather than drifting into the air as you'd hoped, you find yourself plummeting through a dark empty space.

Then a hand reaches out, like a parachutist joining you mid-flight. You clasp it gratefully, this rescuing hand, and find yourself dragged into a room that has a lino floor and a fold-out table stacked with columns of pennies.

'Come here you thieving little brat,' snarls the hag, spraying spit through the gaps between her rotting pegs.

With an almighty heave of the ruler, she brings a vicious blow down onto your hand.

The ceiling, at this moment, opens to a thunderstorm of coins.

'Now take a penny to the butchers and fetch us some sausages!'

And the fierce little witch hauls you over to the door.

***

Maggie woke up so violently she kicked the duvet clear of the bed. She was gasping for breath and her heart was pounding as if she had just run a sprint. She was in the middle of a dream, something about...

A sharp rap at the door interrupted her thoughts. With a groggy head, Maggie stumbled from her bed and held herself steady with the bannister all the way down the stairs. Before she could contemplate who it might be, she unlocked the door and opened it to Elaine from work, still dressed in her ward uniform.

They both paused. Maggie brought her hands to her eyes, blinking in the acid sun.

'Are you OK?' Elaine asked.

'Oh, sure,' said Maggie, 'I was just dreaming about when I was a little girl in Cork and the shopkeeper made me... made me...'

***

It happens like this.

You expected Gable home hours ago. At 3 pm to be precise, and it's now past seven. The chicken dinner has long since cooled in the oven, you have already polished off a bottle of Spanish red wine and you're playing Motown classics on the stereo.

Earlier in the afternoon you'd put on your favourite party dress and some new hold-up stockings, and had spent a good while doing your make-up. You didn't usually bother with make-up, but this is the Guild, it's almost your second wedding anniversary, it's an occasion.

Despite all this, you find it difficult to be angry at Gable's absence. He never stays out late. He doesn't really have any friends. This, you understand, is a one-off.

It's just a pity that you've both missed your Guild dinner.

Although, after a couple of glasses of wine you hadn't felt like eating anyway. You felt like partying. You've been dancing in front of the mirror ever since, with music thundering from the stereo.

You are well into the Motown classics when suddenly you stop. Was that a knock at the door? You wobble as you go to turn the volume down on the stereo. At the door you make out Bob's shape in silhouette through the frosted glass.

'Oh, am I interrupting...?' Bob stands awkwardly at the doorstep, his eyes shining.

'No,' you answer, holding on to the door frame.

'I'm off to t'Big House for a pint, do you two wanna come?'

You pause, you fancy being out amongst a crowd. You explain that Gable's not back yet. He may turn up at any minute. So how will he know where to find you?

'Why not leave him a note?'

'OK. Give me a minute,' you say and go inside to write it.

You like Bob and feel safe in his company. He's a dependable neighbour, always keeping a look out for you and Gable. And you enjoy being out with him, downing beers in the Big House. That is until the conversation gets around to Gable. You're both laughing, making fun of him, when Bob has his slip of the tongue.

'And he took pictures of me fixing the outside tap. You know, me hands,' he chuckles.

'I wouldn't mind, if someone would pay good money for them like he says they will!' you joke.

'Yeah, what can you say about him, the no-hoper.'

'What?' you pull up sharply.

'Sorry, what I meant to say was... that he's a dreamer. A dreamer,' Bob stammers.

You are silent.

'Not a practical man, you know...'

You concede that this is true. Gable couldn't even fix a plug. But something in Bob's words makes you feel uneasy. Your tongue has loosened enough to explain something.

'Bob Atkins, I'll have you know that Gable is the only person I have ever met that I can trust. All my life I've been treated like I'll amount to nothing. From my mother, to my teacher and all. He is the one person who sets me free, so let a man have his dreams.'

You light a cigarette to end the speech.

You feel like going home, and try to finish your remaining beer in one gulp. Out of the corner of your eye you see a commotion brewing as lads begin to rush towards the pub door. Bob looks agitated, staring directly at you while frisking his jacket pockets for his cigarettes.

'I can't believe anyone could treat you badly,' he says.

'I'm going to the ladies.' You get up to push your way past more lads being drawn towards the front door. They are excited, they don't notice you as you struggle through them saying, 'Excuse me, excuse me...'

When you finish in the toilet, you leave the pub via the fire exit and head straight out on to the side ginnel. You can hear fight sounds from the street, guttural roars and grunts of pain. You have heard these sounds many times before but tonight they shock you, they make your knees wobble and knot the pit of your stomach.

It all seems to happen in slow motion. You feel glass, or coins, crunch underfoot. You take a step, holding the wall with your left hand for balance, when you are suddenly grabbed and yanked backwards.

'I knew you'd be out here.' You can barely see Bob against the strip-lighting from the fire exit. His voice sounds strange. The light is blinding. You hear deathly screams from the street, and a succession of bone-crunching thuds.

'Let go!' You try to shrug him off. You can hear a siren in the distance, getting closer.

Eee aww! Eee aww!

He laughs, whispers provocative words in soothing tones. You hear the sound of panic – running feet and heavy breathing. The slap of trainers on wet cobbles. A door slamming shut.

Again you try to yank your arm free but he continues to resist. Is it him, or is it the toilet that smells of carbolic soap?

You have felt this grip before, this immobilisation of your right arm. But where? A memory, a fleeting image comes to you of a punishment you once received.

Without thinking you bring your left knee up violently, connecting with full force into his groin. You follow this with a right uppercut, brought from below your belt-line as soon as he lets go of your wrist, and it lands square against his chin.

Within a moment he lies kicking on the ground.

You stumble towards the haze of an orange street-light, a haze busied by misty rain, and you reach the end of the ginnel at the same time as the police car brakes up. As you look along the street towards the cattle sheds, you see the body. It is twisted out of shape. You feel a physical reaction – it's like an electric shock combined with a fast-working anaesthetic. You see his camera bag lying in a puddle, a good three feet away from his head.

Your face is wet.

Miles Away

November 1992

There's just a clock ticking on the wall. For a minute, maybe more. Tick, tock, tick, tock – regular as a steady heart, and then a question interrupts it.

Well, Mrs McGrath, can you tell me of another occasion when you experienced a change as profound as this?

Followed by a long pause, into which creeps the clock, louder and louder. Tick, tock, tick, tock – until the conversation resumes.

Yes. Yes, I can. Again, it was to do with Gable. But this time it was when I met him.

Ah yes, your marriage. But would you say that was as profound a change as your loss? Especially such a brutal and tragic loss?

There may also be the sound of breathing in there. Slow, deep breathing. But it's difficult to tell for sure.

I honestly don't know, but for me it was about meeting him, not marrying him. When we first met it was much more than love and romance. For me.

Oh? In what way?

Well, I was escaping the clutches of a weirdo, for one thing. In fact, I had just left him that day. And in the evening, when I was out with some friends, I met Gable.

Really? That's interesting. Tell me more.

***

'Here's to a good New Year for us all!' Elaine raised her wine glass.

Maggie and Marie held aloft their beers and, with the jukebox playing *Fairytale of New York*, they cheered and laughed and drank and in amongst it, a second toast was proposed.

'To the single life for Maggie!'

They were occupying a corner table in a side room of the Black Horse, all squeezed onto the window bench. The pub was crowded out with Friday night revellers and a fog of cigarette smoke drifted from bar to booth.

'When did you leave him then?' Marie asked.

'Today,' said Maggie.

'She dropped her suitcase round at mine,' said Elaine. 'Pulled out a party dress, put some slap on and here we are.'

'Well, take my word for it,' said Marie reaching for Maggie's hand, 'you won't be single for long.'

'Get away!' Maggie rapped Marie's knuckles sharply.

'Ah, I don't need to read your palm to know. You'll be married before the year's out.' Marie looked into her eyes, nodding wisely. 'And he won't be your last.'

'Now then, the poor lass is only nineteen!' Elaine shrieked. 'She's got plenty of time! And she's only just got rid of one!'

'Was he a creep?' asked Marie.

'You could say that.' Maggie took a gulp of beer. 'But aren't they all?'

***

Is Marie a psychic? Is she a palm-reader?

All these questions in this bare room, with this bare table. And, of course, the clock. The air buzzes as well as ticks and the atmosphere is stifling, motionless – made more so by the strict counting away of time. And whatever it is that's making that damned buzzing sound.

I don't honestly know. She was a ward nurse at the time,

218

like me. Moved on now. But she thought she knew a thing or two about the gypsy ways, you know.

Ah, the gypsy ways. Yes, of course... Go on.

***

Maggie felt like she needed to get up and out of the pub for a while. The place was airless and choked with the smell of beer, cigarettes and bodies. And the pitch of the general babble was making her feel dizzy. The patterns in the carpet were beginning to zig-zag up at her.

Marie set another round of drinks out in front of them. She had a stain the shape of a mountain down the front of her dress, the result of a collision in the struggle back from the bar.

'One for the road!' she shouted. The scene behind her looked like the deck of a pirate ship in a storm. The Smokin Joes song was playing on the jukebox and a group of lads were jumping about like maniacs.

Maggie lifted her shot-glass and downed its contents in one pick-up and swallow, and she was about to get to her feet when Elaine brought up the subject of travel.

'My Rob says he'll book us a trip to Venice for our summer holiday,' she announced. 'Imagine it – the canals, the gondoliers, and all.'

Maggie tried to imagine it, but all she could think of was the film with Donald Sutherland and the murderous dwarf in the red mac. The setting for it all seemed pretty enough, but while Elaine talked of history and romance, Maggie pictured collapsing masonry, blind old ladies and vicious, cut-throat killings.

'And the rooms have tiled floors and shutters on their windows, to keep them cool. Can you picture how it would look at sunset? With the shutters hooked open, pigeons flapping by and the sound of voices and laughter from the cafés on the street?'

Maggie had half an eye on the lads as they reeled about and

bumped heavily against a table. She watched as the glasses slid off it and then smashed, one by one.

'I was thinking of Ibiza, this year,' said Marie.

'Excuse me,' said Maggie, 'I just need some fresh air.' And she stood up suddenly, steadying herself by the lip of the table. Then, with her balance restored, she strode chin up into a swirl of smoke and swaying drinkers and out towards the exit.

***

You're playing an avoidance game, are you not? Distracting yourself from your story.

What do you mean?

And anyway, a room like this should have a water dispenser. In fact, isn't it a legal requirement? Either way, the gurgle of each drained plastic cup would work neatly with the buzzing and the ticking. If there was a water dispenser. But there's only a table that resembles school furniture, and a counter laid out with three foil ashtrays by a reinforced window.

You were telling me about Marie and her gypsy ways, and you mentioned the weirdo that you'd just left.

Is that so?

But you haven't told me anything about this weirdo, what's his name?

Ken.

Ken. So tell me about Ken.

If the room was busy, everyone stopping at the water dispenser for a regular drink, then the gurgling sound would add a bubbly bass layer to the drone of whatever was buzzing and the beat of the clock. This would become a room with its own music.

Wouldn't Gable have been proud of me for thinking of that!

As it is, the drone and the beat continue as a maddening duet.

***

Once Maggie had bolted the lock on the cubicle door, she allowed herself to think about what had happened to her today. She let herself properly feel the fear, and the relief of her escape. She felt it through her breathing and she focused on keeping it deep and steady. Just let it all go. Let it be exhaled into history – to join the other bad memories.

She drew in and blew out forcefully until, a short while later, she could hear a discussion by the sinks and mirror.

'What d'you make of Jack, then?'

'Oh, he's gorgeous.'

'Isn't he just?'

'And he's in my sights. I'm having him tonight, whatever it takes!'

'Good for you, lass. He won't know what's hit him!'

Maggie tried to act naturally as she opened up the door of her cubicle but she felt conspicuous, and could see their faces reflected in the mirror as they exchanged a little glance while adding touches to their lipstick. Then she took a handful of paper towels, wet them in the sink and set about scrubbing her face free of any trace of make-up.

She rubbed until her skin glowed and then, once done, and ignoring the stifled giggles of the two next to her, she fluffed her hair up before stepping back out of the ladies.

***

Tick, tock, tick, tock…

And he'd be waiting for me. No matter what time I got home, Ken would be there, slouching in an armchair. It didn't matter whether I was coming home from a night out with the girls, or from a late shift on the ward, he would be waiting. He was a control freak.

The buzzing sound seems to have shifted pitch, almost up to a school bell, and now the ticking has been joined by a dull clunk. Like the bony knock of an unwelcome visitor.

But perhaps he was just being caring and concerned?

Hah! That's the way he'd like you to see it. But it was about dominance and control. He knew it and I knew it, once the front door shut behind us.

I see, so it was a sexual thing...

Why do you people always leap to that conclusion? Although as it goes, in my case, it's partly true. At first I thought it was just playing about. You know, a game. But that wasn't the whole picture at all.

The dull clunk is gaining in frequency, almost falling into time with the clock. It sounds like an old man hurrying across a wooden floor.

What kind of game?

Role play.

What kind of role play?

Use your imagination, pervert.

And then the clunk stops.

***

Maggie stepped out of a side door into the alley alongside the Black Horse. She felt the cold air sting her scrubbed face and she was dazzled by a bright light.

'Oh, beg yer pardon,' a voice called out from beyond the glare.

Maggie shielded her eyes. 'Who's that?' she asked.

'Ah.' The light was switched off and Maggie blinked. She saw a dishevelled looking fellow, holding a bulky camera with a long lens. He wiped his right hand on the seat of his pants and offered it in her direction.

'Gable,' he said. 'Gable McGrath.'

'Maggie McCarthy.' She took his hand and raised a smile. His hair was a mess.

'What were you doing?' she asked.

'Oh,' he held up his camera, 'thought I'd try a shot of the pub from the alley.'

'At 10.30 on a Friday night?' Maggie laughed.

'Ah, well, it was getting a bit rowdy in there.' He looked directly into her eyes, 'Truth be told, I was more worried about this little baby than myself. It's too precious to risk getting damaged.'

For some reason Maggie found she was speechless and it threw her. She wasn't normally one to dry up. He was talking about his camera, of course. It must have been the tool of his trade.

'So I just thought I'd take a photo,' Gable carried on, filling the silence. 'While I was out here, you know.'

Maggie became aware, all of a sudden, of the vapours drifting up into the alley from their breathing, but she didn't look away.

'Sorry, I didn't mean to take the shot as you opened the door. It was an accident.'

'No, that's all right!' she blurted out. 'Don't apologise, it's fine.'

They heard the Orchard Street door creak and bang open amid some muttering, and then footsteps stumbled away down the road.

'I'll destroy the negative if you like.' Gable sounded concerned.

'No, don't do that.' Maggie stepped forward, letting the alley door shut behind her. 'It might turn out to be a good photo.'

Gable smiled and began to unscrew the lens from his camera.

'So, what are *you* doing out here, then?' he asked.

***

We had the photograph blown up and framed. It's still hanging on the wall opposite the fireplace to this day. I'm just a silhouette in the door-frame. You know, blacked out. Like a shadow.

I know what a silhouette is.

There. Breathing. A clear, undeniable rise and fall of breath.

223

Holding the whole ticking, buzzing, dull clunk cacophony together. It's been there all this time, it's just taken some homing in on.

Is that it, then? Don't you have any more questions?

This isn't a question and answer session, Mrs McGrath.

Isn't it? Well, in that case, what is this? What's the point of all this?

We're having a conversation. It's an opportunity for you to express your feelings.

But the breathing is completely out of sync with the ticking, which begins to sound like castanets and the buzz has switched to a high-pitched whine.

'Maggie McGrath!'

Out of the blue, a shout invades the whole disjointed tune and each breath draws in the whiff of wood-chip and glue. I open my eyes to see I'm screened off by my hair spread about me.

'Maggie McGrath! Dr Brown is now ready for your return to work assessment!'

And I realise it's my own boot making that clunking noise, as I pull my face off the table and kick the leg of the chair I'm sitting on.

'Oh. Jeez. Sorry, I was miles away.'

The Lyric of Maggie's Christmases

December 1992

Maggie is on the way back from her latest return to work assessment when she thinks of the song...

> *And a Blacksmith courted me, for nine months and better*
> *He fairly won my heart, wrote me a letter*

...while the bus vibrates at a stop and she watches people stepping off, fastening their hoods against the weather. She's watching them through sleet spitting at the windows, spreading across the glass like spiders' webs. And all of a sudden it feels as if it's her first Christmas as a wife again and Gable is waiting for her to get home from work so they can begin celebrating together.

And then, as the bus pulls away from the stop, she thinks of the Christmas before that. She thinks of Ken, who she spent it with.

As she teeters to her feet, some lads wearing baggies and hooded sweatshirts start the giggling and cat-calling, which she puts to a stop with a scornful glance – and they all turn to each other, red-faced, sucking at their roll-ups while Maggie thanks the driver at the door. Then she steps out into the night and feels an icy whiplash across her face, blurring the festive lights of the Rose Tavern into jewels.

And all of a sudden there's something else about that Christmas with Ken she's reminded of...

***

'First of all, he made me take my clothes off, you know, slowly and provocatively,' said Maggie throwing back the bed sheets. The elderly man underneath didn't twitch a muscle. Elaine was stripping down the other side of the bed and she paused to raise her eyebrow.

'Kinky,' she said. 'Go on.'

'And then, once I was standing there completely naked, he handed me a parcel.' Maggie didn't look up, she was tearing open packets of hot cloth for the body wash. 'You see, he likes to buy me little outfits to wear,' she continued, 'and this one was a French Maid.'

'He enjoys a girl in uniform, then,' said Elaine.

'You could say that.' Maggie was lifting the patient's arm and rubbing the cloth with a firm, massage-like grip, through the bicep and armpit.

'So I try to squeeze into this little frilly outfit, and it's a devil of a job getting my boobs tucked in – they keep spilling out of the cups.'

Elaine was washing the man's torso. 'With your figure, I'm not surprised,' she said.

'I'd been wriggling about in this thing for ages,' Maggie continued, 'and he was sat there pleasuring himself, when I noticed the blinds had been open all the time and the man across the way was standing at his window.' She had worked her side of the wash right down to the leg and foot. 'And he was pleasuring himself too.'

Elaine drew to a complete halt at the patient's left calf.

'And I was gob-smacked, I can tell you,' Maggie was ready for the lift and turn-over. 'I couldn't shut those blinds quick enough. Then both me and Ken fell about laughing.'

They gave his backside a once over and flipped the patient back onto some fluffed-up pillows.

'There you go Mr Irongate, right as rain,' said Maggie, and she smiled at the poor man. His eyes were certainly alive now and then, but the rest of him...

'I hope you have a restful night,' she said before spinning on her heel to catch up with Elaine who was already wheeling the trolley back to the station.

***

And... and I hope... you do too.
  I'm a man. I'm still alive.
  I am... still alive.

***

'He'll be due for the morphine pump tomorrow,' said Elaine, pouring out the coffees in the tiny galley at the nurses' station. 'Poor ol' bugger.'

'Shh! He can still hear us y'know,' whispered Maggie and she glanced over her shoulder, even though his bed was just out of view around the corner. It was as if she expected to see him craning his neck to look out at them.

The doctors knew very little about him, except that his name was Peter Irongate – a drunken destitute who'd been found collapsed in Avenham Park. Scans and biopsies had revealed, amongst other things, some metastasized tumours, so he had been moved off the men's ward to the little private room next to the galley. The previous occupant had, only hours earlier, completed his four days on the pump.

'Shall we nip down to the smoking room for a quick cig?' Elaine suggested. 'I want to hear more about your Christmas break with kinky Ken.' And they tiptoed out of the ward, winking at Marie, who was barely awake at the station. She had been on shift since the previous morning and was due off in fifteen minutes.

***

God help me, where am I? I swear there's an angel by me, I can hear her sweet voice singing. A voice like streams of whiskey, washing over ice-cube rocks. And she looked down on me earlier with a benign smile.

Maybe it's Irene. Come back to tend for me in my sick-bed. Though why would she do that? After all I put her through?

Shush! Here she is again...

***

'So after we had our Christmas dinner, he brought me upstairs, poured me a bath, lit some candles and made it seem romantic...'

'And?' Elaine prompted.

'And when he led me into the bedroom, the first thing I noticed was that the blinds were wide open again.' Maggie drained the last of her coffee and paused her story to wave goodbye to Marie as she trudged out of the door.

'So?'

'So, it turns out that Ken has taken a payment from the guy across the road to set up these viewings.'

'Unbelievable.' Elaine's mouth fell open.

'I tried to get mad at him, you know,' said Maggie, quietening her voice. 'But d'you know what he said to me?'

'No,' said Elaine.

'He said, "Where do you think the money came from to buy your presents?"' Maggie picked her mug up again, even though she knew it was empty.

'And then you'll never guess what he made me do...'

***

It was time for Mr Irongate's meds and Maggie opened the blinds to the yellow, box-shaped room even though it was still dark outside. The room had bare walls except for a cheap trade painting of a rural scene – an old cottage in the foreground and a few others scattered in the hills beyond.

Elaine was rolling out the trolley and a radio was on, playing easy listening music. Maggie cupped the back of the old man's head, his knotted hair tangling in her fingers, and she tipped the little plastic tub to his lips.

'This'll be the last time I do this for you, Mr Irongate,' she said and there was a reaction in his eyes, but she couldn't tell exactly what it was. Fear, maybe.

'He'll be happier on the pump,' said Elaine, as she brought in a fresh bag of saline solution.

It was the strip-light that made the room yellow. Maggie realised later, when she looked in and saw it had become dark with the stony-grey skies of the day. She brought in a miniature plastic Christmas tree from the nurses station and dressed it with battery powered star-lights to brighten the place up. She wondered how long those batteries would last.

It turned out that they would outlive Mr Irongate.

***

And the angel whispers to me, she tells me of her plight. Poor angel Irene. With belts and ropes – terrified, thrilled and outraged all at once.

And I recognise her story because she is talking about me. But, in my defence, those were raging days. It wasn't good or bad, it was just necessary. I roared at the world, and my Irene was the one waiting in for me at night.

So, as much as she describes her humiliation (there's someone else here, she might be telling them too), I can't help but feel a longing for that arrival home to our little house (though I see it now as a country cottage), for those creaking steps up to the bedroom and the heavy breathing of her fear and anticipation.

It's a memory that refuses to die. Even here, at the gates of Heaven, waiting for judgement.

***

Three nights later, Maggie and Elaine were on their last shift of the year.

'At first it was kind of exciting.' Maggie tried to keep her voice to a whisper but she knew it still carried into the ward's quiet, early hours.

'You're not kidding,' said Elaine.

'But now it just creeps me out, he scares me sometimes,' said Maggie, and she stood up from her chair at the station as if to make for the galley. Elaine said nothing.

'It's like he's claiming ownership, the way he's obsessive about it,' Maggie paused, still standing by her chair. Elaine was staring up at her with a tired looking face. The long shifts and the festivities seemed to be taking their toll and tomorrow was New Year's Eve.

'Put the kettle on while you're up,' she said.

Maggie stayed where she was.

'The way he pounces on me as soon as I put a foot through the door.' She was talking to herself now. 'It's pure manipulation,' she said. 'He's trying to mould me into something I'm not.'

'Well, love, you will go and move in with men you've only just met,' said Elaine, in a weary voice.

'Meaning?'

'Meaning, you either decide to enjoy life as a porno queen, or you get yourself out of there before it gets any weirder.' Elaine was still looking at Maggie.

'So go on, put a sugar in mine this time.' She offered her mug and Maggie scooped it up, along with her own, before making her way thoughtfully to the galley.

***

She flew our little nest, that sweet old cottage beyond the sparkling fir trees. She flew away to find her freedom. She left

230

me there to collapse on my own, while she went after the happiness she deserved. And yet she has come back to tend for me. She's been visiting every day, while they keep me here on the threshold of judgement.

Maybe this is a sign. Okay, I may have badly injured a few fellows in fights – I enjoy fighting – and I may have robbed and plundered when I could, but if Irene can absolve me of the crimes I committed upon her person, surely, dear God, I can be given your blessing?

Please, God.

I don't want to be alone.

***

They were mid-way through Mr Irongate's body wash.

'Anyway, those are my plans for tonight. What about you? Fancy coming along?' Elaine helped Maggie do a half turn-over and then tore open a fresh cloth.

'No plans especially,' said Maggie. She'd noticed Mr Irongate's lips – he was able to move them today, as if he was mouthing whispers. 'Staying in, I guess.'

Elaine laughed, 'I know what kind of cork-popping you'll be doing!'

'But I don't want to leave him behind, you know, I'd like to be with him until the end,' said Maggie gesturing at the poor tramp, who was wheezing loudly as they held him on his side.

'Will he last till midnight? That's the question,' said Elaine, and Maggie gave her a sharp look.

They pulled his robe back down and tucked him up in his bed and he sat staring straight ahead, occasionally making an O shape with his mouth, his chest rising and falling like an injured bull.

'Some people just keep on living,' whispered Maggie as they wheeled the trolley out of the side room.

***

I walk home through the yellow light of dusk to my little cottage beyond the pine trees up in the hills. Well I say it's my home, but in truth I've never laid eyes on the place before. So this must be purgatory, my place of waiting before the delivery of judgement. That'll be it.

So I walk home to purgatory, in the form of an old cottage, and I hear Irene's voice relating a sordid tale of being strapped across a workman's bench and beaten with a leather lash. The memories make me choke up with nostalgia. To think I did all that! She said she didn't like it, but I knew she did. Her strict convent schooling wouldn't allow her to admit it.

And, OK, maybe now and again I had to give her a slap across the face. But only when she was resisting me in front of friends, you know, showing me up. Like if she kicked up a fuss when myself and Tom fancied a night's drinking.

When me and Tom went drinking, we liked fighting too. It was no place for a lady.

So it was little wonder she left me in the end. I'd expected it for years. Nonetheless it was still a terrible walk up those stairs, on that night, to find my bird had flown the nest. I don't think I ever really got over it.

For all that, she's here by my side. I can feel her now. She's holding onto me as I make this last arrival. She's holding my hand as I pause at the cottage door. And I look all about me – at the evergreens glistening in the frost, at the bright yellow world before I step out of it – and then I see her eyes looking into mine. Her soft, forgiving eyes.

And I choke up with the memory of it all...

***

Maggie hustles through the gusts with one hand holding onto her hood and the other a swinging, rattling shopping bag. She hears kids' voices half-heartedly singing carols, scrounging at a doorstep nearby. Along Lytham Road all the houses have decorated front windows with glittering trees and Advent candles.

She can't help but wonder who Ken would be waiting for now. She can picture him sitting in his dark front room, just a few candles, with a small wooden bench in the middle of the floor. And, in the shadows, he would be slapping a folded leather belt in the palm of his hand.

She would have to unbutton her work dress down to her navel, fetch a toy stethoscope from the kitchen and pretend to check his heartbeat, leaning over him like a *Carry On* nurse. Then she would have to slap him hard across each cheek. And that would be just the beginning of the lengthy foreplay that increasingly led to the same conclusion. He would work her over that bench like a craftsman shaping his prize piece.

From the top of her road, Maggie sees the sleet blowing in waves under the dull-orange street lamp opposite her front door. And she stares at that door when she reaches it. She stares at the frosted glass reflecting the warm light from the street lamp – and she sees her own jumbled face in amongst it all. Then she thinks again of Mr Irongate and the night he died on the pump.

He had been looking at the painting on the wall opposite, a cottage on a country road winding through the hills, and his lips were moving the whole time, which must have been for fifteen minutes, maybe more, while he heaved his final breaths. Then he turned his head, slowly and jerkily, until he looked at her with the empty diamonds of his eyes and said, 'Fly... angel of light.'

It was the only time she'd heard him speak.

Three days later she walked into work with a packed suitcase, leaving behind a pile of burning costumes in the back-yard.

***

Maggie smiles, pulls back her hood and steps inside.

There's Gable waiting for her, and she catches a waft of roast chicken in the air as she shuts the door behind her. Gable's smiling, holding out a glass of wine and she can hear soft, jazzy Christmas music playing in the front room. He leads her in and she sees the table laid out for dinner. There's a huge Christmas tree strung with decorations – it's appeared since she left for work the previous day.

And Gable takes her gently by the shoulders and swivels her round to face the wall opposite the fireplace.

'Do you remember the night we met?' he asks.

Maggie sees a framed blow-up of the photograph Gable took of the pub that night. It was the first time they laid eyes on each other, just hours after Maggie left Ken. It had been a complete coincidence – Maggie stepped outside at the very same moment as he was taking his shot. The flash had dazzled her and they got talking and now, almost a year later, they had been married three months to the day.

'Yes, 'course I do.' The effect of the flash, and the back-light from the pub interior, had made her a silhouette between the old, panelled windows of the Black Horse. The detail of the stained glass and the blood-red brickwork, the worn out sign, the hanging baskets – it was the moment they first met and yet they were both anonymous within it.

'It's... brilliant, thank you,' she says, and steps into a hug.

His cheeks are like roses and she thinks again of the song:

If I was with my love, I would live forever.

***

Only this year she isn't arriving home to Gable. Maggie wipes her eyes and looks again at the jumbled lights in the frosted glass. Then, with her head in a blur, she turns the key to open the door to her empty house.

Jack and Mick and how they Change Maggie's Life

December 21 1992

Maggie closes the front door behind her and leans against it. She can feel the texture of the frosted glass through layers of winter clothing. Her ears ring with the dull hum of her empty home. Lately, since Gable's gone, it's been as if the house has developed feelings. From a place of music and conversation it has, like Maggie herself, settled into a troubled silence.

She opens her eyes and she's looking upwards to the top of the staircase. There's Christmas music playing somewhere. She strains to hear if it's coming from the top front room – Gable's old workshop. Of course it wouldn't be. But she is open to her mind playing tricks on her. It's a source of comfort. She has been signed off work for so long – as 'unfit' – that she needs the reassurance, now and again, that the diagnosis is correct.

It's Roy Wood singing *I Wish it Could be Christmas Everyday*. It's coming from Bob's house next door, along with the occasional whoop and burst of laughter.

***

5.30 pm and the Black Horse is quiet, just a few drinkers – two perched on stools and one on his feet at the bar. All three are occupied with their own contemplations. One does the crossword and another reads the sports pages. The bloke standing up stares straight ahead towards the optic rack, mouthing the odd thought.

The clock on the wall ticks loudly between songs from the jukebox.

All very innocent, on the surface, but little does anyone here realise that soon this will be the scene of high drama. The Friargate door will be thrown wide open and everything in this pub will change. It'll be a biker gang arriving for a night's anniversary celebrations, or a couple of drunken, irreverent comedians on their way to Blackpool. That'll shake 'em all up.

'Another one, lad. When you're ready,' says the crossword puzzler.

And the Robinson's Ale hand-pump becomes a piece of world war two rocket launching hardware. Six firm pulls, a volley over St George's Centre, and there's a pint frothing up on the counter before him.

All of which prompts the standing man to order another.

'While you're at it,' he says, pushing an empty pint pot across the counter. 'It's a Guinness in there.'

'I hope you're not expecting me to pay for that, you crafty toad,' says the puzzler.

The standing man turns to face him. He's dressed in a shiny suit from the 1960s, with drainpipe trousers and winkle picker boots.

'Mick Finnegan always pays for his own drinks,' he says.

'Oh aye?' contends the third one, holding his empty glass aloft.

All of a sudden there's a bit of a rush on.

***

It's the beginning of the Christmas season, and there's still no tree up. Maggie looks about the walls as she peels her coat off and lets it drop to the floor. Maybe she should put up some decorations. She hears another burst of laughter from next door. Bugger it, a bottle of wine seems a better idea and she heads for the kitchen, pulling off her jumper at the same time.

She finishes half a glass in one gulp.

There's a message on the answer phone from Elaine. She wants to meet up at Yates's this evening. Elaine would still be on shift and had probably, by now, heard the outcome of Maggie's assessment. Instead of being back on the ward for the Christmas shifts, she's been signed off for another month.

Maggie refills her glass.

How is she going to keep herself sane for another month?

***

Patrick Michael Finnegan left his house in Fishwick at the usual time, 4.30 pm, and walked down to New Hall Lane. He had made this journey almost every day since moving into his red brick, two-up two-down in the early 1970s.

His first port of call was William Hill's bookmakers. For once, his small treble bet had come in and he left the bookies £42.20 to the good. This was a rare day, for sure, and as he stood outside on the pavement fingering the small fold of notes in his trouser pocket, he wondered what other surprises might be in store.

The last time he had a stroke of luck like this was a few months back, during the Guild week, when it seemed as though the whole town was out celebrating his winnings with him. He'd done as he always did. He placed ten pence on three horses to win. There was little science to his choices. Sometimes he recognised a horse's name, both the donkeys and the sure-fire winners – but usually he went on whichever name he fancied.

When he won the bet during Guild week, it was the first treble winner he'd had since 1980. His first horse, Gypsy Jet, came in at sixteens, so he had £1.60 riding on the next, a second favourite at six to one. As it romped home with the jockey giving it the shillelagh up on the stirrups, Mick was punching the air to the radio commentary in his kitchen. The best part of ten pounds was now riding on his final horse. When he'd placed the bet that morning Midnight Dash was also six to

237

one, but Mick hadn't bothered taking the odds and, to his utmost joy, it drifted in the betting before winning by a nose at twelve to one. He walked out of William Hill's feeling like a million dollars.

Today he felt equally as thrilled, even though this success had come so quickly on the heels of his previous one. Today was December 21st, the longest night and the start of the Christmas season, and to have a bonus in his pocket was like a gift from God. Or the Blessed Virgin Mary, whichever one was giving out the benevolences.

***

The bottle looks to be about a third full. It only took two glasses to reduce it this much. There's been no need to put the TV or any music on, the noise from next door has been background enough. The voices have been getting ever louder through the wall and the Christmas music has been bouncing. While, at the same time, hearing these songs – Chrissie Hynde, Jona Lewie and John Lennon – gives her the shivers.

Maggie looks again around the walls, thinking about decorations. On this very night last year they were dressing the tree with bells and tinsel. Gable enjoyed the ritual of decorating the house at Solstice. They listened to corny Christmas music, got drunk and had sex next to the fireplace with the smell of pine and candles in the air.

At the time they hadn't the slightest notion about the future. At least, not Maggie – she was living in the moment. Never could she have imagined the following Christmas would be like this.

It's been three months since Gable was kicked to death on the street. Manslaughter, they said – a brawl that got out of hand. Although, they still haven't found anyone guilty – just a few lads charged with affray.

She looks down at her glass, follows its stem with her gaze, up into the bowl half filled with blood red wine. They must have been thinking of the patients' welfare, not hers, when deciding she wasn't ready to return to work.

How was she supposed to get through another month of this?

***

With everyone resettled, the contented rustle of newspapers and muttering resumes and the jukebox, which appears to have a life of its own, scratches its way across *I Will Survive* by Gloria Gaynor. No-one here would have put that on. Surely.

The Orchard Street door opens to a rush of cold, wet air and in steps a small man huddled in a parka. He yanks his hood down at the doorway before staggering across the tiles to the bar counter, against which he falls heavily. It's a tall counter at the Black Horse and he rests his head on his forearms. He looks like a night-shift security worker asleep at the desk.

The sports page man looks over, muttering his disappointment.

'It's the same every Christmas, fuckin' small-time drinkers...'

The man in the shiny suit is very carefully peeling the cellophane off a fresh pack of Woodbines.

'And I suppose you're big time,' he says.

'Seasoned.' The other replies, finding his glass without looking up from the paper.

The drunkard slumped across the counter is slowly lifting his head. It's like the raising of Tower Bridge.

'I just...' he begins.

'Ehup!' says the crossword puzzler, shifting on his bar-stool, slipping a pencil behind his ear.

The jukebox whirrs back into action straight after Gloria Gaynor finishes – *It's Raining Men* by the Weather Girls follows. Without doubt, an unlikely choice for any of the present company.

'I'm the advance party,' the drunkard continues, swaying

239

like a mime artist. 'A stag do – the rest are following behind.'
He buckles from the knees and slides into a heap on the floor.

Everyone looks to the Orchard Street door, waiting for some sort of stampede.

'And I suppose you're a gambling man too,' says the bloke in the shiny suit, cuffing a zippo and letting out a cloud of smoke. He stands with his back to the bar, elbows on the counter.

The sports page man chuckles and glances over at him.

'You could say that, pal.'

'What odds would you give for antlers on all of them?' The little man stands up straight to look down on his seated adversary while taking a drag on the Woodbine, which he holds between his thumb and forefinger.

***

Manslaughter is how they describe it, which sounds worse than murder. More prolonged – like being hung, drawn and quartered. And yet, not a soul arrested to this day.

All the voices from next door sound like women. Bob and a houseful of women and the Christmas party favourites on the stereo.

What the hell, Maggie fancies a cigarette. She has the occasional smoke and she bought a pack earlier, on her way to the assessment interview. Rather than rummage in her bag, it's easier to empty the contents out onto the table. Lipstick, wet-wipes and a mirror end up on a small mound of bag junk – a photograph wallet lands in amongst it all. Her ten Embassy filters have fallen in such a way as to be standing up.

Once she's lit up and had a few deep draws, she knocks the wine bottle over. She was reaching for it without looking, her attention drawn to the photo wallet.

'Damn!'

She catches the bottle before it empties but in doing so, wine sprays across the room.

***

On the occasion that Mick Finnegan found himself out celebrating his fortuitous Guild wager, he had a second surprise that compounded the whole experience for him. He called in to the Black Horse dead on opening time, as was his custom, arriving just moments before the bolts were pulled back on the Friargate door. Inside he found two drinkers sitting at the bar in full throes from a lock-in. *Somewhere Over the Rainbow* was playing on the jukebox and it was dark inside.

Mick ordered his pint and took a low stool next to a small, round table near the door. There was something a little unusual about this scene but he couldn't determine what it was. At least not until he was back at the bar twenty minutes later for his second pint and he overheard the elder of the two talking about a boxer. When the fellow, who looked like a fighter himself, finished his story, he threw his head back and laughed and then he turned and Mick looked straight at him. They held each other's stare for a moment.

Mick smoked a cigarette back in the shadows of his table and tried to remember who this was. It was a familiar face. The lad with him must have been his son, he looked about the right age.

He was a boxer...

Then it came to him. It was twenty years ago. In fact, it was twenty years ago pretty much to the day. Jesus, Mary and Joseph, what a throw of the dice this was! It was like the big fellow, perched up there on his bar-stool, had returned as a ghost to haunt them all again.

***

She pushes the contents of her bag to one side with her arm and then fans the photos out on the table like a deck of cards. She'd been making do with the light from the kitchen, but now she switches on the standard lamp to see the pictures clearly.

She hasn't looked at these since the day she picked them up from Boots in a haze of anti-depressants.

They were mostly taken at the Guild parades, on the morning of the day Gable was manslaughtered. He had been particularly keen on photographing abandoned placards and balloons emblazoned with Preston Guild insignia. She fingers through a fair few of those. Then there are some shots of the parades, most of them with herself smiling and waving in the foreground. And the last half dozen are of an old man taken at the bar of the Black Horse – where she'd left Gable, while she went home to prepare the dinner. And that's it. Forty-eight photographs and there's no sight of him here in the final hours of his life.

Do They Know it's Christmas? is playing next door and she drains what's left of the wine into her glass.

***

We're between songs on the jukebox, which increases the tension as all eyes are on the Orchard Street door. Everyone's waiting for a scrum of antlered piss-heads to burst in at any moment. Their first man is lying in a heap at the bar.

The clock chimes the quarter hour, and then Wham!, *Wake Me Up Before You Go-Go*, bangs out of the jukebox. Looks are exchanged between the three men, and the little one, standing on his feet in a shiny suit, turns to order another Guinness.

'Why not break with tradition once in a while?' he winks. 'I'll have one more.'

Still nothing through any of the doors into the pub. All in all it's been a slow start to the holidays.

'Did you put this feckin' shite on?' the little man enquires as he waits for his pint.

The jukebox plays itself, obviously. Once explained, most wonder why they'd never realised before.

'Maybe they've been mistaken for reindeer,' says one, putting down his newspaper to roll a cigarette.

242

'Meaning what exactly?' says the other, sliding the pencil out from behind his ear.

'Meaning,' says the first, rubbing his chin, 'simply, that they may have gone astray.'

'A habit of reindeer...?' says the puzzler, dabbing his pencil at the grid.

The sporting man takes a smug swig of his beer.

'They may have been commissioned, for a show or a shop promotion,' he says.

Everyone goes quiet for a while. The clock ticks and the doors stay shut. The jukebox stirs to life again. An unmistakable tune – *Tainted Love* by Soft Cell. The man lying on the floor groans mournfully.

***

The living room looks gloomy in nothing but kitchen light and the standard lamp. The three-piece suite sulks in the shadows. It should be bright and cheerful in here, with berry lights and candles. That said, she should either do something about it – and pull some boxes of Christmas decorations out from under the stairs – or she should face up to her problem.

Although to be fair to herself, she's bearing up as much as possible, it's just that she can't think of a solution. Gable has been gone for over three months now. She would surely recover and begin functioning normally again soon.

She has been spreading photos across the table like it was a toddler's game. One is stuck to the palm of each hand, face down. She turns the first over and it's a photo of herself standing in amongst the crowd as the Printers' float passes by. She is looking over her shoulder at the camera. The wind was blowing that morning, her hair is across her face, but the rain held off for the parade.

She turns over the other and it's a close up portrait of the man in the bar. His hair is silver, his eyes grey and he appears to be in his mid to late sixties. He is looking away, more or less in profile, up towards the ceiling past Gable's left shoulder. There's a row of optics behind him and he must be leaning on the bar counter with his right elbow. He has the expression of someone who is miles away – 'up there with the birdies', as Gable used to say.

Maggie brings the picture up close to her face. Why would Gable have been photographing this man? Might this old fellow know something about what happened that night?

***

For Mick Finnegan, chancing across a face from the past wasn't the last of his surprises during Guild week. He rushed through his pint that evening and left the pub without saying a word. What was there to say?

Tom Ballindine, the fellow's name was. Heavyweight champion of the Home Fleet in 1955. Mick knew little more about him, except that he lived the high-life, supposedly. And that it was after a party at his house, during the Guild of 1972, that one of Mick's work colleagues committed suicide.

Rumours spread through the sorting room as to why Roy had topped himself. Most of them sounded fanciful, although he was a quiet, withdrawn fellow – so who knows? Apparently his wife was involved. She was made to sound like a nymphomaniac.

All opinion however was agreed that Ballindine was in it up to the neck. He moved away from the area soon after, with stories circulating that his wife had divorced him.

So when, on the evening after his Guild win, Mick stepped into the Black Horse, ordered his pint and opened up the Lancashire Evening Post, he was intrigued to read of a murder on the front page and then astounded to see that the victim resembled the lad he'd seen drinking with Ballindine the day before. It turned out that it wasn't his son after all. It was a fellow named McGrath – kicked to death outside the Big House pub on his way home from the Black Horse.

Mick was amazed. Was this just a coincidence?

***

Maggie pushes open the Orchard Street door. A carriage lamp throws light onto the stone step and the hanging baskets creak overhead. Cold rain is beginning to whip down Friargate. She half expects to see a bar full of Christmas party revellers, but it's empty, save for three elderly men at the counter who let out cries and groans as she holds open the door.

She considers stepping back out again. She glances over her shoulder, back up Friargate, and sees a large, drunken gang staggering their way down the street towards her. To hell with it, she makes her entrance to a small ripple of applause and some whooping. One of them at the bar is wearing a zoot suit and trilby, the other two look like characters from Cheers. The barman, at least, seems sane.

'I wonder if you could help me?' she asks him, and he looks almost embarrassed, as one of the fools gives a whistle. Once the barman stops giggling, Maggie pulls out the photo, bent from her pocket. She bends it the other way, before holding it up in front of him.

'Would you happen to recognise this man?'

The barman gives it a careful eye-over with a strange expression on his face. The three men at the counter strain to get a glimpse and Maggie parades it before the lot of them like a round-board girl at a prize fight.

'That's Tom,' says the barman.

'Jeesus feckin' Christ,' says the little one in the flashy suit. 'Him again – Tom Ballindine.'

The other two look utterly disinterested, having not recognised him.

'He lives in Ireland, West Cork, that's all I know,' says the barman while Maggie stares at the little man, who's in shock after seeing the photograph. He is bent double, holding his chest with one hand on the counter. Maggie is concerned he may be having a cardiac arrest.

'Are you all right?' she asks, resting her hand on his back.

'You'll not impress the girls with that, you old toad,' says one of the others.

All of a sudden both doors slam open and in spews a dozen drunks, some with their shirts off. They are cheering, a few needing to be held upright, others raising fists of defiance. And all of them have antlers on their heads.

'So, can anyone tell me why they're having a stag do this early in the day?' says one of the men, slipping his pencil behind his ear.

'They combined it with a works Christmas party,' says the little one, making a full and fast recovery. His eyes are wild and bright and Maggie can't help but look into them. He has the expression of someone who has earned his reward.

'They're reindeer stags. They started at lunchtime. That'll be forty pounds – please.' He spits in his right hand and rubs his palms together, looking keenly towards the other, silent man.

A few of the stag party are hovering around Maggie and the barman leaps into action.

'Please move to the back!' he says, over again, with enough authority for the lads to shuffle, sheep-like towards the snugs and jukebox. One of them is dragging their unconscious friend along the tiles.

Out of the blue there's an amplified crackle and up starts the Eurythmics through the wall-mounted speakers – *Miracle of Love*. The barman looks about conspicuously, face by face, at everyone in the bar.

It's time to go, thinks Maggie, and she backs away towards the door. She's discovered as much as she's likely to this evening.

***

Mick Finnegan unlocked his front door much later than usual. What an evening. A very rare one indeed.

He could hear the neighbour's TV set, the street was that quiet. After he shut the door behind him, he pulled his shoes off on the mat and left his keys on the telephone table in the living room. The answer phone machine was beeping.

He hit the play button and threw a bundle of five pound notes next to it.

A fine day indeed. Although, it was strange that Ballindine's face should make another appearance.

'Hello...?' said the voice on the machine.

And there was something about the girl who came in with the photo. Something that was nagging at him.

'Hello...?'

For starters, she looked familiar – where had he seen her before? And then, why was she looking for Ballindine? She disappeared before anyone could find out. They had all been distracted by the arrival of the stag party.

The caller hung up, leaving a dial tone for a few seconds before the machine switched off with a click.

He'd probably never find out now.

Jessie's Journal
Part 3

Girls on Screen

January 5 1993

As you've probably worked out, I'm not in a market café writing this. I'm actually sitting in a small room at the top end of Cleveland Street, with the sash window pulled up to try encouraging some air through. Even though it's a cold, foggy evening out there, in this little flat the air is stuffy – maybe because it's over a laundrette.

Anyway, that's part of the deception of writing a journal – locating the action. That said, I can still clearly recall how I felt while drinking that coffee, looking out at the beggar shambling around the stalls on Chapel Market. It was like I was standing on the edge of a cliff. I was the fool about to step into the abyss.

And now here I am, a week later, in Victor's flat which is less than five minutes' walk from work – my first real job beyond a bit of waitressing. Although it doesn't seem like a job. It's more of an education, and several times over the past few days I have to admit to feeling like a school-kid again. A school-kid in a strange country with a whole new language to learn. At the same time I now have a licence to write. Formulaic stuff, a bit like a kinky comic strip, but I get to play with the scenarios as much as I want. I decided to base my first one on my prize-winning short story.

I've been cutting out some segments from the print of my first draft with a pair of scissors. I'll paste one here.

***

When Janie opened the door to find a small, buxom girl with a shaved head and big spectacles standing on the front step, she knew this would be no ordinary visitor. Kim would move in. She had the look of a stayer.

Kim had come to see if anyone was in the market for leather (a shoemaker's college was nearby), and by the end of the night she found herself handcuffed to Janie's bedstead in the frenzy of a first date.

They soon gained a reputation, Janie and Kim, but just amongst a select few. Most of the Bush Road folks saw them as nothing more than a band couple. Those in the know, however, saw a completely different side to them.

They weren't really into drugs, or getting roaring drunk like most of the Bush Road crowd – they enjoyed dressing up and nightclubbing. Theirs was a world of fetish and kink. They went to role-play bars near Old Street, or private clubs in Soho, and brought home girls and boys alike. Their favourite in the street was Mona, the French photographer – but more about Mona later.

It was one evening, while they were both enjoying a particularly convincing cross-dresser, that an unexpected visitor came knocking at the door – a visitor that would take their lives on a new turn. Janie unbuckled the strap-on, put it to one side and snatched up her dressing gown.

'I'll see who that is,' she said.

***

It was Victor's idea to make it a strap-on scene.

'No-one would believe it was the receiver of a hallway payphone anyway,' he argued, and he was right. what's more, the act of using a strap-on made for a more dramatic piece of action when it came to Janie trying it on the unwitting visitor. It was a useful tool to convey the surprise element of what was to follow.

Although I had been writing it more or less as I'd originally heard it, as an anecdote, I have to admit that the energy of the tale was fuelled by my own bout of passion in a store cupboard with Victor, ten minutes prior to typing the first lines. I had just about got to grips with the word processor on the office Macintosh when Victor suggested a quick run through some technical procedures. His voice was as weak as his ruse.

It was one of those 'panties round one ankle, up against the wall' fuck sessions that always leave me feeling galvanised. I stepped out of that store cupboard ready to roll out a sizzling piece of erotica.

So when Victor stopped me to read the first draft, he baulked at the scene with a phone receiver. I had to agree that it was a difficult image to visualise.

'What about a courgette?' I suggested.

'I prefer the idea of a strap-on,' said Victor, and that was that. The strap-on won the day. I made the change using the word processor's find and replace function.

It was all my invention, it must be said, to have a cross-dressing boy in there.

***

For a good while now, Janie and Kim had shared a fantasy about one of their neighbours in Bush Road – a Louise Brooks lookalike from Manchester called Helen. They both wanted to prise her away from Max, her unhinged boyfriend, but for different reasons. For Janie it was to draw her into another, more worthy form of bondage. For Kim it was to liberate her. They would occasionally discuss this with each other, but mostly they carried around their own private thoughts of Helen.

It was therefore a surprise for Janie, once she'd discarded the strap-on and opened the front door, to find Max standing there in a state of agitation. He looked like a stylist's advert in i-D magazine – with a pink mohican and his fists clenched, wearing a denim jacket, drainpipe jeans and calf length boots.

'Is Frank here?' he demanded.

Of course, thought Janie, he's looking for the street dealer. She opened the door wide.

'No,' she said. 'Why don't you come in and see for yourself.' And in an instant Max was past her and up the stairs. Before she had even shut the door, she could hear his surprise as he came upon the scene in the front bedroom.

'Fooking what!' he shouted. Janie joined him by his side and together they looked at the scene on the bed. Both Kim and the transvestite were handcuffed to the gothic headboard. Their feet were bound to the bedsteads with rope and their mouths were gagged. The boy was still in his dress, but it was hoiked up to his midriff as he shifted his weight from one knee to another.

Kim, on the other hand, was lying on her back naked, and could see Max standing and staring at her. She didn't enjoy the feeling in the slightest. This was as exposed as you could get. She wondered what the hell Janie would do next.

'I wouldn't mind, y'know, getting a taste o' some o' that,' Max suggested, edging about on his feet. Janie looked him up and down. Here he was – a bully-boy, macho and homophobic – seeking her permission to be filthy, as if she were a schoolteacher. She resisted the urge to ask him which piece of trussed-up action he fancied most.

'Sure,' she said, 'but only if you wear handcuffs too.' She dangled a set in his direction.

'Rules are rules,' she added.

And he held his hands out like an obedient schoolboy, wrists pressed together, expecting and deserving of the punishment about to come his way.

Janie couldn't believe her luck.

***

I got the character for Janie from the Valley Dolls bass player in Bush Road. That said, I live a lot of my fantasies through her. Janie is someone I can relate to, if not live up to. I admire her sure-footedness. When it comes to writing my own character, I can never give proper voice to her. I portray her as a weak person or refer to her in passing, in other people's tales. That way I can be harsh and objective. But with Janie I can let the imagination go. That's why I have chosen to become her in this new life I'm leading.

Kim, on the other hand, is more or less how I remember her. In full flower, before she left Janie and our part of town for Spain.

Today, when Victor sat down to discuss scripting a few scenes from the action, it made me feel slightly sick to think someone would have to play the part of Kim. Or anyone else in the tale for that matter. But then I thought of Anaïs Nin and figured this wasn't any different when it came to it, just that times had changed, and I quickly began to feel comfortable about my new line of work. So I took my first lesson in storyboarding – for erotic videos.

Then, when my final draft was done, I spent two hours in a small recording booth doing the voice overs into a stand-up microphone until Victor gave me the OK sign through the window. For a while there I felt like I was Dan on stage. Which is when I realised that the main reason I was struggling to write my own character was because one of the hottest tales I had, the one gagging to be told, was one of mine. It was the story of the day I was caught out in some style. It was the day Dan came home unexpectedly when in fact he was supposed to be on tour.

It was the story of how an era was brought to an end.

***

Who would have thought it? The phone started ringing just as Janie snapped shut the cuffs on Max's wrists. She tugged down his jeans before skipping to the hallway payphone and then spent some time trying to convince whoever it was that Mona was out. Janie even called out theatrically – 'Monaaa!' – although she had to draw the line when the caller persisted.

'No, am I fuck going to knock round the street looking for her!' She shouted and slammed down the receiver.

When she finally made it back up the stairs, Janie was presented with a startling spectacle. Even with his hands cuffed behind his back, Max had managed to work his way across the bed and tangle himself amongst the ropes tethering the transvestite's stockinged legs. Max's own legs were restricted by his trousers round the ankles, and his arse was rearing like a donkey in season. What with Kim wriggling in her binds next to them, it was all too much for Janie. She reached for her ultimate buckle-up accessory.

This was an occasion for her studded, black Bishop – the one with the multi-speed, revolving Mitre.

***

The thing is, when I stepped out of the little recording booth and back into the narrow corridor, I walked past the room outside which I originally met Victor. The door was open and I could see banks of TV monitors in there. It was like a traffic control room, except all the cameras were watching parts of the building: offices, corridors, the reception – and then I saw the store cupboard. I saw the very shelf I held onto, twenty-four hours earlier, while Victor took me through some technical procedures. I could picture the pair of us in shot.

It didn't take long for the penny to drop.

'So how does filming us in the store cupboard fit into the scheme of things?' I asked him later. I was quite calm when it came to it.

'Ah,' he hesitated. 'That's genuine voyeur action. It'll be a massive niche market sometime soon.' And sure, I understood what he meant straight away. I could imagine writing up the scenarios. But it still didn't feel right, I'd presumed that those ten breathless minutes were our secret – so where would the line get drawn between the job and real life?

This prompted an unexpected sermon from Victor. He said

he'd only just realised it himself, but the world was about to change.

'Everyone will be making their own media within ten years,' he said. The tone of his voice was different. He was whispering, almost conspiratorially.

'And, with this new internet engine, everyone will have the means to broadcast.'

Of course, I understood the purpose of all this writing and videoing that I'd now joined in with. They'd shown me a prototype 'magazine' on one of the office computers and I could see the appeal immediately – a hybrid of words, images, sounds and even some jerky video. But I still couldn't imagine how this was going to mark the dawn of a new age.

'Oh yeah,' I scoffed, 'everyone will have gear like this.' I gestured towards the cameras and editing desks. Victor was collapsing a tripod and he looked up.

'Yep.' He was sure. 'Just take a walk around the City and the West End. Cameras on every street corner. Look at the private porn trade in magazine ads – that's home video cameras. Everyone's a star of one sort or another.' He zipped up the case and stood up straight.

'Surely there must have been home cameras about when you lived with the band?'

I thought of Monica and her bulky video camera at gigs and events, and Dan with his Super 8 around the house. I recalled the few times I'd sat down to watch any of it. Once, all of us in the house did – that is except for the drummer in the attic, who never appeared for anything but drumming. But the rest of us were there, one night in a twilit room, and we all fell silent as the footage rolled over. First Monica's, through the TV, and then Dan's short films projected onto the wall.

They had me spellbound and squirming at the same time – I have no idea what anyone else felt about them. Monica's videos were loud, raw and real. Dan's Super 8s were, of course, silent.

Victor was looking at me pointedly.

'Just let me know when it's for filming and when it's not,' I said.

***

Janie was mopping off the sweat with a full-size towel, looking down at Max's quivering butt and, beyond it, at Kim's gagged and startled face. She was feeling pretty pleased with herself. She felt in command.

But earlier, while Janie had been grinding away and whooping on Max, Kim had been thinking of Helen. She'd been imagining how it would feel if it was Helen restraining her, instead of Janie's ropes. She shut her eyes and felt the weight of Helen's body and imagined Janie's dirty talk to be hers, whispered hotly in her ear.

Kim and Helen had been meeting for some weeks in fleeting, often daring situations. Once, in a laundrette, they joked about being kept prisoners like Cher. While for Helen this was pretty much true, Kim had simply grown tired of being Janie's plaything. But they both laughed at the notion and then fell into some serious heavy petting, attracting one or two window peerers. They only stopped when a middle-aged lady in a raincoat waddled in with two bin liner's full of washing.

Of course it was the last thing Kim expected, to find Max here, hand-cuffed and sprawled across a transvestite while Janie gave him a vigorous back-door slam. She knew straight-away that this was it. This event would be the opportunity Helen was waiting for. Once she got wind of this, and Kim would make sure she did, Helen would have every reason to pack her bags.

Little could Kim have known that Helen was, at that very moment, naked from the waist down and bouncing around like a rodeo rider on the lap of the local drug dealer – a guy called Frank. Helen was making her own plans.

Janie threw the towel onto a chair which was hung all over with abandoned underwear.

'Enjoy that did you, big boy?' she mocked. 'I know Kim did.'

***

Tonight is Twelfth Night and someone nearby is having a bonfire party, the sky is full of car-horns and explosions – and then there's a sound like the restless ocean that never leaves London. Wave after wave of tyres on tarmac.

The time I have spent jotting down these thoughts have been rare minutes of stillness in a frantic ten days. In a short while Victor will walk through the door and we will both head out for a restaurant in Goodge Street, where Swinford Mason is laying on a company party. And so the ride will continue.

There's barely been time to think about what I've left behind – nor have I thought much about Dan. Someone told me today that they heard he was moving to Ireland. I will need to make one last trip to Yorkshire soon, to pick up my things and let him know what I'm doing. I'll find out about his plans then.

And now it's come to it, I'm surprised how easy this has been. And to think that a few weeks ago, when I realised my period was well overdue, I actually paused to consider getting all domesticated.

I will never forget slithering down the snowbound lane to the phonebox in Yorkshire and shivering as I called the Harley Street clinic to book an appointment. But now this step has been taken there's no going back. The last eight years, and all the characters who populated them, will remain forever golden. It was a fragile and precious era for me and now I won't have to watch it end. Thankfully, I managed to leave the scene before it was too late.

***

It was around midnight when the sirens woke Janie up. The exertions of the evening had worn her out and the nap she'd taken had turned into a couple of hours. There was no sign of Kim. She hadn't come to bed yet.

Janie caught sight of the blue flashes in the curtains and

hauled herself up. She was tired. She pulled up the sash window with a struggle and stuck her head out to see two fire engines turning into the street. A small crowd had gathered and there was smoke coming from a house near the railway bridge. Maybe it was Max and Helen's?

Shouts broke out amongst the onlookers and then, from out of the crowd, Janie saw Helen striding defiantly with a rucksack on her shoulder.

'Yaay for the sisters!' Janie called out as Helen walked beneath her window and she looked up, punched the air and threw a beaming smile. Janie watched her reach the corner and head off in the direction of the tube station and then she shut the window and turned to look at the bed. It was a scene of utter debauchery. She ought to be ashamed of herself.

Kim and Helen couldn't keep their hands off each other all the way to Victoria. They didn't care what the other passengers thought. Their little plan had found the perfect night for executing and they were both amazed they'd pulled it off. The excitement had made drunks of them. In less than an hour they would be on a coach to Barcelona.

'What made you do it?' Kim was laughing, holding onto Helen's shoulders.

'Do what? Frank?'

'Yes, OK. Let's start with Frank,' said Kim.

'He's hung like an elephant,' said Helen.

***

So that's it. Well, it's a sketch at least.

It's been a strange and eventful couple of weeks. I'm sure I'll keep finding different ways to write about it for years to come. But this will have to do for now – Victor's here and it's time to go and party.

Part 6
Three Endings

Frank, Maggie and Tom Meet in a Blur

December 31 1992

Not until Mr Ballindine asked the question, did it dawn on Maggie that she was pregnant. She'd felt ill for weeks and her cycle was completely messed up, for sure, but she'd put it down to the anti-depressants.

She was still amazed at how easily she had found him – the man whose photo she'd been carrying around for days. It had become important to search him out. She decided to fly to Cork with the scant information she had. Then all of a sudden, she happened to be standing next to him at the airport bar. What were the chances of that? On top of which, for him to ask such a pointed question took her completely by surprise. She swivelled on her stool to face him again.

'Yes, I suppose I am,' she said.

He was a perceptive old bugger, even if he was a drunkard. They'd hardly spent five minutes together.

'It'll be a fitting tribute,' he said, raising his glass. 'After all's said and done, it's the best outcome.'

***

Once I'd ascertained that the ol' geezer was Dan's pot and pan, my mind immediately began working overtime. If I could get him over to see his son he might be able to talk sense into him. In fact the shock'd probably bring the little fucker round. The fact that the old man was with an intriguing looking bird made it all the more important I got my plan right.

263

I know I should have been thinking about Monica. About how, when I waved her off at the departure gate, it would probably be the last time I'd see her. But, to be honest, as soon as I walked into the bar to mull it over with a snakebite, the gypsy-haired bird and the old feller caught my eye. So what a turn-up to discover this was Dan Ballindine's daddy!

It was when their conversation got onto spirits rattling about their homes that I started properly listening in. I'd felt the same thing in Bush Road after Dan and Jessie left. The house emptied and, for a few weeks, I rattled about with those spirits. And Monica of course. Me and Monica and the echoes of the past eight years, all shifting about in an empty house. The studio had been stripped bare, and even Keith slunked out with his keyboard. But I swear the kitchen still chattered and buzzed with activity, and both of us heard guitars and drumbeats a few times from the basement.

The girl up at the counter was talking about hearing music too.

'But it's more than that,' she said. 'He's always there, in the house. I can feel him as if he were a part of me.'

'He is that now, for sure,' said the old man.

They were sitting on high stools at the bar and I couldn't help giving her legs the eye over. She was a well tasty bit of skirt. It was distracting me badly when I should have been considering the poignant nature of what just happened with Monica.

'You know,' said the old man after a lengthy pause. 'Your fellow Gable, reminded me of my son Dan.'

***

What odds would you get on this happening? While flying over Wales (where Tom traditionally liked to visit the toilet) he heard someone mention that the flight was bound for Manchester. He thought that he'd boarded the wrong plane until he was told that heavy fog across southern England was forcing flights to make alternative landing arrangements.

He'd just about got used to the idea by the time the plane touched down. And, once through customs, he headed for the bar. He needed a little thirst quencher before wandering off in search of the trains. He wasn't even sure, at that point, whether it was worth trying to get down to London anyway. The truth of the matter was that Angela wasn't expecting him to turn up. Up until that moment in time he'd figured it would be a nice surprise, but in fact it was probably a fool's errand. Especially now he was so late – the delay at Cork had been bad enough.

Yet even as he ordered his pint, a young woman was asking his name. She was beautiful and for a moment Tom couldn't believe his luck. Then she showed him a photograph. It sent a shiver up his back. It was a portrait of himself perched up at a bar somewhere. He hadn't a clue when it was taken, or why this girl should have it. The shock took the strength from him and he reached with his hand for a stool to sit on.

It turned out she was the wife of the lad with the camera that was killed during Preston Guild. The photograph was taken while Tom had been drinking with him in the Black Horse. It must have been one of the last he took before he was murdered.

***

'Excuse me,' said Maggie. She realised her voice was shaking. She'd lost control of it all of a sudden. 'Are you called Tom Ballindine?'

She'd pulled the photo from her purse dozens of times during the last ten days but now it came to it, she couldn't find the damned thing.

'Jeez, am I that well known?' Tom turned around, looking astounded.

'Wait, I'll explain,' said Maggie, rummaging frantically in her bag. The photo finally came to hand.

'Here!' she said, holding it out with her right hand. He

stared at it for a while with his mouth open before he sank onto a bar-stool.

'My name's Maggie.' She offered her left hand. 'Maggie McGrath.'

***

It was typical of Monica to jump on a plane back to Holland at the drop of a hat. She wanted to search out her mother and I tried to talk her out of it. What was the point? Even if she managed to find her, which would be no easy matter, it'd more than likely end up being a complete bummer. Her ma would probably be on the game, or a junky, or both. But what the fuck did I know? Monica's mind was made up.

After I'd seen her off, I was riled enough to head to the bar for a drink. On the face of it, I'd taken a risk driving with no licence in the first place, so why not have a snakebite too? It usually helped clear the mind.

So I was thinking about how Monica had changed. I was thinking about how much she'd hated the hippie house during her visit. These were my thoughts up until I looked along the bar and saw the two of them on tall stools. The girl looked like she was straight out of the flake ad – green eyes, scarlet lippy and black curly hair. And there was something interesting about the duffer she was with. He could probably tell a good story. He looked like he'd lived a bit.

By the time I sat down with my pint, I'd lost my whole train of thought when it came to Monica. I was wondering about those two up at the bar – father and daughter, most likely.

Although I did pause for a second, to think about whether Monica leaving like this was a message in some way. That maybe I should leave the hippies behind, give up on Dan and head home. Jessie had already done it – and who could blame her? Dan was off his face pretty much all of the time. He was in his own world these days.

Things weren't the same, that's for sure, and I was living off memories and whatever wits I had left.

Then I heard the girl at the bar say, 'I feel his spirit like an echo through the house.'

***

'I'm sorry for what happened,' said Tom. 'He said he was alright when he left the pub.'

He looked at Maggie. She had a kindly face.

'I should've walked with him.' Tom turned on his stool to look towards the bar.

'Was he happy?' Maggie asked. 'When you saw him.'

Tom smiled.

'Yes, he was happy enough,' he said. 'And very proud of his beautiful wife.'

Maggie sat down on a stool while she mopped the tears from her cheeks with a handkerchief.

***

What possessed me to think that Angela would be glad to see me? She never liked it when I turned up. She would always find an excuse to get rid of me quickly. She didn't need me hanging around. She didn't need any man. I must have been mad catching a flight over to see her. It was probably just as well I'd ended up in Manchester...

Tom's thoughts were interrupted by a girl at the bar who had the look of a femme fatale, full of smouldering stares and lipstick.

'Are you Tom Ballindine?' she asked, and Tom put his glass down carefully on the counter. He couldn't believe his luck. The bar was virtually empty, just some scruffy punk loitering at the entrance trying to make his mind up about coming in. A flight to Amsterdam was being last-called over the PA. Tom pulled himself upright and drew in his chest.

'Am I that well known?' he quipped.

***

Maggie was drying her eyes, her chin trembling with sobs.

'Now, now,' said Tom. 'I'll get you a brandy.' He moved to give her a comforting grip of the shoulder, but something made him draw back and instead he patted her arm. She smiled and blew her nose.

'That's OK. I'm fine,' she said, and Tom looked at her closely.

'Ah. You're pregnant aren't you?' he said and she turned her face away.

Tom didn't say anything more. He waited for her to reply and took a long gulp of his pint while he did.

'Yes, I suppose I am,' said Maggie, finally.

'It's the best outcome,' said Tom. He saw her doubtful look.

'You can't bring the poor lad back.'

***

How many times had she pulled that creased up photo out of her bag this last week? And now, the one time it could be shown to the fellow who was in it, she was buggered if she could find it. Bloody typical.

Up to that point, she had discovered this much – the fellow in the photo was called Tom Ballindine. He was a Preston man of old, a boxer and the only one of his family to go to university. He had a career but gradually, after his wife left him, he and the career broke down. Nowadays he lived in Ireland. And, unbelievably, here was Maggie, standing next to him at the bar in Manchester Airport.

She remembered stopping in here during the summer, after she'd seen her friend Elaine off on her holiday to Sardinia. She'd loaned Elaine a suitcase, to carry most of the contents of her dressing table, and at the last minute the dizzy mare decided not to take it after all. So Maggie lugged it to the bar, fuming, and sat down for a coffee.

She had an odd feeling then, and she experienced something similar, like déjà vu, when she glanced over at the elderly man alongside her. He looked drunk and a little unhinged, though nothing you wouldn't see on a normal weekend at the Royal Preston.

When she asked him, he told her about the afternoon he spent drinking with Gable – the subjects they talked about. And that would be the last conversation Gable had. There was nothing unusual in there. He was as Maggie had last seen him, outside the pub a few hours earlier.

'But he was pissed when he left,' said Tom. 'I should have walked with him.'

And then Tom asked her if she was pregnant with Gable's child and, it seemed impossible, but he must be right. It would account for the strange feeling through the core of her lately – on top of all the rest.

'Yes, I suppose I am,' she said, but then it crossed her mind that maybe she wasn't. She shouldn't leap to conclusions.

'But I might not be,' she said.

'You are.' Tom leaned forward to whisper. 'Believe me, I used to be a doctor.'

***

'Sometimes I feel as if he hasn't gone away,' said Maggie. 'I mean, it's like his spirit is still in the house.'

'A loveless house is just bricks and mortar,' said Tom, looking at his pint.

'I feel him as he were part of me.'

'He is that now, for sure.'

'I hear it as music a lot of the time.' Maggie was stirring her coffee for no reason. She didn't take sugar. 'He's like an echo through the house.'

Maggie looked up at Tom. 'Music was a big part of our lives.'

Tom paused from lifting the glass to his lips. 'You know, your fellow Gable reminded me of my son, Dan,' he said. 'He's into music too.'

***

Ghosts were what we had all become. We'd left our spirits to inhabit No. 1 while we all slipped away like Fagin's kids. The band was nothing without Dan after all, and with no band there wasn't any point to anyone being at No. 1.

Monica insisted on sleeping in her old room once everyone had left. Although I was pretty sure she didn't sleep much. She didn't have much to say either, beyond some garble about Dan and the baby she snatched...

And then my thoughts were stopped mid-flow. Father and daughter, I figured. It would make sense of the match-up. You couldn't imagine those two giving each other the time of day in any other situation. But then he went on to mention a son of his called Dan, coincidentally enough, and he described him a bit – so she couldn't be his daughter. A shabby millionaire and his escort?

I ought to have been giving more serious thought to Monica's situation, but the two at the bar were fascinating me. And then something the girl said stopped me in my tracks.

'Why d'you think Gable wanted to photograph you, Mr Ballindine?' she asked him.

That's when it dawned on me that maybe this was Dan's old pot and pan. It was like a handful of bombers kicking in. All of a sudden my mind sprung into action. If it was him, I'd have to get him to come back to Dan's house with me. That might just bring the little fucker around.

***

'He was in a pop band, until recently. Now he's way off the tracks.' Tom was eyeing up the barman, while finishing off his first pint.

'On drugs and all sorts,' he said, fishing in his pockets. 'Can

270

I get you another coffee or something?'

'I still haven't finished this one, thank you.'

'You know he turned up at his grandmother's funeral in a shocking state, last I saw him.' The barman was striding over in their direction.

'He was definitely on something.'

'If you don't mind me asking, Mr Ballindine, why do you think Gable took photographs of you?' Maggie lit a cigarette from a packet she'd bought a week or so ago. Tom finished his transaction with the barman before he answered.

'I suppose he thought I was a memory worth keeping,' he said.

***

As soon as she held the picture in front of his face, Tom felt dizzy. He almost lost his balance and had to reach for a stool to park up on. It was a good photo, it somehow captured the spirit of the pub without showing any of it – just the optic racks, slightly out of focus in the background. He could tell straight away it was the Black Horse in Preston. It must have been taken the last time he was in town, during Guild week, when he was there for his mother's funeral. He'd been on a fair old bender that visit, but the occasion was coming back to him. And then the woman introduced herself.

'Maggie McGrath,' she said, offering her hand, and the mention of her name helped the penny drop. He was a young fellow, around Danny Boy's age, who could barely afford a round but he had an expensive looking camera. They'd drunk together all afternoon. He said he preserved memories, when Tom asked him about his photography. He was called Gable McGrath and he was beaten to death by thugs on his way home that evening. It was all over the Evening Post the next day.

And this had to be his widow.

'I'm very sorry for your loss,' said Tom, accepting her handshake.

***

'How are you getting by? Do you have a job?'

'Oh, I'm a nurse at the RPH...'

'Ah! My ex-wife Angela's a nurse. And I was a ship's doctor once,' said Tom. 'Well, pill-pusher would be closer to the truth.'

'Although I'm currently signed off.'

'I know the feeling,' said Tom. 'I was struck off – for being an alcoholic, they said.'

Maggie took another drag from her cigarette. She'd left it so long since the last one, a long, curly tube of ash fell onto her lap. She felt a little nauseous anyway, so she stubbed it out.

'But a psychiatrist told me I get bouts of mania every now and again. He said that losing my family brought it on.'

'Really? Is that what they say?' she asked.

'Well,' said Tom. 'Some doctors thought it was boxing that did it – that I took too many punches.'

He drained his pint glass.

'Whatever they think the problem is, I refuse to take the medication.'

'I've taken so many pills lately, I feel like I'm rattling,' said Maggie.

'You should stop that now.'

'I will,' she promised.

***

Now that it had come to it, Maggie wasn't sure why she'd sought Tom Ballindine out so keenly. She'd thought of little else this last week. She wanted to know about him maybe, get a sense of Gable's last few hours, for sure, but there was more. There was something else, something she hadn't even considered because of finding him so quickly.

She'd started out expecting to spend a week at it, to have to stay with her mother, to ask around all the bars and hotels in West Cork armed with the photograph. Instead, she found him before she even set off. So now what was she to do?

And then for it to dawn on her that she must be pregnant. It would account for all the sickness lately, and the confusion. She'd put it down to the pills.

Her head was in a spin. She certainly didn't want to be getting on a plane now.

'Are you OK?' he asked.

'Yes,' said Maggie. 'Just feeling a bit heady.'

'His spirit will always be with you,' Tom whispered as he leaned forward on his stool.

***

'So where are you off to now?' asked Tom

'What?'

'I mean, do you have a flight to catch?' Tom glanced down at her suitcase.

'Oh,' said Maggie. 'I'm not sure now. I was planning on flying to Ireland.'

'Home to see your family?' asked Tom.

'My mother,' said Maggie. 'She lives near Clonakilty.'

'Ah, a coincidence. I live towards Bantry at the moment.' Tom smiled at her. 'And your pa?' he asked.

'Never met him,' said Maggie. 'A little man called Mick, that was all my mother ever told me about him. She never married, it was a bit of a scandal.'

'A little fellow called Mick – that narrows it down,' laughed Tom.

'I was going home to look for you,' said Maggie and she pulled the photo back out of her purse.

'Oh.' Tom reached for his pint.

'I guess I wanted to meet the last person to talk to Gable,' she said, looking at the photo.

***

Dan had got himself into a right state just lately. It had all gone tits up after the scene at this very airport, six months back. He packed himself and Jessie off to the Yorkshire moors, got a couple of dogs (to get her broody, he said) and proceeded to hit the booze and drugs like there was no tomorrow.

Just this morning, when I last saw him, he accused me of shagging his missus. More or less. Given I was probably the only geezer in Bush Road that hadn't, I was a little affronted by the suggestion. But I calmly assured him that I had, in no way, shagged her, although I might as well have not bothered. Dan was on another planet. He told me he hadn't gone to bed since she'd left.

The old man at the bar had definitely mentioned his son being out of it all the time. And I was sure I'd heard him talk about a band earlier, so when the girl called him Mr Ballindine it hit me like a bolt out of the blue. What a turn up! I had to think of a way to butt in on their conversation and convince the old feller to come back to Dan's. And the girl, if I was lucky.

It was tricky because it sounded like they were talking about personal things. She'd already burst into tears a couple of times. Other times they both laughed. I'd have to catch them during one of their light-hearted moments and come up with a cunning ruse.

Then I pulled myself up. I ought to think about this a minute. Putting myself in Dan's shoes, would I want someone dragging my old man round to see me when I was fucked up? Who was I to judge if someone had got so out of control they needed help?

I got up to buy another snakebite. This needed a little more thought before jumping in there.

***

'Will your ma not be expecting you?' Tom asked.

'My ma? Nooo!' laughed Maggie. 'She's no telephone. I just turn up. It's better that way. She's a bit batty.'

'So it's back to Preston, then?' Tom returned to his pint.

'I suppose it is,' said Maggie.

'Maybe I should go and see my sisters, and then have a pint in the Black Horse for New Year,' said Tom.

'Where else would you be going?'

'I had this idea to visit my ex-wife in London,' said Tom. 'But like you with your mother, I haven't told her about it.'

***

If all had gone to plan he would have been at Angela's by now, and they'd have enjoyed lunch together. As things were panning out, he'd be lucky to get there much before 7 pm. She may already have taken herself off somewhere. She'd probably made her own plans. It was New Year's Eve for fuck's sake.

Tom looked around at the young widow. He realised he'd been hunched up at the bar for a moment, lost in his own thoughts. He should return to the conversation. They were talking about Gable and Dan and the spirits of the departed. It made him think of Angela's spirit, which had always remained with him.

'If you don't mind me asking, why did Gable take a photograph of you, Mr Ballindine?' she'd asked.

His pint was almost finished. He'd have to get another now, after this. And she just asked a strange question – it deserved some consideration.

The barman was good and on the strength of a nod brought over a freshly poured Guinness. Tom remembered what the lad said to him about his photography.

'I suppose he thought I was a memory worth keeping,' he answered.

She started to cry and her chin was trembling. All of a sudden Tom felt badly sorry for her. He recalled that the lad was broke. He couldn't help but worry for her welfare.

'How are you getting by?' he asked.

***

'Neither of us remarried, and that's the way it's been – sometimes on, mostly off.'

'And what about your boy? What's his name again?' asked Maggie.

'Dan,' said Tom. 'He lived mostly with his grandparents in Fulham, Angela always worked long shifts. Sometimes he stayed with me – wherever I happened to be.'

'And now he's in a pop band?'

'He was,' said Tom. 'He told me he'd given up, last I saw him. But to do what, God only knows.'

***

Of course, she'd have to stop taking the anti-depressants now. She was only having the occasional one these days, but she'd have to stop altogether. And she'd have to book herself a check-up and scan just to be sure.

These last few months had been spent in a haze. It turned out to be a good idea stopping in at the bar for a coffee. Maybe she had to find Tom before she could let herself recognise her condition? This was probably just what she needed to snap out of it. It was time to face up to life.

Maggie looked at him while he studied the photo again. He held it in his hands, rubbing the surface with his thumbs. He was squinting at it, he probably needed glasses.

'You can have it, if you want,' she said to him and he turned to look at her.

'Are you sure?' he asked.

'Sure. Why not?' she said.

The old fellow smiled.

'Thanks.'

Maggie would be glad of the company travelling back home. She felt safe with Tom, even if he was a drinker. He reminded her of someone, probably a patient, she couldn't remember who. But it was someone who was cut from the same cloth. A drinking, fighting old-fashioned bloke.

***

'What was the name of the band?'

'They were called the Smokin Joes, they had a hit a couple of years back,' said Tom, raising his near empty glass.

'Hmm, rings a bell,' said Maggie. 'They were the ones that did that song, what was it called…?'

***

After all I was no saint.

But in the end I was the only one looking out for Dan, now Monica had gone. It was typical of her to just up and fly off like that. And where did it leave me? I was hoping she'd move in to the hippie house and help me talk sense into Dan.

Although I couldn't really blame her for not considering it. After the lives we led in Bush Road, the hippies were pretty comical. It was like being in an institution, with the house rotas and strict diets. I was tired of it myself. A month had been long enough.

Since Jessie had gone, I'd tried talking to Dan a couple of times about coming back to London. But with no luck. He said he wasn't ready for it.

And it seems this Christmas did for Monica too. She'd been living mostly at an arty squat near the Angel since I shifted up here in late November. She didn't take to the idea of Yorkshire gloom or commune life but, for whatever reason, she turned up for a seasonal visit with her worldly goods in a suitcase. And I thought she'd come to stay.

As usual, things couldn't have been less straightforward. Dan and Jessie threw a party on Christmas Day and everything that could have gone wrong, did: Jessie ended up wrapping herself around one of the hippies from the commune, Dan upset Monica before passing out in the kitchen and Monica, in turn, threw a bucket of water over me after I was discovered in one of the upstairs rooms shagging a cute, spiky-blonde groupie on her sleeping bag.

Jealousy wasn't something I'd expect from Monica – even if we'd been together in the romantic way – so I was puzzled as to why it should freak her out to catch me at it. Thinking about it, it was probably what happened with Dan that got her goat. She didn't let on, but I guessed that she'd made her feelings about him known and got short shrift in return. All she would say on the subject was that Dan had upset her, and that he was an arsehole. Or *asshole* as she put it, in her Dutch accent.

Two days later she'd made her mind up about finding her mother – and here I am, having waved her off, maybe for the last time, only to find myself sitting next to Dan's old man. Shame she hadn't stuck around. And it's true, Dan is an arsehole – self destructing, beyond any help I can offer, or Monica for that matter. I'd tried everything I could think of. Now I was tired of it all and wanted to go back home to London.

That's why I had no choice. It was time to involve Dan's old man. I'd had enough. So what was needed was a plan. I had to map out how to squirm my way into their conversation and make all this happen. That'd be half the battle won – visualising it all. It'd be as good as dealt with once I'd managed that.

***

'Jeez, it must be some life, being a musician,' said Maggie.

'I guess it probably is,' said Tom. 'With Dan, it's mainly meant he's either too broke or too busy to see anyone.'

'That's a pity.' Maggie felt for Tom, she could hear the emotion in his voice.

'But on the odd occasion I have seen him these last few years, we've had a fair old craic together,' he said, finishing his Guinness. 'I succeeded in teaching the lad a thing or two about having a good time.'

***

It was while his shoulders were heaving with the laughter that he felt the tap. And he turned around on his stool, wiping his face dry with the back of his hand, to see the scruffy looking punk standing awkwardly next to him.

***

'Sorry to butt in, but I couldn't help hearing some of what you were talking about.'

Maggie looked him over. He was probably her age and had the look of a gypsy about him, with a hooped earring and his hair in a messy, curly quiff.

***

So this is how it works out.

I finish my drink and stand idly at the bar, as if to buy another, when I hear them talking about Dan and use that as an excuse to interrupt them.

'Sorry to butt in, but I couldn't help overhearing what you were saying about Dan Ballindine.' I sidle over to them before they can reply. The girl's eyes and lips look moist and inviting. Whereas the old man has his hackles up.

'And I'm a personal friend of Dan's. About his only one, right now.'

And then they're both caught in rapt attention. I have to keep talking.

'I'm just off to see him now,' I continue. 'To be quite truthful, when I saw him yesterday, he didn't look very well.' I maintain the demeanour of a concerned friend, frowning and slightly bowed.

'What do you mean, "didn't look well"?' says Dan's old one.

'A little malnourished, you know, probably not getting enough sleep,' I say with a bit of mystery.

'I can't help wonder if he doesn't need a little care and attention, you know,' I add, wringing my hands.

'Seems like you were right to be worried about him, Mr Ballindine,' says the bird, swapping her legs over as she sits on the high stool. She has an Irish accent. It sounds like morning rain.

'I appreciate that you're bound to be busy right now, and not able to come back with me,' I say. 'But if you happen to have a pen and paper to hand, I'll write his address down for you.'

'How far is it?' says the old feller.

'Oh, under an hour from here,' I say, throwing my hands up. 'Train station's on a line direct to Preston.'

In no time they're in the back of the car, 'Young Maggie here's a nurse!' he announces as we pull away, and not once during the journey do they ask me about my legal status with the driving. By the time we're weaving up the A646, I'm considering my job done. I'm thinking about having a fry-up in the café on London Fields. I'm thinking of starting again, in territory I'm used to. And I already have a place to head for, the squat Monica stayed in down Angel way. Maybe I can talk the nurse into coming with me.

The snow thickens and the road has become a lot trickier with each mile. The car begins to slide along stretches. But I get us going again, with a bit of a push, and eventually we slither to a halt at the bottom of the street that angles away up to the terrace where Dan lives.

There is no star-light above and the snow makes the visibility poorer. I lead the trudge up the hundred yards or so to Dan's steps. My breathing is hard, with fear and exhilaration. I can hear the dogs howling at the door.

And this is the moment where it all changes for me.

***

So I finished my drink, stood up and tapped the old bloke on his shoulder. The girl looked up at me with alarmed eyes.

'Sorry to butt in, but I couldn't help overhearing you talking about Dan Ballindine.'

Monica's Flight

December 31 1992

'Would you like a drink?' A stewardess hovered above me. I'd been lost in my thoughts. I barely even noticed her rattling up the aisle.

'Does it cost anything?' I asked. I had only ever flown once before – when we first came to the UK around ten years ago. I wasn't sure what the deal was.

'Drinks are complimentary, madam,' said the stewardess, a pretty girl probably about the same age as me.

'Oh, excellent,' I said. 'In that case, I'll have a beer.'

She poured half the beer into a plastic glass and left the rest of the can on my fold-out tray.

'Cheers!' We swapped smiles and I took my first sip of lager since the party at Dan and Jessie's on Christmas night. As the stewardess pushed her trolley onwards, I thought about my final conversations with those two. They weren't good ones.

With Jessie it had quickly turned into a row. She said she was going to London to have an abortion and I told her she was mad, which she didn't like. Especially coming from me. And then when she said she hadn't told Dan, I almost exploded. I can't remember exactly what happened but I almost broke their front door slamming it shut behind me.

I shouted, 'If you don't tell Dan, then I will!' and I stormed out of the house. That was Christmas Eve.

Then there was the hopeless talk I had with Dan at the party. We were sitting on the sofa and he looked completely wrecked but I still tried telling him about the baby. This was the first chance I'd had to speak to him out of anyone else's earshot since I escaped from the hospital. I wanted him to know that I knew it was a mistake. That I knew it was wrong. That I did it because of Ruth.

And then I told him that I loved him. I said that Jessie had no intention of staying but if he wanted, I would be there for him. I laid my soul bare and he looked horrified. His face was pale. He passed me a joint and shook his head. He said something about waiting for someone, it was too quiet to hear above the music and shouting. His body language told me everything I needed to know. It was at that moment that I decided I was going to straighten myself out. It was time to ditch the drugs and reorganise my priorities.

Dan had little more to add this morning. I'd called around to thank him for buying my air ticket. He wished me luck and scooped me up into a hug. But it felt like he was holding his body as far away from me as he could. It was like he wasn't really there.

'Has Jessie told you?' I asked and looked him in the eyes. The light had gone from them. She must have told him.

'I don't think she's coming back,' he said.

'You need to get out of this place as well, Dan,' I advised and then I waved him goodbye.

***

It was a shame about how it all ended at Bush Road. It's as if I was still being punished for taking the baby. I got home to find the band had split up and it was chaos. Dan and Jessie left for Yorkshire before I even had a chance to see them. Keith stormed about the place punching holes in the plasterboard walls. Only two of the most devoted groupies stuck about, and a sixteen year old acid casualty called Justin. They weren't being useful in any way, it was more like they had nowhere else to go.

Frank was the one person who noticed I was back. He looked after me, and wanted to sleep with me (but I said no), and we were the last to leave the house – a few months later. Keith eventually came to terms with what was happening and he packed up and left – to join a band in Camden, so he said. In the time I'd been back, he barely spoke to me.

And along with Keith went the last of the hangers-on.

Me and Frank led a strange, almost reclusive life for the final few months in the house. It felt like the place was haunted. We often thought we could hear the band playing in the basement.

And then one day the police came. I answered the door, and maybe I should have thought of a way of holding them up, but they flashed a warrant and were in the house before I could speak. They were after someone called Jason Lupus.

Frank had enough time to swallow the last of the speed, which was just as well because the coppers searched the place from top to bottom. We were pretty pleased with ourselves, sitting in the kitchen chatting to a couple of officers, when one of them stooped to pick up the wedge of paper we used as a door stop. When he unfolded it, he tapped his colleague on the shoulder and they both peered at it. I looked over at Frank and saw sweat breaking out on his forehead. One of the policemen looked up.

'And why would you be in possession of a plan such as this?' He held up the sheet of paper which had diagrams and instructions on it. 'Mr Dobro, is it?'

'Listen officer, we only just squatted this place last week,' Frank blurted out. 'It must have been whoever was here before us.'

'Do you have any identification – something to prove you're not Jason Lupus?' he asked.

Frank leaped for his jacket and pulled out his UB40.

'Here you go, mate,' he said and the two policemen looked it over carefully before handing it back.

After they had left, Frank went into a panic. He wanted to pack up and go that night but I talked him into leaving it until the next day.

I'd made friends with some artists in Islington who shared a big squat, so I could head over there. Frank tried to persuade me to come up to Yorkshire on Dan and Jessie's tail, but I resisted. It didn't seem right following them. But Frank wanted to get as far away as possible. He told me that the police had just found some bomb-making plans that should have been burned.

'Not only that,' he said. 'When they run a check on my name any number of pulls could come up.'

So Frank skulked away into hiding, up to a hippie commune in a valley next to the moors.

I only went up myself after my attempts to track down Ruth came to nothing – although I did discover that her parents had discharged her from hospital and taken her away. I tried to find out where that was, but they wouldn't tell me. Nor could they tell me whether she was pregnant or not. When I finally gave up, I felt lonely and wanted to see Frank and Dan.

He looked sad when we said goodbye at the airport earlier. He stayed where he was and watched me walk down the gangway for a long while. Each time I turned to look back, I could see that he hadn't moved.

Frank needs to get out of that place as much as Dan.

The Tannoy brought me out of my thoughts. It was the Captain's announcement. We were ten minutes from landing. I finished my beer and looked out of the window while we dropped through the clouds. The plane bounced around a little and then all of a sudden field patterns and strings of lit buildings came into view.

I was back in Holland to find my mother. But first – here I was arriving in Amsterdam on New Year's Eve, twenty-five years old, clear-headed and ready to face the unexpected. I buckled up, shut my eyes and prepared myself for whatever the future was about to throw my way.

Dan's Plan

December 31 1992

His eyes were like fucking dinner plates, and he had the cheek to suggest you were overdoing it. It's come to something when the man who has spent the best part of ten years supplying your drugs says you need to slow down. Unbelievable. And what's more, he's probably sleeping with Jessie.

Dan put the film reel down and turned up the volume on the radio. He needed to hear a conversation, any conversation, to stop the one he was having with himself. Instead he got studio laughter, probably some comedy panel show. So he hit the play button on the cassette machine and turned the volume up so it drowned out the radio. It was a tape someone passed on to him recently – the Valley Dolls had finally got a big record deal.

He sat down on the kitchen sofa and rolled a cigarette. These women churned out a weird wall of sound but there was something in it, something he could definitely learn from.

What the hell are you thinking, mate? You have just walked out on a band with a sound you crafted for eight years – one that's now out of date. Forget it Danny Boy. You grabbed yourself a fat goose and cooked it for all it was worth. Only Keith has what it takes to keep going. For you, it's all over.

Both dogs were asleep on a tatty rag rug in front of the stove, so Dan reasoned he might as well leave them be. They probably needed letting out for a walk, but why bother them when they looked so peaceful? The music, on the other hand, needed changing. The discordance was beginning to jar with his own rattled thoughts. He wanted to be reassured by something old and familiar He switched off the tape player and the discussion on the radio was about Saturnalia and the 'non-days' at the end of the Roman calendar. He left it at that. He could relate to the idea.

And now, not only have you driven Jessie away, but Monica has upped and left. You even dipped into your dwindling savings to pay her fare back to Holland. The scene at the Christmas party probably helped make her mind up. She was trying to tell you what Jessie's intentions were but you weren't in the mood to hear it, even though you knew it was probably true. You were slumped on the kitchen sofa at the time and she was sitting next to you. She was talking about when she snatched the baby. Her voice drifted in and out of range, like she was speaking through a phaser. And you, Danny Boy, hugged a bottle of vodka like it was your best friend.

Voices were speaking with authority about the Pagan mystery of the dark days, while Dan collected a few more split logs from the wood-shed and stacked them by the stove. His bottle of Teacher's was empty so he opened the Tullamore Dew to refill his tumbler. The dogs raised their heads to look at him. They kept watching until he returned to the films on the kitchen table. He opened up the shoe box and picked out another small reel. It looked like one of the films from the 70s Guild. He put it down and rummaged through the papers on the table for a pill bottle. A little booster was required.

And the kitchen needed a good clear out. Enough letters and newspapers had gathered on the table to fill two sacks. He found a Lancashire Evening Post, one he'd picked up a few months back at his grandma's funeral. Jessie had kept hold of it for some reason. There was a story about a murder on the front page, and a photograph of the victim's wife. Her face looked vaguely familiar but he couldn't bring to mind where from. Not that it mattered right now. He'd use the paper to light the stove next time it went out, and he threw it on the sofa.

Well, these days it's part sofa part bed because you haven't even been able to sleep upstairs since she left, have you? You haven't been able to bring yourself to it. Instead, you've more or less moved into the kitchen this last week. Just you and the dogs, holed up with the stove and the radio – while outside, snow builds up in the valley.

You've only been back up to the bedroom twice, to get clothes. Monica was right, Jessie had no intention of sticking around. Her life was in London. Going back upstairs made you realise.

And you realise how perfect Jessie was when you first met – how right for you she seemed. She was like a part of your soul, the part that allowed you to be Dan the performing artist. Despite all the warning signs, you could never have prepared yourself for this to happen.

Once he felt the ephedrines kick in, Dan set up a small whiteboard and marked up the words: Dan's Plan. It was time to figure out the next move. At least he could now do so without having to consult company managers or the guys back at No. 1. And he didn't even have to check in with Jessie any more. He was in control of his own destiny. He was his own artist again.

That deserved a toast, and he left the whiteboard to fetch his Tullamore Dew. He poured half a tumbler and downed it in one. The chat on the radio seemed to have moved on to sacrifice rituals. Dan found a tape to drown it out with.

He decided the plan could wait. He needed to get this film reel finished. It was time to see what kind of disjointed show he'd made of a lifetime of Super 8s.

***

An open door that looks along the valley side, thick with snow – the air is full of dog's vapour and the sound of padding paws and panting faces. And then the door shuts quickly, of its own accord, and you retreat as if you're standing on a conveyor belt in reverse. But you're not standing, you're sitting, splayed on the kitchen sofa with your head tilted backwards. The stove has reduced right down to glowing embers, however the oven is on and it keeps the chill from the room.

You threw a newspaper on the sofa earlier in case you needed to relight the stove, but it isn't obviously about. It was the Lancashire Evening Post, with a murder story on the front page and a photograph of the young widow. The dog must be lying on it.

You can hear an earnest discussion taking place somewhere within earshot and the sound of singing voices in the distance. Icicles are hanging off the wood-shed guttering, and the projector wheel is turning and flaps the loose film with a metronomic beat. The house creaks loudly enough to expect it to shatter at any moment. And there's more singing, like a heavenly fanfare to begin with, but soon it becomes clear it's a triumphant chorus of soldiers outside a besieged city. The air hisses and crackles with rifle-fire. It's anyone's guess what the conversation in the foreground is about but the voices sound panicky.

There's something about that murder in the Preston newspaper. Something nagging at you that you can't, for all the world, place.

'It's a story within a story within a story.' That's what Jessie said, when she looked up at you from her manuscript. Her smile is angelic, so much so the light is dazzling and you want to shield your eyes. It's just that you can't, so you blink fiercely. It's her parting smile you can see, the one that feels like lemon juice in your eyes. It stings like the chilly draught that came with it when she opened the door to leave.

The panicky voices have turned into whimpers now, whimpers and snuffling about the ears. It feels like being scrubbed by your grandmother. Then the whimpers are replaced by howls of laughter, or maybe it's a pitiful wailing. You can't be sure.

The howls remind you of Monica, the strange, mournful cry she let out when you told her you didn't feel the same way as she did. Would it have hurt to show more sympathy? It was self-protection mostly. You offered her your spliff, but kept hold of the vodka bottle. You needed the drink and she needed to deal with her issues.

She sat down next to you on the sofa. She was wearing shades. You hadn't noticed before how beautiful she was. All these years and you hadn't realised. And you could never have guessed she felt that way about you. But with a few words, she was dismissed and she howled and walked away with the spliff, but you held onto the vodka bottle as if it were an infant.

Out of the corner of your eye, when you glanced into the living room, you saw Jessie curled all around someone. But you kept walking to the kitchen. It was probably innocent party play.

There were plenty of people there. You didn't know half of them but hasn't it always been like that? As you bobbed through a crowd of bright and wasted faces, a feeling like anaesthetic took grip of your limbs. You knew deep down that wasn't party play. What you saw was not innocent. And you excused your way to the sofa.

The sofa. Viewed from above it's the shape of an L, with thick arms and a big cushion wedged into the corner. Currently it has one of the dogs curled up on the short end. And it has you, spread out like a starfish with one boot practically in the stove. The little table to your right is spilling over with bottles and cans, and the ashtray looks like a model volcano made of butts and matchsticks.

You can't remember what music you heard playing before you passed out at the party, but tonight, the last thing you knew, Pink Floyd was on and you were watching the Super 8 home movies. It had reached the one of an old boxing match (what was the occasion?) and now here you are, out for the count. Typical, but worse than that. Maybe this time you really have overdone it. Maybe you should write some sort of parting note. There's no way you could make it to the phone-box in this weather, in this state, to call for help. You're not even sure you could lift a pen.

***

Her smile is bright enough to sting like acid. You can feel it chilling your skin and then the door bangs shut and you rush backwards into this slump across the couch. Trying to catch your breath has become like chasing a hat in a stiff breeze.

The valley is so steep, Frank is at a funny angle as you face him down – the double-crossing bastard. And there he is, sliding away along a sharp incline, probably a bit too soon. You could have done with him sticking about today.

Shouldn't have called him a sad, wife-stealing fucker then. The dogs are running through and around you, padding across the snow with their breath rising up in a cloud.

You're surrounded by the whiff of cigarettes and electricity and ganja. While all the time in the background, there's something musty – thin, stained carpets and plaster mouldings – and that's what it's like at No. 1.

The first three or four rows were all you could see, whenever you looked. Writhing, sweaty, hair-lashed faces. Those and the bobbing party people, half of whom you will never know. As well as all the faces at No. 1. Every one of them, the house itself, as vivid as the day – Keith tipping his hat and Frank thumbing his waistcoat. The thud in the ceiling above, the creak of the floorboards and Monica skirting in and out wispily – Jessie floating through it all like a perfect little cloud.

Then all of a sudden there's your dad, shouting and shadow boxing, throwing those hooks from a crouch. Lift a glass to the old man! At which point you make to rise up, and the smile you're looking into is blinding yellow – and you keep squinting until you realise it's a corridor of light.

A box-shaped shaft of light that you arch yourself up into, whereupon you're met by a round dark face, one that becomes more distinct the closer you get. She is an angel, with clear green eyes, her hair falling in long, black ringlets – so close you can feel the tickle on your cheeks. She leans in and peers. She's asking if you're all right.

'Yes,' you can hear your own voice speak. One of the dogs is barking.

Your dad sounds choked up with emotion. 'Thanks be to Christ, you're all right,' he's saying.

'Where's the stop-cock!' shouts Frank. 'There's a fountain pissing out the front room wall!'

The chimes of Big Ben echo from the radio and all of a sudden, clear as the day, you can picture three cards laid out on a table inside a billowing tent.

'This is your future,' said the gypsy woman. 'You and your wife, and a little lad.'

And that, Danny Boy, is how you got here.

StreetBooks

StreetBooks is an Oxfordshire-based micro-publisher.

'My interest is in artisan publishing: which involves high quality, regional fiction, marketed locally in person and globally via the Internet. An analogy I like is that of the micro-brewery: a combination of tradition, passion and the opportunities offered by new technology.' Frank Egerton, editor, StreetBooks

http://www.streetbooks.co.uk

Lightning Source UK Ltd.
Milton Keynes UK
UKOW01f0847271016
286226UK00001B/1/P